THE CALM WITHIN

CRYSTAL A. BLANTON

Crystal A. Blanton

The Calm Within

Published by Crystal A Blanton

Copyright © 2018 Crystal A Blanton

All rights reserved

The Calm Within

First Edition 2018

ISBN: 978-1-7320072-0-8

Cover Art:

Breakaway Designs

(www.facebook.com/breakawaydesigns)

Editing:

Edit for Content

(www.editforcontent.com)

Formatting:

Formatting Done Wright

(www.facebook.com/FormattingDoneWright)

Poem:

J.R. Rogue

(www.jrrogue.com)

Table Of Contents

Dedication

To everyone who has supported me in all my crazy endeavors.

Let me in,

to the places your past

has pushed and pummeled you.

Lay it all on me,

the last breaths,

the names lingering

on your lips.

Place the pieces

of your history

still present,

still repenting,

into these palms.

For I am the one

who gives

you strength,

I will be your calm.

J.R. Rogue

Chapter 1

Kinsley

"It's our birthday, Kit," Ryker says softly through the phone. It's midnight on the dot and I know he hasn't slept a wink with the way the rasp grips his words.

"It's *my* birthday, Ryker. You turned seventeen six months ago." I pull the cover over my head and put the phone on speaker.

"Exactly six months ago, which means it's my half birthday. *That's* just as important."

I smile at our familiar words, my eyes remaining closed so I can imagine him by my side. "Ryk, one year I'm going to surprise you and say something different."

Our laughter coincides, dancing together until it's dispersed into thin air.

"I'm holding you to it. We only have forever." A contented sigh passes his lips. I can feel how he has more to say. "I hope you enjoy your day."

That wasn't what I was expecting.

"Will I not see you?" We've spent all of our birthdays together—at least all the ones we could.

"You will," he hesitates, "I just don't know when."

"Oh." It's barely a word, but I know he can hear the frown in my voice. A minute goes by, the faint whisper of our breathing the only sound.

"Well...I'll let you get back to your beauty sleep." He rustles with the phone. "Lord knows you need it more than me." His words are lighter, yet I hear no smile.

"Ryk?" I pause. Not for his response—for my own courage. "Fall asleep with me?" The words are not the ones I was going to say and he knows this but gives it no attention.

"Always."

"Mr. Liehmann?" The voice over the intercom rings into the class. "Could you please send Kinsley Carmichael to the office with her things to go home?"

Mr. Liehmann looks to me, making sure I heard. I nod once as I gather my books to shove into my satchel.

"You didn't tell me you get to leave early," Jenna whispers across the aisle. She's used to my parents doing something crazy and fun for my birthday. Perks to being an only child.

I shrug my shoulders and lean closer to her, "I didn't know. They were already gone when I got up this morning. Their case-loads have been heavy lately."

Mr. Liehmann clears his throat, bringing the classes' attention to where I sit.

"Flamingos!" Liv shouts from the back of the room causing everyone to look her way. I hate being the center of attention, which is the reason for her outburst. She's saving me. This is one of the many reasons I keep her as a friend.

"Miss Carlson, what do flamingos have to do with statistics?" Mr. Liehmann asks.

I stand and quietly make my way toward the exit of the room, hearing Liv's response before I'm out the door. "Because, statistically, flamingos are the most badass birds in existence. Being all pink and shit."

I shake my head as I make my way down the hall. *She's crazy.* Teachers don't even get to escape Liv's colorful mouth. Some still give her detentions hoping to persuade her ways, others have become used to it— ignore and move on. Mr. Liehmann, however, usually gives it right back to her, in a philosophical way, of course.

I'm almost to the stairs which lead me to the main floor, when a hand encircles my wrist, catching me completely off guard. Spinning around, I jerk back and let out a tiny yelp.

My best friend stands before me, head cocked to the side, his gray eyes shining with mischief.

"What the crap, Ryk? You scared me half to death." I give him a playful shove. "What are you doing here?" It's the middle of fourth period. He should be at work right now, qualifications to be in the schools work release program.

"I got Logan to cover my shift. Told him I had a very important meeting to attend today." A slow smile spreads across his lips.

He takes a step closer and grabs my hand, sliding his fingers through mine as he starts walking us the direction I just came from.

"I was headed to the office," I state; my legs keeping in sync with his strides.

"I know." He glances at me from the corner of his eye.

I halt my steps, my grip on his hand stopping his as well.

"What do you mean, you know?" His hand goes to the back of his neck as he turns to face me.

"I was the one to sign you out."

What? He can't do that.

"Bridget Henson," he continues, "was covering the desk." I laugh at him as he dips his chin down, hiding from his own admission. *It all makes sense now.*

"Bridget Henson, huh? The girl who's been pining for your attention since the fifth grade?" It's amusing to see how uncomfortable he is right now. "Please don't tell me you decided to start dating her just to get me out of class." The thought of him doing such a thing makes my stomach queasy.

He brings our joined hands to his mouth, his lips pressing against my knuckles.

"I...would...never...do...that." He kisses each knuckle between the words, making sure not to leave one out. I give him a pointed look. "I just flirted with her...turned up the swagger a bit."

My eyebrows rise with his confession. Ryker's naturally flirtatious, so I can only imagine what 'turning up the swagger' means to him.

He turns on his heel without another word, pulling us both to the exit sitting at the end of the hall. These exits are locked during school hours unless you have a particular keycard which lets you out.

Ryker just happens to have one.

As I sit on the tailgate of Ryker's truck, I stare out across the still waters. He's brought us to Bush Wildlife, Lake 33, which is the best lake for catching largemouth bass. Only today, he didn't bring a fishing pole.

"You know, this is not what I thought we'd be doing when you pulled me out of class."

Another stone slides from his hand, skipping across the water, leaving ripples in its wake. I lean back on my hands, tilting my face toward the sky. It's a warmer winter day with it being only sixteen days into March. It feels more like the middle of spring.

The truck dips as he jumps up next to me to sit down. His body seamlessly seals to the side of mine. Ryker's an affectionate person, especially with me. There's rarely a moment when we're together where he's not touching or holding or caressing a part of my body.

"And what did you think we'd be doing?" He nudges his shoulder against mine.

"Hmmm...skydiving, bungee jumping, hang gliding." I laugh at myself knowing these are all things I would never do. I wouldn't necessarily say I have a fear of heights, just a fear of dying from falling from those heights.

He puts his arm around my shoulder and pulls me to his chest. He kisses my forehead and leaves his lips there as he says, "next year, Kit. I will get you to do all three of those things for your birthday."

Ryker's the only person who calls me Kit. When we were little he couldn't pronounce certain letters. 'S' came out as 'T'. We could never figure out how he dropped the 'N' in my name. Somehow, Kins came out as Kit and has always stayed the same.

I sit up and he takes my hand. "Let's go to Mandy's party tonight," he says.

"Heh. And how do you suppose we'd get away with that?"

Mandy Newton and her older brother Trexton are part of our close circle of friends. Her family bought twenty-five acres, of the old McMillon farm, a few years back and built an eighty-five hundred square foot house, or mansion, or estate. I don't know what to call it, except huge.

Shortly after they moved here, we all learned they will literally use any excuse to throw a party—social gathering is the term they prefer to use. They usually have alcohol, and regardless of if their parents are there or not, my parents won't go for that.

"We can tell your parents were doing something else."

I look at him, incredulously. I'm pretty certain he doesn't even believe the words that just came out of his mouth.

"Okay, yeah, I know," he says like he's trying to explain his reasoning. "We can't lie to them, per say. I'm sure I can work my charm and convince them to let us go."

There are many people I could lie to and get away with it. Frank and Karen Carmichael are not a part of those people. Growing up with parents who happen to be top detectives in your town has its many perks. It also has its downfalls.

"Mmhmm, sure." My consensus is barely believable. "I guess it doesn't hurt to ask, but you get to do *all* of the talking."

He gives me his megawatt smile, causing my stomach to do a flip.

How did I get so lucky to have him in my life?

Chapter 2

Ryker

4 years old

"Hi Sweetie, what is your name?" The nice lady in the police outfit asks me.

I keep trying to count how many there are, but I don't know if they're all police or just some more of Erin's, I mean Mommy's, friends. I have to remember to call her Mommy. She gets really mad when I forget.

"I'm Ryker Elliot Pritt. I four." I try to show her how many that is with my fingers but my hands really hurt.

"Ryker is a cool name. I really like it. My name is Officer Alisia Stevens. You can call me Ms. Ali. Ryker, I want you to know how brave you are for calling for help. You are such a big boy! Can you tell me what happened before you called for help?"

"Um, my mommy had a birfday party for me and there were lots of big people here."

"Oh wow. I like birthday parties. So you just turned four?" I nod my head.

"Now Ryker when you say big people, are you meaning adults like me and your mommy?"

"Mmhmm, there were tome kids like me. I don't know them and they didn't play with me."

Ms. Ali is writing stuff in a little book with a pen when I talk. I hope I don't get anyone in trouble. Mommy says it's not nice to tattle and is always telling me to keep secrets.

"Okay, Honey. Can you to tell me what happened to make you call nine one one?"

"I woke up cause I needed to go potty. I tried to go back to weep cause Mommy don't like it when I bother her. I weally had to go. I was being weally quiet. When I went into the bathroom Mommy and the man were on the floor. I couldn't get to the potty. I tried waking them up. They wouldn't wake up and there was tomething hanging out of their arm. My mom and dad always told me if tomething bad happened to me or if I thought tomeone else was hurt, then I need to find a phone and press nine one one."

"Well, Ryker, you did an amazing job." She writes some more stuff in her book and I try to look at it. I can't read yet so I don't know what she's writing.

"I'm just writing some notes for my boss. Can you read Ryker?"

"I can read my name."

"That's great! We all have to start somewhere." She looks at me and smiles. She's pretty. "I have just a couple more questions for you. Is that okay, Ryker? You are doing a really good job." Before she can ask me another question a policeman comes over and says something in her ear. I can't hear him so it must be a secret. She nods her head and looks at me. She's not smiling anymore. I hope he didn't say something mean to her.

"Who's that?" I ask

"That there is Officer Shou. He's my partner and he was just telling me that your mom is at the hospital and they were able to wake her up."

I shiver. I think I'm cold. Ms. Ali must notice cause she grabs the blanket off the couch and puts it around me.

"Ryker, you said your mom and dad taught you how to call nine one one. The man who was in the bathroom with your mom, is he your dad?"

"No, ma'am. I have a different mom and dad I used to live with when Mommy wasn't feeling well. I haven't teen them in a long time." Thinking about them makes me feel sad inside. I'm not going to tell Ms. Ali cause I don't want Mommy to find out.

It might hurt her feelings.

"Is Mommy getting sick again? Will I get to go back to my other mom and dad to live?"

"I will have to find out for you. Let's talk about this bruise and cut you have by your eye. Can you tell me how you got it?"

I forgot that was there. It's a good thing she can't see my butt. It still hurts to sit sometimes. I probably should tell her what Mommy told me to say.

"Ryker, Honey, you can tell me what happened. Did someone who was in this house hit you with something or with their hand?" Ms. Ali has her hand on my shoulder now, but all I can do is think about what happened. My belly hurts now.

"Ryker, did your mommy do this to you?"

I look Ms. Ali in the eyes wondering how she would know.

"No, no I fell and hit my eye on the table." I hope she believes me. Mommy made me say it a few times so I could remember in case anyone asked.

"Okay. Can I share something with you that I've only told a few of my really special friends, which will make you one of my special friends?" I nod my head cause I want to hear her secret. I don't tell her that I don't need a special friend since I already have one. Ms. Ali leans in close to me.

"When I was about your age my mommy hit me because I made her mad about something. She told me to tell people I hit my head on my bunk bed I shared with my sister or I would get into more trouble. I did tell people what she said and they all believed me. The thing was my mommy hit me again, many times, and every time I wished I wouldn't have lied for her. So, I'm going to ask you again and please tell me the truth so I can make sure it doesn't happen anymore. Did your mommy hurt you?"

I look down at my hands, which still hurt, and wonder if I do tell Ms. Ali the truth maybe I will get to go back and live with my Mom and Dad again so Mommy Erin can get better.

I start nodding my head to tell her yes. Maybe if I don't actually say the words then I'm not really tattling. She doesn't move or say anything, so I turn my head to look at her.

"I need you to use your voice and tell me exactly what happened, okay?"

I guess I'm going to have to tell her.

"Mommy let me call my best friend who lives by my other mom and dad's house. Her name is Kit and I miss her. Mommy heard me Tay." I stop talking. I don't want to say the words. It makes my belly hurt when I think about it.

"It's okay, Ryker. You can tell me anything and you only have to say it once. I'm a really good listener."

"I-I taid I love you to Kit. Mommy got reawy mad and told me not to tay it to anyone but her." I whisper that part. I hope Ms. Ali heard me so I don't have to say it again. My belly really, really hurts now.

"Is the bruise on your eye the only thing that happened?" She looks at my hands. Mommy didn't hurt my hands.

"I got a lot of pankings on my butt and my legs and my back. It hurts when I tit down." Ms. Ali kind of looks like her belly hurts now.

"And what about your hands? Tell me what happened to your hands, Honey."

I look at my hands. They don't have any bruises on them so I'm not sure how she knows they hurt so badly.

"I can tell they are bothering you by the way you hold them and won't use them."

I try to move my fingers a little. I stop cause it just makes them hurt even more.

"Remember Ryker, you only have to tell me one time."

"The man that was in the bathroom with Mommy was titting at the table last night with more men like him. They had a funny looking hammer. The whole top was black and not hard like a real hammer. They made me play keep away. Mommy told me it would be fun."

"I haven't heard of that game before. Can you tell me how you play it?"

"You put your hands flat on the table and you have to move them before the funny looking hammer hits them." I move my hands again hoping the pain will go away. It doesn't. "I'm not very fast. I lost a lot and they made me keep playing cause they thought it was funny."

Ms. Ali asks me to put my hands on hers so I do. She looks at them and slowly turns them over to look at the other side.

She looks at the boo-boo on my eye, but she looks away quickly when a voice calls her name from the front door. A voice I know so well.

I turn my head in the direction and I see an angel. It's Kit's mom! I run to her. She gets on her knees and opens her arms for me to slam into her chest. I take a deep breath to smell her cause her house smells much like my Mom and Dad's house. She smells like home.

I won't tell anybody this, but I kind of hope Mommy Erin's sick again so I can go to my real home. I miss my mom and dad. I miss Kit more.

Chapter 3

Kinsley

"I still can't believe Ryker was able to convince your parents," Jenna says, as she loops her arm through mine.

We're standing in front of Mandy's bedroom window watching the sun begin its descent into the Western hemisphere, giving daytime to the other half of the Earth. Its rays paint a beautiful scene of brushed yellows and oranges and a few hints of blue across the sky.

I give her a pensive smile as I think about the amount of effort it took Ryker to convince my parents, and then how quickly he disappeared. He didn't say where he was going or why he had to leave, just that he would meet me here, at Mandy's. His abrupt departure almost made me change my mind about coming to the party at all.

I pull my phone from my jacket pocket and click the side button one more time—*no new notifications*. A pit forms deep in my stomach.

Jenna lays her head against my shoulder and rubs her free hand up and down my arm. It's soothing, comforting, the way a parent consoles a child. She's my closest friend, outside of Ryker. Her father moved the two of them here when she was six, one year after her mother died in a car accident. We didn't meet until we were nine.

"So, what do you think is up with him?" she asks. Jenna's perceptive. She's a watcher, an observer. Her quiet, reserved nature keeps her in tune with the people and the world around her.

"I have no clue." I rub my fingers across my forehead. "Our relationship has been so weird lately, distant. I mean, yeah, he's been working a lot of extra shifts, except even the texting and calls have many days between them."

I look down to the backyard and watch the Newton's gardener adjust the rock which lines the fire pit. He starts stacking pieces of wood in the center, making them stand in the form of a teepee then douses lighter fluid on top. He lights the end of a rolled-up newspaper and tosses it into the wood. Even though I'm two stories high and away from the fire, I can feel the burning flames, the heat licking my skin.

"It's like he's drifting out into the open waters and I've lost the rope to pull him back to me."

Jenna looks at me, her honey-brown eyes searching, assessing. She always takes a moment to gather her thoughts before she voices them. "I don't think that's it at all. Your relationship is changing, yes, but if you take a step back and look at it from a distance, you'd see the real direction it wants to go."

Confusion floods me as my mind replays what she's said.

"Are we ready to head down?" Mandy asks, not giving me time to analyze Jenna's words.

"Fuck, yes!" Liv shouts as Jenna grabs my hand and pulls me out the door.

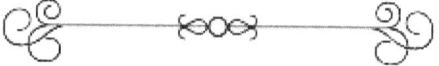

The Newton's backyard is expansive. A broad staircase leads us from the deck down onto the beautiful stone patio, which is currently being used as a dance floor. The bonfire sits further out in the grass. Rectangular haystacks, with thick blankets on top, are scattered around the yard.

Jeremy, the tenth grader known for playing sick beats, is positioned behind an elevated table, headphones hanging around his neck, his hands working old school turntables, pumping music through speakers into the open air.

Strung white lights twinkle under the pergola, giving us our own version of a starry sky.

I'm a little shocked by how many people have shown up. I've always heard they're the best parties in town. With Trexton away at college now, I'd assumed they wouldn't be as large.

Mandy slides through the crowd effortlessly, leading the four of us to the middle of the patio. Bodies dance all around us, some I'm familiar with, a lot I've never seen before. Mandy and Jenna dance before me, their bodies moving as one with the tempo. I'm not as confident as they are, so I move just enough to not seem out of place. I search the crowd of people, curious to know where Liv ran off to and hoping to see the person who hasn't left my mind since he left my home hours ago, except he's not here.

I stiffen as arms wrap around me from behind. A familiar voice, one I wasn't expecting to hear, speaks words of encouragement into my ear. "I know you can dance way better than this, Red."

There's only one person who calls me Red because I flush easily and it's my favorite color. I went through a phase where anything I wore or owned had to have red in it somewhere. I spin around and take in the smile spread across his face, before slamming into his chest, wrapping my arms around his lean body. He squeezes tightly, lifting me inches off the ground. "Trex! What are you doing here?"

"Did my girl miss me?" he asks, his words playful and teasing; always calling me 'his girl'. He once told me it drives Ryker crazy, something I've never witnessed. He's wearing a powder blue button-up shirt which makes the blue of his irises almost clear against the olive tones of his skin. His mouth turns up on one side as his gaze glides over my body, leaving a streak of heat in its path. I've pushed myself out of my comfort zone with the dress I'm wearing.

"Eh, it's hard to miss you when you haven't been gone very long." I giggle as his eyebrows rise to his hairline. "I thought you weren't able to come back until spring break?"

Trexton is studying business and finance at Cornell University, a good nine hundred miles away. He came back during Christmas break, except I didn't get to see him.

"This is the start of my spring break. Mine's one week ahead of yours," he says.

Liv shows up out of nowhere, five full shot glasses held carefully in her hands. Jenna and Mandy each give Trex a hug then take a glass from Liv. I hesitate before reaching for one. It's the one thing Ryker promised my parents I wouldn't do. *Well he's not here now, is he?*

Liv has yet to acknowledge Trex, the last three glasses held firmly in her hands. She's like this anytime they're in front of people, acting like she can't stand him when it's the furthest from the truth. They have a love-hate relationship where Liv loves pretending to hate him. I'm uncertain of what all or if anything has happened between them. What I do know is Trexton has made it very clear that they both can live their lives and do their own thing, for now, and he'll be patiently waiting in the background for when she's ready for more.

One of Trexton's hands goes to the small of Liv's back as the other slides a glass from her grip. The glare she gives him sends shivers up my spine. It doesn't phase Trex one bit.

"It's good to see you, *Oliviana*," he says, stretching out each syllable of her name.

"You really want my fucking knee in your balls tonight, *Charles*?"

Trexton is the fourth in the line of Newton men who all bear the same name, however, the only one who is called by his middle name.

"Oh Muñequita, if I have a choice in the matter, I'd much rather have your mouth on my nuts instead of your knee," he replies.

The one thing which sets Liv off more than calling her by her entire first name is Trexton calling her by the Spanish pet name he's reserved only for her. If looks could kill, he would've been dead long ago.

Mandy takes this moment to raise her shot glass, looking at each of us to follow suit. "To enjoying the night," she says as the clink of our glasses is lost in the bass of the song.

I bring the shot to my lips, throw back my head and empty the contents to the back of my throat. The taste is not what I was expecting. In the movies, people always cringe or cough after a shot, but this one is sweet, like cotton candy.

Looking up, I come to the realization I'm licking the inside of the empty glass. Trex is staring at me, one eyebrow raised and the right side of his mouth cocked into an incredibly sexy smirk.

Damn, he caught me.

Damn, he's sexy.

Damn, I want more.

Trex takes my glass right before Jenna grabs my hand and twirls me around in a circle. Mandy and Liv join us as we sway our bodies to the music. I feel warm and light and happy.

I'm finally having a good time, truly enjoying myself, when I feel it—a shift in the atmosphere. Even in the night's warm air and through the thin layer of sweat sheathing my skin, goosebumps rise on my flesh, and a chill runs through my body.

Ryker's here.

Jenna spins me again giving me a chance to take in my surroundings, secretly searching.

I spot him.

He's watching me but isn't aware I just saw him. Or if he is, he hasn't made a move. I continue to dance, moving my body with the flow of the song, in ways I've never moved before.

I see him in my peripheral, he's not alone. There are two guys I've met once before, not long enough to remember their names and some girl...*Bridget? What the hell?* Her arms are wrapped around his waist, pinning herself to his side. She looks like a thirsty leech searching for blood.

I feel his glare—piercing, searching, seeping into my skin. I have the urge to look at him, straight at him. To ask why he's even here? What's the point of showing up now, and with Bridget...*really*? Mostly, I want to tell him to leave.

Kinsley, don't look. Don't let him know you care.

My mind says one thing, my heart says something else.

I have to look.

I want to look.

I need to look.

I turn my body and dance next to Liv, which causes me to face where Ryker stands. Mandy is before me, dancing and singing, unknowingly using her body as a barrier. The unfocused distance shows his silhouette. He hasn't moved. His arms are crossed tightly over his chest now, causing the leech to disconnect from his body. It doesn't stop her from touching him, though. Her hand massages his bicep as she speaks into his ear.

Shit!

My eyes fail me, connecting with his glare. We're in a stand-off, a stare-off. Who will be the one to look away first?

"You ready for another shot?" Liv says, leaning into my ear. I nod my head and feel her leave my side as my focus remains in place—on Ryker.

My friends all know he's here. I've seen them glance over there from time to time. None of them have acknowledged him though, something I'm grateful for.

I know when Liv comes back as Ryker looks her direction. *Ha! I win.*

I turn to face Liv, except it's not Liv, its Trex. He holds a shot glass, filled with amber colored liquid, in each hand. "I was told to make you feel...good." He says 'good' as he glances over my body from head to toe, again.

He extends one hand to me, offering the glass. I reach out and take both, throwing back one right after the other. The cinnamon smell permeates my senses. The taste sweet and spicy, the temperature a contradiction of hot and cold. The burn it left inside my throat somehow feels smooth, inviting.

I bring my head down to find Trex staring at me, one eyebrow quirked, that damn, sexy, smirk back on his face. My tongue skims across my lips. His focus follows its path before darting back up to my eyes. I watch his Adam's apple bob as he swallows.

He gets rid of the shot glasses, then steps closer to me, his hands on my hips, his cheek pressed against mine. He says, "let's dance," as he sways our bodies to the song. I glance around. Jenna, Mandy, and Liv are dancing with their own guys. Liv's eyes meet mine and she gives me a slight nod, encouraging me to keep going—so I do.

I pull Trexton's body closer and run my hands up his firm arms to his shoulders. I'm not sure of the song playing, but the melody flows so smoothly through our bodies.

Feeling brave, I turn around and tease him with my ass. He grabs my hips tightly and pulls me so close my back is flush against him. "You're killing me, Red," he says. His voice a thick rasp in my ear.

"What. The. Fuck. Kit?"

Standing before me is Ryker, and he's pissed.

I take a step forward so my body's no longer against Trex. He grips my hand and squeezes, letting me know he's here if needed.

"Oh Hi," I say, "I see you decided to show up," I look at everyone except Ryker, hoping to portray that he's bothering me.

"Why wouldn't I show up?" he says, as he glares over my shoulder at Trex.

I ignore his question, "Where'd your...*friend* go?"

His arms cross over his chest. He looks around like he has no idea what I'm talking about. "I promised your parents you wouldn't drink."

Apparently, we're holding two different conversations.

"Oh my God, it was two shots!" I throw my hands in the air. *He wasn't here for the first one, so I'm won't bring that up.*

He reaches for me. I'm quick to dodge his advance. *How dare he?* I straighten my shoulders and peer into the storm brewing within his eyes.

What gives him the right to be mad? I deserve to be mad with how he's treating me like he's my handler. Mad at how he left me earlier, without another word. Mad he came here late, and with Bridget of all people, on his arm.

Not that I have any claim over him. I'm not trying to make a big deal about her. This is about him, Ryker Elliot Pritt, and the simple fact that on all of my birthdays, and all of his, it's always been us. Just us.

Oh, I'm mad alright. I'm pissed.

I turn around and find Trexton. I smile. Two steps presses me against his body. One movement puts my hands around his neck. Half a second has passed and my lips are sealed firmly against his lips.

Holy hell, I'm kissing Trexton.

The alcohol must have really done something to my confidence because this is my first kiss. Well, okay, technically, Ryker was my first kiss. We were kids who had no clue what we were doing.

Trexton's arms wrap around me tightly as his tongue slides across my bottom lip, silently asking for entrance. My lips part, allowing him to take charge. He tastes like spearmint. His smooth tongue sweeps across mine and suddenly I feel a hard metal ball jut out from the middle. *Is that a...no way, it can't be.* Trexton has a tongue piercing.

Wow, he sure has changed since leaving home. Of all the people in the world, I would've never guessed Trexton to be the one with a tongue piercing.

As the song switches from one to the next, there's a break in the noise. I hear Mandy's say, "Ryker, you need to calm down. You flipping out will not help things between you and Kinsley."

"Fuck this!" Ryker yells. And before I know what's happening, he spins me around, lifts me over his shoulder, and carries me off toward the Newton's basement.

I'm absolutely mortified.

I cover my face with my hands, shaking my head. I won't put up a fight. No need to draw any more attention to the situation at hand.

Trex tries to head after us only to be halted by Mandy and Liv. I overhear them reassuring him how I will be fine. "Ryker would never hurt Kins," Mandy says.

"And it's about time they figure their shit out," Liv adds.

Whatever the hell that's supposed to mean.

Ryker swings open the basement door and then trudges through the rec room. He's headed toward the bedrooms located off to the right. Not sure why he's going there when all the rooms are locked. I'll let him figure that out by himself though.

One of Mr. and Mrs. Newton's rules is that all these rooms stay locked unless deemed necessary to be opened by Mandy, or Trex when he's home from school.

No one stays in the rooms for obvious reasons and when people do go to sleep it's in the open rec area, all together.

Ryker stops in front of the last door. He removes his hand, which was holding my dress down over my rear, and digs in his pocket.

You've got to be kidding me. Mandy seriously gave him a key to the door? Oh, she's going to hear an earful from me whenever this...whatever this is, is done.

Ryker makes his way to the bed and gently puts me on it. I feel off-balance, my head's foggy, and all the blood that rushed there is now going back to its rightful places. I tug at my dress making sure nothing's exposed and fix the collar on my jean jacket.

I watch Ryker's feet as he paces back and forth across the hardwood floor. His favorite blue chucks, already worn thin, can barely take the beating.

I'm not ready to look up at him just yet, so I watch my finger as it outlines the lace flowers running throughout my dress. I bought this dress a year ago on impulse. I have never worked up the courage to wear it until now.

"What the fuck was that, Kit?" I flinch. The voice I normally enjoy is full of anger, distaste, as he spits my name out like a bad taste.

My mind's reeling, spinning in circles over how to respond. What am I supposed to say? *My impulses got the best of me with Trex and I wanted to make you jealous. Although, how could you possibly be jealous over me, I'm your best friend and nothing* but *your best friend if that.* Yeah, I can't say that.

My head is still down, my lips sealed. I'm weighing my options of feeding him a lie or high-tailing it out the door. Would it seem too childish?

"Answer me Dammit!" he shouts. *I should've chosen the door.*

"What do you want from me, Ryker?" A sigh passes my lips as I finally look at him.

He's standing still, his hands on top of his head. His fingers are laced through the strands of his baby fine hair, interlocked within each other. He's wearing my favorite pair of jeans—a hole in one knee, a rip on the other thigh—and the Shinedown t-shirt I bought him at the concert we went to last summer.

"How long have you and Trex been a thing?"

Huh?

"Trex and I are not a *thing*," I scoff, "you of all people should know that."

"Seems like I don't know shit." he says through clenched teeth, "You might as well have fucked him out there. Hell, maybe that's where it was headed if I hadn't stopped you."

"How dare you! It was just a kiss, one kiss."

"There's no way!" He's pacing again, his head shaking back and forth. "You can't sit there and tell me that was the first time you guys have kissed." He stops moving, putting his hands on his hips and looks at me.

"When did you start keeping things from me?" Defeat strangles his words.

Heat rises toward my cheeks, embarrassment and anger tumble through my blood. I would *never* keep anything from Ryker. He knows everything about me...*everything*. He knows my moods so well he's the one telling me when Aunt Flo is coming to visit. If anyone should be questioned about secrets, it's him.

I stand and move in front of him. I want him to see my eyes while I speak, "It was the first and only time. I haven't seen Trex since the charity float last summer, a week before he left for college. And you were with me the *entire* time. Secrets are not on my end."

He stares at me, unblinking, but barely for a second more. His hands slide back in his hair, gripping and pulling causing random strands to stick up everywhere. He turns around and makes his way to the door. Instead of reaching for the handle like I thought he would, he places both palms flat against the white wood and hangs his head.

It makes no sense for him to make such a big deal about Trexton. Ryker's had plenty of girlfriends, which I know he's not all innocent with.

I'm frustrated and hot. The temperature of this room is increasing with the angst and turmoil our bodies are producing, and the heat is enclosing on me. Turning back to the bed, I'm caught by the gleam of the moon shining through the rectangular window which sits at least six feet off the ground. *Maybe the full moon is to blame for Ryker's craziness.*

I slide my jacket off my arms and lay it on the lighthouse covered duvet. I can feel him behind me before I hear him.

"Kinsley," he says.

Every muscle in my body contracts as fireflies light up my insides and flutter in my stomach. *Ryker just used my full name?* I try to turn around, to face him. I'm halted by his hand on my shoulder.

"This dress..." He clears his throat, "Baby, please tell me you've worn that jacket all night?" It's not a question, it's a plea. And the way he called me baby so naturally, as if it's a term he uses all the time, causes adrenaline to course through my body.

"W-what?" I stammer, pressing my palm flat on my chest to calm my erratic heart. "Of course I have. I wasn't even out there that long before you arrived."

The feel of his finger touching my back, on my *bare* skin, clears the confusion in my mind. My dress is backless. The thought escaped me when I took off my jacket.

Ryker glides the tip of his finger across the top of my back, tracing the opening that forms into the shape of a 'V.' Goosebumps rise in the wake of his path.

He's made it halfway down the right side of the opening, just inches above where the 'V' comes to a point in the most extreme lower part of my back. The sheer sensuality of this movement makes his name fall from my lips in a breathy whisper and causes a groan to rumble through his chest.

"I know you were just kissing Trex outside, but Baby if anyone other than me saw you in this dress, like this, I would have ripped their eyes out."

His voice is primal, feral. He is the lion. I am his prey. The emotions he's stirring within me are confusing. Never in my entire life have I heard him the way he sounds right now, and it has my body reacting in ways which are all too new to describe.

Seconds flow by, feeling like minutes. "Kit, say something, please."

Now he's back to Kit? He has to be messing with me.

"I...um." The way he continues to keep that one finger, resting on my lower back, has my mouth so dry. I lick my lips and try to swallow. "I'm not sure what you want me to say, Ryk. I'm just so confused." After confessing my thoughts my hands go to my forehead, rubbing it with my fingers.

A feeling of loss passes through me briefly as Ryker removes his one daunting finger from my back and places both his hands firmly on my hips. He turns me slowly, bringing me face to face with him. He removes my hands from my forehead and holds them. The familiarity in his grip reminds me that *this* is Ryker, my best friend, the one who knows every detail about me, who lifts my spirits when they're low and has a perspective of no other.

"Why don't you start with the why on Trexton...and I want the truth." His gray eyes capture mine, waiting for my answer. I wish he would just move past this already, it was just a kiss. So what if I finally kissed someone. It's not like he hasn't kissed many girls, if not done more, yet I don't get all pissed about it.

"Honestly, I'm not sure why I kissed him. After you left today, I almost changed my mind about coming. You never texted me like you said you would. You show up late to the part, and then..." *Ugh, I don't want to say her name.* I close my eyes and breathe in deep. "*Bridget* was awfully comfortable hanging on you."

He studies my face and smirks at me. "So you're jealous?"

"No! I'm not jealous. Are you even listening? I'm hurt and pissed off so I wanted to try and piss you off too, I guess. Hell, I don't even know anymore."

"Do you think I'm pissed?" He still has my hands, rubbing his thumbs over the underside of my wrists.

"Seems a hell of a lot like it to me, Ryk. Come on, you want the truth from me, how about you give me some truth." I'm so frustrated. I feel like he's playing head games with me and I just want to scream. His grip tightens as I try to remove my hands from his.

"Fine," he grits out, "you want truth, Kit? I'll give you truth. You wanted to piss me off. Sure, I can admit there was a tiny bit of anger, except it was masked by pure jealous rage." He stops there and stares at me like that explains everything.

41

"Is that all you're going to say, cause *news flash,* I can't read your fucking mind!" I'm so sick of this shit. Of us going around in circles. Catching him off guard, I yank my hands from his grip and make a break for the door.

"Please don't go."

I ignore him and grip the handle of the door, the only barrier keeping me within the confines of these walls. Before I can turn it, one word annihilates my escape.

"Skittles," softly whispers past his lips, wraps around my entire body, and cements my feet to the floor.

It's a word which creates a rainbow-colored image for most yet has a much greater significance to us. It's love and trust, security and hope. It stands in place of three little words which if said, would do more harm than anything else.

For us, Skittles means I love you.

It may seem like a funny or juvenile word to have chosen in its place, but when you're four years old and share a favorite candy, strange euphemisms come into play.

I was almost out of here, but he's playing dirty. Ryker knows how much that word is my weakness. He doesn't say it much, usually handing me a bag of the candy in place of the word.

I'm stuck, frozen, planted firmly facing the door, wondering if my ears deceive me.

"Say it back," he says, confirming he truly said our word. "Why aren't you saying it back, Kit?"

Stubbornness has overtaken me and even though my heart is hurting from the broken tone in his voice, nothing has come out of my mouth to soothe his pain. I have never not repeated our word back to him.

"Are we changing, Ryker?" I ask, knowing it's not what he wants to hear. I need to know if this is a start to an end for us. If this is where we drift apart. When we realize it's time we go our separate ways. I'm not ready to lose my best friend just yet, but it will be easier for me to know now.

"I'm hoping one of us is." His voice breaks with emotion.

I turn around so I can see his face, gauge his reaction. I'm exhausted with the cryptic messages he's been throwing at me since he brought us into this room and it's time I start demanding answers.

"You hope one of us is? What does that even mean?" I bite the inside of my cheek. "You are so damn confusing, saying things that make no sense, and not finishing your thoughts. Here I am worried how we hardly see each other anymore or talk like we used to, feeling as though we're drifting apart. And here you are...you carry me in here like a petulant child, and then call me 'Kinsley' and 'Baby' when you've only ever called me Kit." I pace the room back and forth. "As if that's not got my head jumbled enough, you tell me you're jealous of Trex!" I stop and throw my hands up in the air. "Can you please, for the love of the almighty, stop with the fucking head games and just tell me what the hell is going on?"

I'm panting and out of breath from the charade I just produced, but it was coming to a head and I needed to let it out. I look at Ryker, his limpid eyes impale me. He's the epitome of calm, the settlement after a storm, or maybe before.

"Kiss me," he says.

"W-what?"

"Kiss...me," he repeats, in more of a demand.

Ryker Elliot, the boy I've known since birth, has just demanded me to kiss him. *He can't be serious right now, can he?*

"I just want answers, Ryker...nothing but the truth." The exhaustion in my voice is evident.

"I'm trying to give you the truth, but you can't even kiss me! You were just all over Trex outside and..."

He thinks he can give me the truth through a kiss? Do I want to kiss Ryker? It's a stupid question. Of course, I do. I've wanted a repeat since we shared our first kiss when we were merely ten. Both of us were so nervous, and the slobber that was left all over our mouths from the lack of knowledge made it less than pleasurable. Yet, the way he picked me a handful of wildflowers and handed me a bag of Skittles on our way home from the park, made me think we were destined to be together.

Unfortunately, our lives don't always go down the path our head and heart desire. As we've grown older,

Ryker's protectiveness toward me has only grown stronger, and I know he loves me probably more than anything or anyone else on this planet. Once he started dating other girls, I knew his love was only of a best friend, so I quickly pushed my feelings aside. *Why the change of heart now?*

My focus falls back on Ryker. He's pacing, again, his hands clasped through the strands of his hair, again. Every sign that shows he's struggling to deal with his emotions is laid out before me, awaiting my calm. A play that happens from time to time, but never broaching this subject. He's still talking, even though I haven't heard a word he's said.

"I'd planned on staying away from you today, I couldn't. The mere thought of not seeing you, touching you, holding you in my arms already breaks me in two. But for it to happen today...my favorite day, the day God brought you into my life, I'd likely shatter." He's facing me now, intently staring into my eyes. "The distance you feel," he pauses, "it was supposed to make your feelings grow stronger, to make you notice me. Like *really* notice me as more than your best friend, because Kit, I don't want to be *just* your best friend anymore."

He exhales loudly after the last line, sounding like a balloon deflating. His hands drop to his sides, shoulders hunched over, neck slightly bent. He looks weak, defeated, and it hurts me so much. His eyes are trained on the floor as though the wooden slats hold all the answers. I step once, twice, three times until mere inches keep us apart.

I lay my hands flat against his chest, one splayed directly over his heart. Its beats are a pattern, Morse code, speaking straight to my soul. His breathing evens out as he watches me intently, waiting for my next move. The longer I take the faster his heart begins to pick back up with anticipation.

It's ironic how I've been the only person that has ever been able to calm Ryker and now I cause his heart to go into a frenzy.

I slowly slide my hand up his chest to his shoulder, up his neck to his jaw. The stubble on his face is rough against my palm. He studies me, searching, watching my every move. His nostrils flare slightly as his chest presses into mine, releasing the air he had trapped in his lungs, his breath sending tingles down my spine.

"Kinsley," he says, using my full given name, instead of the childhood nickname I've heard all my life.

He didn't say it with a question mark, inquiring my intent.

He didn't say it with an exclamation, his excitement depicting where this may go.

He didn't say it with a period, an ending to a plain old sentence.

He simply breathed it, allowing its escape on the exhale of his breath, once a part of his soul that was ready to be released.

A fire ignites deep within my core.

With one hand gripped in his shirt, I pull his head down with the other, our mouths melt together. His lips are as soft as I remember, and I have to remind myself we are no longer curious ten-year-olds.

Neither of us has made a move to push past this lingering peck. Self-doubt creeps into my conscience, wondering if he's changed his mind. I withdraw slowly, releasing his shirt from my grip, removing my hand from his neck.

As I pull my lips from his, the connection nearly broke, I'm caught off guard by his arms wrapping around me, disintegrating any space our bodies once had. A gasp escapes me, my mouth falls slack, his tongue delves deep inside, dancing and caressing, making me clench my thighs.

The world has stopped spinning, the clocks no longer count. We are floating, drifting, in a space between time. I feel his heart beating wildly, mimicking mine. I never knew a kiss could feel so divine.

My hands find their way under his shirt. My nails skim across his soft skin. The hold he has on me loosens as his hands move to the backs of my arms. He pulls me forward, step-by step. The kiss never faltering.

I know we've reached the bed as I feel him begin to sit. Hesitation hits me, I'm unsure of what to do. His hands slide up my arms until they're cupping my neck, his thumbs rest upon my cheeks, coaxing me to continue the kiss. I reach for his shoulders to steady myself and climb onto his lap, my legs straddling the outside of his thighs.

Our kiss is tender, gentle, and full of passion. It's a lifetime of friendship and hidden desires pouring out all at once. Sliding my fingers into his hair where the length is longer on top, I pull the strands slightly, granting me full access to explore his mouth.

A thunderous rumble comes from deep within Ryker's chest, vibrating me to my core. The grip he has on my hips tightens and rocks me against him. I can feel how much he wants me as his arousal strains against the zipper of his jeans and presses into the center of my thighs.

This time I rock against him while his strong hands guide me. The movement causes a friction I've never felt before. The sensation is overwhelming and consumes me causing conflicting emotions to course throughout my body. I have a need to finish what I've started, and a want to stop it now. Sweat beads on my forehead, goosebumps cover my skin. The euphoric state I'm encountering takes me to a place I've never been.

I rip my mouth from Ryker's, trying to catch my breath. He looks at me through his long dark lashes and lust filled eyes, and its then I notice my body is no longer moving. He has stopped me, gripping me tightly to keep me from shifting even an inch. A whimper escapes me, sounding more like a needy cry. My gaze shifts, involuntarily, to the bulge that's no longer pressing against my heat.

"Kinsley...Baby, please don't look at me like that. Trust me, I want to keep going. If we continue like we are, there will soon be a mess." I give him a shy smile as my forehead meets his. I'm slightly embarrassed for not thinking about how this was affecting him. If a flush didn't already cover my body, I know I would feel it rise across my skin.

His hands are resting on my thighs, his tentative fingers edge under the hem of my dress. Once he reaches midway up my thigh, he stops and chuckles.

"Are you wearing boxers?" he asks before pushing my dress up to see for himself. They're *his* boxers I kept from a few years ago. He let me wear them when I had to sleep over at his house while my parents went on an emergency call.

I shrug my shoulders and bite my lip. "What can I say, they're comfortable."

His hands torture me, tickling my waist as he flips me onto my back. I'm laughing hysterically, trying to fight him off.

He finally stops and crawls up my body, holding himself up with his hands. He pecks my lips once, twice. "God, you're beautiful," he says.

My heart melts into a puddle.

Chapter 4

RYKER

13 years old

I slide the marker diagonally across the square box. Red ink absorbs into the paper, slicing through yesterday's date. Another day is gone where I feel like that box—cut in two.

The bell rings and everyone jumps from their seats, pushing and shoving to get through the door. I shove the marker into the spiral of my notebook and make my way to the hall. Trevor and Ashley are propped against the lockers, waiting for me to join them for our walk home.

"Hey Babe," Ashley says, wrapping her arm around my waist, snuggling up to my side. I switch my notebook to my other hand and throw my arm over her shoulder.

I give her a quick peck on the lips and look her over. Her hair has purple streaks in it today. The color never stays the same. "What are the plans for the weekend?"

"My brother got us an invite to Dillon York's house party," Trevor says, as he tosses the football in the air.

A high pitch squeal pierces my ears as Ashley bounces with excitement beside me. "Oh, em gee! We have to go. I've heard his parties are the best."

"Of course his parties are the best," Trevor says, "He lives in an actual house instead of the projects we live in."

I smack the back of his head. "We don't live in the projects, you fool."

"Projects." He holds up one hand. "Meth-infested trailer park." He holds up the other. "It's all the same."

Okay, sure. The trailer park we live in isn't known for being the best in town or the safest, but I think meth infested is going overboard, right? "Well, it can't be too bad since it passed the CPS visit." My mother's a recovering addict. We were living in a nice apartment on the west side of town. Mom said she wanted something of her own. At least that's what she told me.

"Dude," Trevor says, "CPS is shit. They ignore the whole back half of the neighborhood." He throws and catches the football some more as we walk the half mile home. "Did you know there were two explosions near Ashley's trailer about three months ago?"

Trevor knows we've only been living here for two months, so no, I didn't know. I look at Ashley. She's staring at the ground, watching the gravel we walk on. We walk the rest of the way in silence. When we reach the front of the neighborhood, Trevor turns left to head to his place. "I'll try to come by later," he says to us as he walks backward, "If I can't get out, meet me at the entrance tomorrow night by eight. We'll head to the party together."

I give him a nod and turn right, Ashley still tucked under my arm. We stop in front of my trailer and her arms go around my waist, her tits push into my chest. "You wanna come over?" she asks, "My mom won't be home 'til late."

Ashley's been pushing for more, lately. We've been hanging out for a little over a year and in the beginning, she kept asking me what we were. A year ago we were twelve-year-olds that had no business worrying about being boyfriend-girlfriend. I told her that, and she told me I sounded like her grandpa. This past birthday I made out with her for the very first time and she said it changed things. The same question came from her, after that kiss, 'what are we?'

I told her the only thing I could, 'I don't like labels.' A partial truth she believed. What I couldn't tell her was how sick I'd felt all day, because it was another year without my best friend. I had no way to see her or even call to hear her voice. I couldn't tell her how every thought I'd ever had was always about Kit; no matter where we were or what we were doing, it was always Kit. Even while I kissed Ashley, my thoughts were about Kit. I imagined it being her. I even got hard.

"Yeah, I can come over. Let me just go tell my mom." I jog up the few stairs and open the door. I set my notebook on the small table and turn to look for my mom. What I see almost knocks me off my feet.

My mom is on the couch, hunched over, head hanging to the side. She doesn't look like she's breathing. I run as fast as I can to her, knocking the coffee table out of the way. I push up her head and call to her. When I let go it falls back down. "Oh God, Mom. Mom? Mom? Wake up...shit!"

Out of nowhere, Ashley appears. Her movements are fast but steady. She presses two fingers against my mom's neck. "She has a pulse." She puts one finger under her nose. "It's light, but she's breathing." I look at her dumbfounded, she shrugs her shoulders. "My dad's been an addict all my life." I didn't even know her dad was around.

Her hands work the belt, I hadn't even noticed, from my mother's arm. She searches the small table on the side of the couch and picks up something plastic. She pulls the needle from my mother's skin and, very carefully, puts the piece of plastic on it, then sets it on the table. What...the...

There are bright white spots in my vision before everything begins to turn black. "Ryker, look at me." I turn my head to where Ashley should be, I don't see her. "You need to breathe." Inhale, exhale, repeat. My vision comes back to me. "Good boy. I don't need you passing out. I'm gonna go get her some water. Keep trying to wake her up." I nod my head as she walks away.

"Mom…Mom." I shake gently. It doesn't work. "Mom!" My hands grip her shoulders, her head bobs back and forth. "Ash, she's not waking. Should we call for help."

Ashley's at the sink, messing with the faucet. She turns the knob, nothing comes out. She looks at me and frowns. "We can. Is she on probation?"

I grab my hair and pull. "She got off a month ago." It's hard to speak. "She was doing so well." *I can't believe this is happening.*

"We need to try and wake her on our own." She makes her way to me. "Her pulse was good. She must've just taken the hit." She's so calm about all this.

I rub my hand down my face. "How do you know so much at thirteen?" I ask as I continue to shake my mom.

She looks at me from the corner of her eye, grabs an old water bottle near the table and opens it. There's barely a sip left. "I'm fourteen. Like I said my dad's an addict. My mom was too, for a while." She empties what's left of the water into my mother's mouth. "Things were real bad when I was eleven. I'd come home, almost daily, to this site." She says it like it's no big deal.

My chest feels heavy. It's hard to breathe. I may be an offspring of an addict, but getting put in a foster home, with the most amazing parents, had me live a very different life. The thought of having to deal with something like this, more than once, makes me sick to my stomach. *I have to get her to wake up.*

"Mom!" I shout, shaking her harder. "Erin!" The use of her name seems to grab her attention. "Erin...Erin, wake up." Her head falls back, her eyes open a little. I'm kneeling in front of her. I pat lightly on her cheek. "Erin, please wake up." As her name passes my lips, her eyes pop open wide.

Smack!

My hand goes to my cheek, the pain reaches all the way to my ear. *Why would she hit me?*

"What have I told you about calling me by my name?" she says.

I stand up to think. She stands and wobbles.

"I-I...I was just try-"

Her hand comes out to smack me again. I'm able to stop her by grabbing her wrist.

"You're worthless," she spits. "I regret the day I had you. You've done nothing but ruin my life."

She pushes my chest with her free hand. She's too weak and I barely move. Tears fill my eyes. I try my hardest to blink them away. "I was just trying to wake you." My chin trembles as I say the words.

I glance over at Ashley. Her mouth is open, her eyes are wide. She takes two steps backward. A creak in the floor makes her cringe. My mom hasn't noticed her yet and I hope she doesn't. Trevor and Ashley used to come over when we first moved here, to the trailer. One day my mom went off the deep end when she found me with my arms around Ashley. Neither has stepped foot in here since.

"I wasn't asleep, you fucker," she grits through her teeth. "I should've let them take my rights away the day you were born, instead of doing all the shit I've done to get you back." Her words are a chisel, carving pieces out of my heart.

I was born with neonatal abstinence syndrome, a result of my mother's heroin usage during her pregnancy with me. I spent thirty-six days in the hospital, detoxing the drugs from my system. Kit's mom was assigned to my case. She was pregnant with Kit at the time, and once told me I was her first living case in the seven years she'd been a detective.

"Those people," my mother says, "your foster parents." She knows their names. She won't ever say them unless she has to. "They once tried to adopt you. You were six, I think." Her body sways as she speaks. Her tones soft, but laced with venom. "A couple of years after the last time I had custody of you." I was four the last time; her custody barely lasting six months. "When you, Little Fucker, ratted me out to the pigs." Tiny drops of spit hit my face on the last word.

The Brownlee's wanted to adopt me? Heath and Colleen Brownlee, my foster parents, have basically raised me since birth. They're the ones that brought me home from the hospital on that thirty-sixth day. Karen and Colleen have been best friends since college and once Karen knew all the details of my case she worked with child protective services to have me placed. The Brownlee's were already deep in the process of being approved to foster and the time it took me to detox was enough time for them to finish being approved.

I'm standing here looking at my mother. No, she's not my mother, she's just the person that gave me a shitty start to life, and I wonder why I thought things would be different this time. I wonder why I ever thought she would actually hold an ounce of love for her child.

I let go of her wrist and watch her sway on her feet. She sits on the couch and looks up at me through her lashes. With how she looks right now you would never guess how much hatred just spewed from her mouth. I will not respond to her, she's not worthy of my words. I have to get out of here before the walls close in.

As we round the corner of Ashley's home, I look at the trailer that sits two doors down. It's a new trailer, compared to the others. The charred remnants on portions of the small lawn and the blackened concrete of the driveway let me know that Trevor was telling the truth. My fists clench. *Why would my mom move us here?*

Ashley pulls a pack of cigarettes from under the stairs. She pulls one out and lights it. I snatch it from her hand after her first inhale. I study the burning stick that sits between my fingers, wondering how people become addicted to these things...to drugs, to alcohol, to anything. My therapist once told me being born with NAS, and to a mother who suffers with addiction, I may be more susceptible to addiction as well. That scared the shit out of me, still does.

I put the end of the cigarette to my lips and inhale. The smoke barely makes it down my throat before I'm choking. I hand it back to Ashley as I continue to cough. "It gets better after a couple of tries," she says.

"What's the point of it?" I ask, "What does it do to make you want it?"

She shrugs as she takes another drag. "It relaxes me, I think. Honestly, it could just be in my head. When I'm nervous about something or on edge, a couple drags takes all those feelings away." She holds the cigarette before her and studies it, the way I did just a minute ago. "It's not a painkiller or a high like street drugs. The nicotine acts as a calming agent, so in stressful situations, I tend to go for them."

I watch her as she puts it back to her lips and inhales deeply. *Calming agent?* That's definitely something I could use right now after what I just went through, except I know a cigarette won't do the trick.

"Do you have a phone I can use?" There's only been one thing in my life that has been able to consistently calm me. Except she's not a thing at all.

"Uh, yeah. We have a pay as you go saved for emergencies."

"Would I be able to use it?" I bounce on my toes as guilt runs through me for asking. She eyes me suspiciously before tossing the cigarette and heading into her house. I follow close behind her.

"What are you gonna do about your mom?" she asks. She probably thinks that's why I've asked for her phone.

"I don't know." I pace across her floor. "I think someone needs to know. I don't want to be the one to tell on her." How my mom says I ratted on her has really messed with me. My stomach forms in knots at the thought of telling someone.

"Skip school," Ashley says. I stare blankly at her as she hands me the phone. "If you miss enough days the school has to report you. CPS will come and check on things. Then she can't blame you for telling." It's the perfect answer to this shitty situation. I need to figure out if it's the right one.

I dial the numbers I've committed to memory, praying the Carmichaels haven't turned off their landline and that someone is actually home. After the fourth ring dread begins to fill me, however, in the middle of the fifth, my heart dances with excitement.

"Hello?" Her soft-spoken voice meets my ear. She sounds different somehow, older maybe. She's spoken one word, yet I already feel relaxed. "Ryker?"

I blow out the breath that was stealing my words and smile. "How did you know?"

"I didn't. I'm always hopeful, though." I can tell she's smiling too. "Is everything alright?" Kit asks, her tone changing slightly.

"Yeah, I just needed to hear your voice." Her laughter fills my insides.

"How've you been?" she asks.

"I'm good...you?" I hear noise in the background. Her line becomes muffled like she put her hand over the speaker.

"Sorry," she says after a couple seconds, "I moved to the other room."

The silence between us thickens because neither of us knows what to say.

"Ryk," she whispers, "six hundred thirty-five." I know what she's saying, but I stopped counting long ago.

She sniffles...she's crying. My heart pauses and the only way to make it restart is to get to my best friend and hold her in my arms.

"Kit, I miss you so much it hurts." She sniffles some more. I don't have a lot of time left and part of me feels bad for using this phone. The other part doesn't care, because I don't ever want to let go. "I'm making you a promise I intend to keep...I'll be back by your birthday."

As we say our goodbyes and end the call, I'm finally certain on what I have to do. Only fifty-six days to go.

Chapter 5

Kinsley

"Let me have your seven," Ryk says as if he already knows what I'm holding.

I have two cards left and neither is a seven. I grab at one like it is. His smile is of victory while I wear a pretend frown until I say the words that deflate his game ego. "Go fish," I smirk at him as his smile slowly fades. It's funny how this is the one game he becomes so competitive with.

I start to move when he grabs my legs. We're sitting on the couch in his living room. He's facing forward and I'm sideways with my legs draped over his thighs.

"I figured you'd want to pick your own card this time," I say. The cards are spread out on the coffee table. With how we sit it's hard for him to reach them. He looks at me like I'm right. Instead of pushing my legs off he holds them closer and leans over to reach for his card.

It's been six weeks since Ryker and I started dating. Forty-two blissful days of being able to call him mine. On my birthday, after we headed back out to the party, Ryker held me close out on the dance floor. Placing my hand over his heart, he whispered the sweetest words into my ear. *"Do you feel that? Kit, my heart only beats for you. In my darkest of times, you bring me light. When I can't breathe, you are my air. You give me strength and reason, and I need you to know it's always been you. You are the only one for me. Can we make this official? Will you be my girl?"*

Things haven't changed much between us since moving from best friends to boyfriend-girlfriend. Ryker's always been a tactile person. Having a constant need for physical touch to show him he's worthy, loved, has made the transition almost invisible. There are a few things which are completely different and sometimes catch me off guard. The obvious being the kisses, and not just the make-out sessions. It's *all* of the kisses...the pecks to my lips, my cheek, my forehead; the kisses on my neck and my shoulder. Those are probably my favorite because he does them when he's standing behind me and holding me in his arms, which is also new. We've always held hands or walked with his arm around my shoulder, and whenever we sit together some part of our body is always touching, even if it's just our feet. But when he walks up behind me and wraps his arms around my middle, or comes before me, his hands cupping my face before kissing my lips, a fire ignites deep within my belly.

Ryker stares at the card he just picked from the pile. A triumphant smile covers his face.

"Goldfish!" he yells, showing me his pair of sevens before tossing them on the table. I smile at his outburst as I stack the cards in a pile.

"Ryk, can I ask you something?" I focus on the cards, making sure they're all in the same order and straight.

"Always, what's up?"

"Um...well," I hesitate, unsure if I should even ask the question; unsure if I really want to know the answer.

He places a finger under my chin and brings my head up, forcing me to look at him. "Babe, you know I'll answer anything for you, besides, I'm not sure there's much you don't know. So stop thinking and ask me."

"Why do you still call me Kit at times?" He breathes out a laugh.

"A seventeen-year habit is a hard one to break. Does it bother you?" I shake my head. "Good, cause I don't plan on giving it up." He narrows his eyes at me. "Now, out with the real question."

I guess if I had a list of cons about dating your best friend, knowing you all too well would be on it. Good thing I'm not into making lists. I set the cards on the table and pull my legs off his lap, bringing them to my chest. I wrap my arms around my legs and rest my forehead on my knee. Ryker's hand is on my ankle.

"O-kay...how was your first time?" I take a second and work up the courage to elaborate. "I know it's different for guys. Was it everything you thought it'd be?"

"What! I've never had sex. What makes you think that?"

I look at him with wide eyes; his look is perplexed. I've always just assumed he wasn't a virgin anymore with the couple girlfriends he's had.

"Well, there was Ashley..." I name the first girlfriend he had while he was living with his birth mom.

"I was thirteen."

"True. Then there was Kate?" In the middle of our sophomore year, Ryker started dating Kate. She was a senior and they were the talk of the school, even though it only lasted two months.

"I told you everything we did."

"It's just, it felt like there was more you didn't want to say." I shrug my shoulders. "And then there was that rumor." Embarrassment runs through me as heat rushes to my face. Kate was the one to break up with Ryker and the rumor was she'd slept with him, wanting to be his first, only to find out she wasn't. It made me feel sick to hear, and even then I didn't want to ask him what all they'd done, however, curiosity got the best of me—good thing I'm not a cat.

"Kit...Babe," He moves his hand to my back and rubs it. "I didn't mean to make you think there was more. Honestly, it was weird to even tell you the little that happened because to me, you've never been just a best friend. Rumors are just that...rumors." He pauses to make sure he has my full attention. "Plus, I only agreed to date her to see if it would make you jealous." I roll my eyes at his admission. The most devastatingly handsome smile spreads across his face. "Want to know why we really stopped dating?"

My eyebrows reach my hairline as I nod my head.

"So, we were kissing." I cringe. I shouldn't have since I already know those details. It's different to hear now that I'm his girlfriend. "Just bear with me. So, Kate and I were kissing when my brain starts thinking about *our* first kiss. You know the amazingly sloppy one when we were ten?" I smile at the memory. "But then I started thinking about how good our kiss would be now, and just the thought of that is what got me carried away." I'm glad he said carried away instead of groping. "The whole time, in my head, it was you my mouth and hands were on. It wasn't until I moaned out your name that I remembered it wasn't you."

"No you didn't, did you?" I say behind my hand that's now covering my mouth.

"Sure did. She was really pissed at first. Then ended up telling me how she knew all along my heart belonged to you. She just wanted to see if she could make that change, she couldn't. No one can."

I can't imagine how Kate felt. Probably how I felt after hearing they'd slept together. Knowing that even Kate could tell his heart was mine fills me with bliss. Ryker walks his fingers up my arm and then attacks me.

"Oh...my...gosh...Ryk!" My laughter breaks up my words. "Why do you always tickle me?"

I've fallen back into the couch, lying on my back. Ryker's between my legs, his hands a relentless torture. I'm squirming around trying to get away from him when he moves forward some more. I feel him...*there.* A moan escapes me and all movement stops. My chest is heaving, I'm out of breath and for some reason so is he. He leans down and kisses my collarbone, his erection pushes into my groin. He continues with a path of kisses until he's next to my ear.

"I tickle you because your laughter is my most favorite sound." I feel his smile when his cheek touches mine. He continues to kiss me across my face and then presses one to my mouth. Our bodies are incredibly close, and the electric charge surrounding us is about to ignite.

"My parents are going out of town this weekend," I whisper.

"I know," he says. The fire in his eyes is smoldering, causing heat to radiate between my legs.

I grab his face and pull him to me until our mouths connect. As I part my lips, ready for more, the sound of a throat clearing stops us in our tracks.

We scramble to sit up and Ryker smoothly puts himself in a position that hides his arousal. Heath is sitting on the edge of the recliner, his elbows resting on his knees and his hands clasped together. He's looking at us with parental discern and trying to disguise the smirk on his face.

He looks back and forth between us and says, "you two are getting awfully close together out here on the family couch," he pauses and looks directly at Ryker, "I'd hate to witness Frank find you the way I just did."

Oh my god, my dad! Just thinking about him or my mother seeing us, the way we were, sends shivers down my spine. And the fact that they're both right out the back door, where Heath just came from, makes me count my blessings it wasn't them.

Our parents try to get together at least once a week, alternating houses each time. They sit outside by a fire, if the weather permits, and discuss life while drinking wine. They say these nights are essential to their well-being as adults.

Heath opens his mouth like he's going to say more. Ryker speaks instead, "I'm sorry, Dad. Things got a little carried away. It won't happen again."

Heath shakes his head and smirks as he stands and heads toward the kitchen. "Oh, I'm sure it will happen again. Just be courteous of where it's happening at." He retrieves another bottle of wine and turns back to face us. "And Ryker? Don't forget about the many talks we've had."

With that, he heads out the back door. Ryker and I look at each other and laugh. I can't believe that just happened. My parents are actually pretty chill, especially with the type of careers they have. Being detectives—my dad over homicide, my mom apart of the special victims unit—their demeanors have to be cold and calculated. With a single look, my mom strikes terror into the hearts of the criminals she has to deal with. At home, they're calm, cool, sweet, understanding, and very funny. My dad can't seem to take anything seriously, yet I have no doubt the outcome of what just happened would've been extremely different if it was either of them discovering us. Heath and Colleen, on the other hand, know how to diffuse any situation. Heath is always the voice of reason and always really cool. No, I take that back...

Heath is legit.

Chapter 6

RYKER

13 years old

I shove the last bit of clothes I own into my book bag. It's sad to realize that it's not even full. When I first came to live with Erin, almost two years ago, my mom and dad sent me with a suitcase full of clothes. Then puberty hit in addition to a good growth spurt and I quickly ran out of them. Erin bought me a few things here and there at the thrift shops. Even before her relapse money was tight. I guess I never realized how little I actually have.

I grab the pillow from my bed and pull the cover off. The pillow is not what I want with it's ripped, stained, and flattened condition. It's the picture taped deep inside of the pillow-case. It's the only one I brought here, figuring Erin's dislike of Kit was still in full force, and I made sure to keep it hidden so she wouldn't tear it up or throw it away, or do both.

The day this picture was taken, Kit and I were playing outside in her backyard. It was summertime and we were ten, sliding down the slip n slide and swimming in the inflatable pool. We were both soaking wet and in fits of giggles about something that'd happened. At the moment the picture was captured, we were laughing. Well, Kit was laughing. Her hand covered her mouth as her smile lit up her eyes. My focus was on her, my arm slung over her shoulder and remnants of my own laughter left on my face. I vividly remember thinking how absolutely beautiful she was…is.

Kit's always been beautiful to me. That day I could feel something change. Ten may seem too young to understand all there is about feelings, how they are and what they do, however, that day I could've been one or one-hundred and I would've felt the same exact way.

"Ryker, are you finished in here?" Barb asks, "It's time to head out."

I nod my head and glance around the small room, making sure I've gathered everything. Besides my book bag, I've filled one small box with my notebooks and little things I've collected since being here. I never had anything of value. Even if I did I'm sure it would've been sold by now.

Seventeen days of missed school is what it took for them to finally report me to the state. I'm sure it would've been faster, except I was only skipping a day here and there, to begin with. After a few weeks and nothing ever done, I started skipping more. I tried to stay away from the trailer as much as possible at night since Erin's drug habit continued to get worse. Most days she was sleepy and wouldn't know who I was. Every once in a while I caught her in a good mood, a noticeable mood. She would get upset because I was gone so much and cry, telling me how worried she'd been or how sorry she was for the way things were; how she was going to make everything better. I never held her to it since it never lasted long. Four different times she shot drugs into her veins while I was sitting in the room with her, not a care in the world or a regret to be doing something so terrible while her teenage son sat on the same couch. The first time I didn't even know it was happening until the needle was in her arm. I was tired that day, falling in and out of sleep. The second time I tried stopping her I was smacked in the face again. I left and slept at Trevor's that night. The last two times I watched her tighten the belt around her arm, and then bolted out the door. Those two times happened on the same day. That's when I knew I had to do something more. I didn't go to school for an entire week after and only then did the school report me.

I make my way through the trailer and out to Barb's car. She looks at me with tired eyes and a pensive smile. She's been my case manager from the beginning and I think she was hopeful this time would be a new start for my mom and me. In the beginning, so was I.

Chapter 7

Kinsley

My parents called at five this morning, earlier than I normally get up for school. They wanted to let me know their flight landed. They took a red-eye to Myrtle Beach, South Carolina for the weekend. It's their twenty-fifth wedding anniversary and they wanted to do something nice for once since they're always tied down with work.

I went ahead and took a shower and got ready for the day. There was no hope for me going back to sleep anyway. I'm shocked I slept as well as I did with these anxious nerves coursing through me. I apply my mascara and then mess with the rope belt on my dress. It's the last week of April and even though the forecast calls for spotty showers, it's supposed to be a rather warm day.

As I make my way into the kitchen, my phone pings with an incoming text.

Ryker: I hope you're awake and decent because I'm coming over.

It's barely past six o'clock which means he probably couldn't sleep. Ryker hardly ever sleeps. If he gets any amount over five hours we call it a miracle. Yet somehow he always looks refreshed.

Before I have a chance to respond another text comes through.

Ryker: Scratch that. You don't have to be either. I'll be happy to wake you. ;)

Me: Good morning, I am both of those.

Ryker: Dream Crusher.

I slip on my sandals, strapping them around my ankles, and grab my bag off the counter deciding to meet Ryker outside. Just thinking about coming back here later, without the possibility of interruption, makes me nervous and anxious at the same time. *I can't believe tonight's finally going to be* the *night.*

Making my way out the front door, I spot Ryker striding toward me. His brown hair is messy in that just-rolled-out-of-bed kind of way, and he's wearing black shorts with a red Hurley t-shirt.

He takes his time admiring my body. I clutch the strap of my bag, twisting it back and forth. The butterflies within me are already on full alert, ready to take flight at a moment's notice. This day is going to move agonizingly slow.

He takes my hand and holds it in the air. I scowl, but he's not affected. His free hand comes between us and he moves his index finger in a circular motion. *Damn.* I spin quickly hoping it satisfies him—it doesn't.

"Uh-uh," he says, "You need to make that *much* slower." His voice is low, his eyes penetrating. I do as he says making my movements deliberately slow. Once I'm fully turned, I'm greeted with a leisure smile and one word that sets me aflame.

"Stunning."

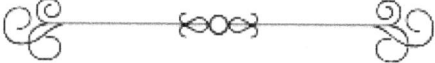

Thankfully, most of the day has flown by. I wasn't sure I was going to survive World History. Being my last class of the day the minutes on the clock seemed to sit still. At moments I was for sure the thing was broken. The final bell ringing was music to my ears.

"So, tonight's the night?" Jenna asks quietly. I look at her through the reflection in the mirror. Her grin is wide and unapologetic as her eyebrows move higher to her hairline. We're standing in the bathroom of the restaurant we just had dinner at, leaving Ryker and Logan back at the table.

"It's supposed to be...I'm really nervous," I tell her as I continue messing with my hair. Those butterflies, who've been hanging out all day, are in full force now wreaking havoc on my insides.

"I think you're supposed to be nervous, at least some. It's a big moment in your life," Jenna says, always wise beyond her years. And she's right, plus I can't blame all the butterflies on nerves. I'm also happy, anxious, and excited.

I stare out the passenger window of my car as we make our way to my house. Ryker's hand rests on my bare thigh, where my dress has shifted. His thumb rubs circles in slow motion—his innocent touch lighting me on fire.

As we turn onto the familiar streets of our neighborhood my phone begins to ring. It's my mom. I answer her call with genuine excitement, waiting to hear how things are going, and relieved that this will be the last time my parent's call for the night.

My mom spends about ten minutes gushing over how the town they're in is so beautiful, and how she and dad are already planning another vacation to bring Ryker and me along with so we can enjoy everything as well. They've always included Ryker in the things we do, even before we were dating.

"I love you," my mom says, to finish up the call.

"Me too," I reply.

My parents know more than anyone the effects those words have on Ryker, which is why we never use them around him. My mom told me, when we were four and he was back with Erin, the day she got the call from

Barb to meet her where Ryker was, she felt she'd failed him. She said she'd made a promise to him, when he was a newborn in the hospital, that she would do everything in her power to make sure he was taken care of. When she'd walked into Erin's trash-filled trailer, and saw the gash above Ryker's eye and how he wouldn't use his hands, she would fight hard to never let him down again. And she did fight hard, which is why it took until he was eleven for Erin to earn back her custody again.

Tucking my phone back into my bag, I notice we're already parked. We're leaving my car at Logan's house, and walking the couple blocks to get to mine.

My attention turns to Ryker, who's staring straight ahead lost in his thoughts. I take this moment to study just how beautiful he really is. I know beautiful is not a typical word one uses when describing the male form, however, that's the word that comes to mind when I look at him. Beautifully sexy is really the best term, with his chestnut brown hair, almond shaped eyes which house the most unique coloring of irises—gray graphite with a thin charcoal outer edge. His nose is long and straight, his bottom lip slightly fuller then the top which acts as a thinking cushion he bites into when lost in thought...like now.

I grab his hand, that is now completely still on my thigh. He looks at me, his stare intense, then attempts a small smile. Something is eating at him and I'm craving to know what. Ryker is not one to ever hold his tongue. Before I can say anything, his words travel to my ears.

"Your parents know we're together."

It's a statement, not a question. I remain silent waiting for him to explain.

"The way you replied before you hung up."

The way I replied? Oh no, I didn't even think about it.

"You know I'll be fine," he says, "if you guys say those words around me. You and your parents should be able to express your feelings whenever you want. Just because I—"

"Don't," I interrupt. He's never brought this up. I'm sure he figured out a long time ago how we don't say them in his presence. It's truly not a big deal. When we were little my parents caught on quickly to us utilizing the word Skittles in place of I love you. After everything that happened they even tried telling me to no longer say those words directly to him. I was too young to understand, however, I remember noticing the way he flinched as I said those words to him, and the way he folded in on himself as if taking cover. That was the last time I ever spoke those words to him.

"Exactly, Kit, just because I *don't* say the words doesn't mean you shouldn't."

I climb across the center console and straddle his lap. I press my index finger over his lips to stop him from completing his rant. His eyes are cast out the driver's side window, while his hands graciously hold onto my hips, keeping me forward so my bottom doesn't press on the horn.

"No more," I say, "I don't want to hear this shit anymore."

Gray eyes flash to mine. The sternness in my features dissipates as soon as I see the amusement scrolling over his. I don't want him to think about things that have no need to be thought about, and I definitely don't want him to think about her—the birth mother that's not even deserving of that title.

I slide my finger from his lips and down his body until I reach the hem of his shirt. I pull up and place both of my hands on his stomach. An intake of air slides through his teeth and I'm unsure if it's from the coldness of my hands or my touch in general. His muscles are taut. His abdomen has begun to take on definition from his vigorous daily workouts. Thoughts of adding a different kind of workout to his routine run ramped through my mind as his strong hands tighten on my hips, deflecting the movement I was about to make.

"Kit," he clears his throat, "I want you...so fucking bad right now, but there is no way I'll have you in a car." A small whine travels up my throat. A chuckle comes from his chest. "Your house is two blocks away. If *I* can wait, I know you can too."

I open his door and climb off his lap. Ryker gets out behind me. We walk hand-in-hand a couple of feet before I decide to take off in a sprint between the houses. I glance over my shoulder and see Ryker shaking his head right before he runs after me. I attempt to pick up my pace. His arms wrap around me, lifting me off the ground. He sets me down and turns me around.

"Don't tire yourself out," he says, "I don't want you passing out before the fun begins." There's no way that could happen with the amount of adrenaline pumping through my veins.

Before I can respond, a loud clap of thunder has me jumping from my skin. The cloud laden sky pours its rain upon us with nowhere to seek for cover.

"Oh-no! I was hoping it wouldn't actually rain," I complain, attempting to cover my head with my bag.

"What? It's just a little rain." He throws his arms straight out to his sides and looks up at the sky.

"A little rain? This is a freaking monsoon!"

Ryker moves in close to me and takes my bag from my hands. The rain tumbles on my head. He puts the long strap over his shoulder making it cross over his chest.

"Hey, I was using that as my shield." I pout.

"Trust me when I say it wasn't helping any, besides I've always wanted to do this." He grabs both of my hands in his and grips them tightly. He extends his arms, pulling mine straight, and begins to walk in a circle. It brings back memories of when my dad would do this with me as a child, except he leaned back to lift my feet off the ground, my little body taking flight. Even though my feet are on the ground now, I still feel like I'm flying.

I tilt my head to the sky and close my eyes, feeling the spin within me. The rain has turned from monsoon to mist, glistening across my skin. We slow down and I bring my head forward. I open my eyes to a smile of content—a reflection of mine.

"Watching you was better than I could have ever imagined."

"You've imagined me spinning in the rain?" I ask with disbelief.

"I've imagined you doing many, many different things in every scenario my mind could create."

My skin flushes. His hands slide against the sides of my neck, his thumbs run along my jaw, and then his mouth covers mine. His movement is slow, fervent, purposeful. A glimpse of what the near future holds.

Chapter 8

Kinsley

My parent's house is a ranch style with a walkout basement. The right side of the backyard moves upward into a hill, shadowing the basement doors from curious neighbors. Ryker's house is a few houses down the street and on the other side so his parents are only able to see the front of mine.

As we make our way inside I remind Ryker not to turn on any lights, "not even the flashlights on our phones in case it shines weird in the windows."

He closes the door behind us then wraps his arms around my waist, standing behind me. "Yeah...good thing your mom has that obsession with keeping the lamp on in the bedroom down here. Otherwise, I would've had to think of a different place for this to happen. There's no way I could even fathom having you naked and under me in the pitch black." I quiver with his words, or maybe it's from the kisses he's placing on my neck.

"She doesn't have an obsession. More like an overprotective-detective-with-a-family kind of th-thing." I stutter on the last word, his kisses driving me wild.

My dad used to work as an undercover agent. I've heard a few stories here and there, but apparently, some of it was pretty heavy. The lamp always stays on in the back bedroom down here. It's the only basement room which has a window you can see from the front of the house. All of our phones, keys, and a few different hidden spots upstairs have a trigger that cuts power to the light. If it's ever off, we go somewhere other than inside this house and contact each other. We also have a code word we use which if said lets us know everything is good. If someone was making us talk we wouldn't say the code word and we would know to find help. Even though it's been years since my dad has been undercover, it still remains in place.

"Am I making you stutter, Kit?" He pushes the strap of my dress slowly off my shoulder.

I turn to face him, pulling my strap back up. I'd rather not get undressed right in front of the doors, even if they only lead to an empty backyard. I grab his face and smack a quick kiss on his lips. "I didn't stutter. I was just making sure you heard me correctly!" I flip around and head toward the guest bedroom when I feel a light smack on my butt.

I look over my shoulder and giggle at his playful smirk. I may have been nervous most of the day, now I feel elated and somehow calm. Giving myself to Ryker is something I know I am more than ready for. He is everything to me. Even if things change for us in the future, this is something I could never regret.

I open the bedroom door fully and am in awe of sight before me. Pink, white, and red rose petals are scattered everywhere. There's a picture frame in the middle of the bed, propped up by the pillows. I make my way over to where it sits and pick it up to take a closer look. It's handmade from wood—three boards glued together with a picture ingrained in the center. The picture is my favorite one and set as the background on my phone. It's from my birthday this year, a kissing selfie.

Words are carved into the wood around the picture. Across the top in capital letters reads Skittles, as though he's shouting out his love for me. Down one side is best friends and R heart K on the other, with a beautiful heart. But, it's what's across the bottom that has me tearing up—my forever, inscribed in cursive.

I press the frame firmly against my chest allowing my heart to wrap around it. Around the love he put into making this for me.

"Ryker, you didn't have to do all of this," I say as I turn to face him. The color of roses rises to his cheeks. *He's blushing! I have never seen him blush.* I set the frame on the nightstand and then wrap my arms around his waist.

"I want tonight to be perfect for you," he says with so much honesty in his voice.

"For us," I correct, reminding him we're in this together. His head nods as a hint of a smile appear on his lips.

I kiss the corner of his mouth as my hands slip under the hem of his shirt. I push up, but the dampness causes it to stick to his skin. Ryker grabs the collar at the back of his neck and pulls his shirt off effortlessly, tossing it to the floor.

Damn.

With a sharp intake of breath, I stop still and just stare. My heart accelerates and I can almost feel the extra blood coursing through my veins as I look at him. The Ryker standing before me is no longer the husky best-friend from down the street who gives me wildflowers and sugary sweets. No, this Ryker is a strong, lithe man who fills my head with lust and my insides with desires. He is the essence of perfection.

I reach my fingers out and touch his chest. It's warm. I place my palm over his heart. The beat is fast, rapid, the same tempo as my own. With the distance between us, I'm able to trace the fine dark hairs on his chest and down his stomach. As my fingers slowly lower, the hair becomes thicker, coarse, and I smile to myself. The Happy Trail, I now understand the jokes.

As I stare into his slate gray eyes, my fingers work on the button and zipper of his shorts. Within seconds they're on the floor. His hands move to the nape of my neck, his fingers slide into my hair. The air around us crackles with electricity as he takes charge. He tilts my head back causing my mouth to go slack and his lips claim mine—the world fades away. He's promising the future with this kiss. A taste of all our tomorrows.

He reaches for my dress, pushing the straps off my shoulders, the belt fastened at my waist keeps it from falling. I pull away and work to untie it. Once it's undone my dress falls to the floor and I unclip my bra, adding it to the pile. All I'm left wearing is my pink lace panties.

Ryker takes a step back, searching every portion of my body. His chest heaves with the intake of new air. His gaze appreciative, approving and ablaze making me feel more beautiful and confident than I've ever felt before.

He clears his throat before he speaks, "God, you're beautiful. There's only one thing that comes close to describing your beauty; the sunset after a warm rainy day, where the clouds are thin and scattered, and the sky is filled with pinks and blues, maybe a little red. Even as beautiful as the sunset is, it still seems dull compared to you." My eyes are half-closed, my legs feel weak. His words intoxicate all my senses. My need to touch him, to feel his skin on mine, is so strong, like a magnets pull to metal.

He uses the pads of his fingers and lightly traces the outline of my face. My flesh raises with tiny bumps as warmth floods my insides.

"Lie down," he tells me, and I do as he says. He sits on the edge of the bed, retrieving a condom from his wallet. I watch him set it on the nightstand and notice a slight tremble in his hand. I sit up and kiss his shoulder, wrapping my arms around his waist. His fingers find mine and slip in between them.

"What's wrong?" I ask, "Are you worried about hurting me?" He pulls my hand up and kisses my palm.

"I'm not worried about the physical pain. I'm going to do everything in my power to make sure you enjoy this as much as possible."

I draw a path with kisses across his shoulder, hoping to bring him calm. "There's nothing to be nervous about," I say.

He turns sideways in my arms and rests his forehead against mine. His lips are tightly pressed together and he swallows twice before speaking, "I can't..." he pauses and takes a deep breath. He rests his hand on the side my face, his thumb caressing my cheek, and exhales. "I can't even say the three most important words that you need to hear before this happens. I can't say them during and I won't be able to say them after." His emotions choke him as he voices his fears. Fears that aren't warranted.

I scoot back a little so he can see my face. I need him to look me in the eyes, to process every single word

I say. I put my finger under his chin and lift up. It takes a moment for him to look at me. When he does I feel his gaze exploring my soul.

"They are words, Ryker, just words. Don't let their meaning hold value over us." I give him a minute to absorb what I've said, but he still looks unsure. I lie back down and pull him with me—I want his body on top of mine. He takes the hint and climbs between my legs. His arms on each side of me, hold the brunt of his weight. "The best ways to show me how you feel is with this..." I point to his chest. "The way your heart races for me." I move my finger to his lips and lightly feather across them. "And this..." I give him a chaste kiss. "Your mouth holds all the power. It wouldn't matter if you never spoke a single word again, because those three stupid little words will never, ever surmount the way you make me feel without them." This time he kisses me. It's a quick peck, yet the smile he gives me when he pulls away makes it totally worth it.

"Even with all of the shitty things that have happened in my life, I thank God every single day for giving me you. From the day you were born until the day that I die, *you* are my forever."

And with that, he tells me how much he loves me without speaking another word.

Chapter 9

Kinsley

The sun shimmers over the clear blue water of the swimming pool as the kids laugh and play, splashing water up on the sides. I observe the area I'm in charge of, making sure everyone is fine, and then take a drink of my water. The humidity is brutal, being the eighth day of July, which is the cause of us being so busy.

I began working here, at my neighborhood pool, as a lifeguard last summer. All my friends started working when they turned sixteen, except for Mandy of course, and I felt I needed something to do, at least during the summer. This year, Ryker's been working a lot trying to save as much as he can for college. Heath and Colleen have a college fund set up for him, except Ryker says he feels bad taking all their hard-earned money.

"Hey Kins, you're up for your break." My boss, Josh, says as he looks up to me from the pool deck. I climb down the ladder then stand and scan the pool waiting for Josh to go up. After he's settled I head to the breakroom. I pull my phone from my bag and see I have five new texts from Ryker.

Ryker: When do you get off work?

Ryker: ?

Ryker: I'm not working a double anymore.

Ryker: Don't you usually get a break?

Ryker: I'm leaving soon. Let me know.

I grab a drink and a snack before sitting down to text him back.

Me: Sorry, you know I can't have my phone out on deck. I get off at 3. What's going on?

I watch the three little bubbles come on the screen immediately. Within seconds, I have another text.

Ryker: Good, I'll pick you up. We'll get your car later.

Me: Everything ok?

Ryker: Yep. Just missing you.

He's missing me, huh? Maybe he wants a repeat of last night.

I'm looking out the window of Ryker's truck. We stopped for a bite to eat before he brought us here to The Field. The Field is a place we discovered when we used to walk the neighborhood as kids. It's a large circle of common ground lined with massive trees. We always thought it was a lost patch of land, as we grew older we figured someone knew about it since it was always mowed. Off in the distance, there's a half-built treehouse we once tried to make. Ryker never wanted to tell anyone else about this place and the two of us couldn't finish it by ourselves. Many times we would come out here and lay in the middle of the grass. We'd spread out to have our space, but our fingers were always connected, our feet overlapped one another, as we let our minds clear of thoughts we had. Out in the middle of the grass is also where we shared our very first kiss when we were ten years old.

I'm not completely sure why he's brought me here now. He's been silent since we arrived, almost fifteen minutes ago. The air in the cab of the truck is cool from the a/c but feels thick from the waves of anxiety rolling off him. His eyebrows are drawn together, his lip between his teeth, and he's gripping the steering wheel so tight I fear it may break. I typically wait for him to start the conversation, however, his emotions right now are beginning to make me feel sick.

"Ryk, what's going on?" I twist my fingers in my lap. It's weird for him not to be touching me in some sort of way, but until I know what's going on I'm going to refrain from reaching for him.

His forehead meets the steering wheel as he takes in a deep breath. "When do you start your period?" he asks, taking me by surprise. It takes me a moment to think of the last time.

"Uh, I don't know. I think in like a week...why?"

His exhale whistles through his teeth and I realize he held it as he waited for my reply. His eyes are shut tight as his knee bounces.

"Ryker, what does that have to do with anything?"

"The...broke...night."

We speak at the same time, his words slipping through the cracks of mine, making me unsure of what he said.

"What did you just say?" I ask.

He squeezes his hands shut and lightly pounds the sides of the steering wheel. A string of profanities comes from his mouth.

I flinch.

He notices.

He turns to me, quickly. His gray eyes, a cloudy storm, wide and apologetic. His hands clasp on top of his head as trepidation seeps through him.

"Kit, the condom broke last night."

The condom broke last night. The condom broke last night? The condom broke last night!

I try to swallow his words. A ball of angst blocks them from going down. My body is weighted, my chest heavy, the sun-filled field begins to turn black. I'm blocked from the path I was headed on, being pulled into a path of uncertainty.

"Breathe," Ryker says in my ear, "Breathe," he repeats, "Kit, breathe, please."

I finally do.

I regain all my senses and realize the weight I still feel is Ryker's arms wrapped around me.

"How?" I don't know why I ask. It seems like a simple question, I know it's not.

"I wish I knew," he says, as his forehead meets my shoulder.

"Why didn't you tell me last night?" Memories of our Friday night play in my mind.

Our parents went to see a movie while we were shopping at the mall. Once we got back to Ryker's we still had about an hour to ourselves. I did everything in my power to seduce him and eventually succeeded. We've only had sex a handful of times since we're hardly ever alone. Plus, his self-control is ridiculous, wanting to wait until I get some form of birth control. Which this is the exact reason why.

"Because my mom texted saying they were almost home. Your face was already flush. I didn't want you freaking out when they got there."

Tears gather at the corners of my eyes, waiting for permission to fall. I let him hold me in silence as my mind tries to figure out where we went wrong, and how he's been dealing with this on his own.

Ryker worries. To the point of making himself sick if he can't talk about it with someone he trusts. His free-spirited, fun-loving nature keeps this hidden from most. It's been said that I'm the only one who can calm him; who can make all of his worries disappear and take away any of his pain.

When we were little he suffered from night terrors which often became intense. There were lots of nights I would stay over at the Brownlees' when my parents had to go out on a call. The first night I can remember, Ryker's night terror woke the whole house. He was screaming and thrashing and crying out in pain. I ran from the spare room to his, finding Colleen and Heath unsuccessfully trying to get him to wake. I couldn't just stand there and do nothing, so I got in bed next to him, wrapped my arms around his body, the best I could, and squeezed. I didn't know what I was doing or if it was even going to work. Once I had a tight enough grip his arms relaxed. I felt his fight begin to waiver. I synced my breathing to him, hoping it would encourage his own to slow down. His strong heart rapidly beat against my arm. I pressed my head to the side of his face putting my mouth next to his ear and repeated 'Skittles' until he was awake.

Whenever I'd stay there again, we would sleep side-by-side on the floor with our fingers and arms interlocked and his terrors far, far away; at least for those nights.

"Last night," he says softly as he lifts his head from my shoulder, "I read that a woman who has a period every twenty-eight to thirty-two days will ovulate between days eleven to twenty-one. That the egg only lives up to twenty-four hours after you've ovulated. If we can figure out what day it was for you, it could let us know if we're in the clear." The information he spouts from memory makes it seem like he just graduated from gynecology school. His knowledge about a woman's menstrual cycle is more than I even care to know.

Tears defy me, staining a pathway down my cheeks. Ryker cups my face, brushing them away. "Talk to me, Kit. Let me know what's on your mind."

"I'm sorry," I say. It's the one thing that comes to mind. He presses his forehead to my cheek.

"Why are you apologizing? I'm the one who's sorry. I should've caught this. I should've inspected the condom. I should've been slower when putting it on. I should've...known."

He's gripping me tightly, so tight, like he's drifting away and I'm the only thing keeping him tethered. Another tear slips down my cheek, this time it's not mine. I grip his hand and turn my head to look at him. My chest constricts as I look at the image before me. Worry, sadness, regret all play like a movie picture across his face. I lean back into him letting his tears mend with mine.

"This isn't your fault," I tell him, as we hold each other and let our worry seep from our eyes.

An hour ticks by as we remain in the same spot, our tears have now dried. I take in a deep breath and notice the air is no longer dense.

"What do we do now?" I ask.

"We wait."

Chapter 10

Kinsley

Every day we waited seemed to bring out new emotions we had to sort through. Often, more than one at a time. After the initial shock of finding out the condom broke, we mapped out my cycle. I was wrong about when I was supposed to start next. Instead of a week, it was actually about a week and a half out. Even then most calculations of when I should've ovulated put us in the clear. We started to feel good about things, a little at ease until I found a site where so many women told their stories of becoming pregnant at all different times of their cycle.

Anger set in at that moment. It was Tuesday morning, I was lying in bed, not wanting to get up and get ready for work. I sent the link to Ryker's phone, even though he was already at work, and then I began searching for ways to make sure I wouldn't become pregnant—I was fifteen hours too late and any other option was out of the question. My anger grew all throughout work. Ryker came to the pool for a swim an hour before I was off and that put me over the top. He works at the carwash and likes to cool off during the summer by coming here. I know that's all he was doing but my brain told me he was just being carefree without a single worry, while I was slowly dying inside. I wish I could say that's where my anger ended. When I finally got off work and we walked outside, Ryker seemed agitated, frustrated even, and I felt it was geared toward me. I blew up at him for being silent and for not opening my door to get in the car. Stupid, I know. When he looked at me with wide eyes, shaking his head as he rubbed a hand down his exhausted face, guilt formed a pit in my stomach. It wasn't until our drive home when he pulled over the truck on the side of the road, got out and screamed into the skies above. I knew then he was feeling every bit of the way I felt.

When your world is tilted on its axis, it's hard to know which way is up. It makes you step back and take a look from the outside. Re-evaluate things from a different perspective. Sure we've talked about kids and having them, how many we want—three. We just thought it would be at a different time in our life. After our careers were already started.

Pregnant or not, I knew the anger boiling inside was not a healthy thing for us, for our relationship. We needed to pull through and focus on the road ahead. So, I had him take us out to The Field where we talked through and channeled everything we felt into one giant, nasty email addressed to Trojan for making a faulty condom. Even though we never pressed send, it sure felt amazing to tell those jerks off.

Two days after I should've started my period, thirteen grueling days after the condom broke, we decided it was time to take a pregnancy test—or four. Ryker's demeanor changed drastically during those two days. He was calm, back to his carefree self, as though we didn't have the weight of a thousand bricks lying on our shoulders. He became besties with acceptance like he already knew the outcome and was at peace with the results. His hands would make their way to my stomach, a grin always highlighting his face. I prayed for his calmness to encompass me, it never did. I know stress can delay your period and the late arrival continued to make me stress. It was a vicious cycle I was trapped in.

Chester City is where we bought the tests, figuring thirty-six miles was a good amount away from running into people we know. The family restroom wasn't the ideal place to take them, but I needed Ryker by my side and there was no way we could take them at home.

Before we started, Ryker pulled me to his chest and held me.

We stayed that way mere minutes before he softly spoke softly into my ear. "No matter the outcome, I'm here, by your side, through every part. No matter what those little sticks tell us, negative or positive, I want you to react how you feel you need to. Don't hold back thinking your current feelings aren't what you're supposed to feel. If you feel pissed and need to hit something, I will be your punching bag. If you're scared and need to scream, I will be your sounding board. If you're sad and need to cry, I will be your shoulder, my shirt will catch your tears. If you're happy and excited, we'll jump with joy together. There is no right or wrong with me. If you need to cycle through every emotion to get to the one that feels the best, then do it. We won't leave until you're ready."

The thought of how amazing Ryker's been through this entire ordeal, makes me smile. As we ride the elevator to the third-floor, excitement bubbles in my gut. I'm almost twenty weeks pregnant, and today we get to find out the gender of our baby.

We didn't tell our parents until it was getting closer to school starting back up. When the pregnancy was confirmed we still had a good month of summer break left, making it easy to stay away from home between working and hanging with friends. I was terrified of being caught alone with my parents, knowing how hard it is to lie to or keep secrets from them. When I told Jenna, Liv, and Mandy they were all equally shocked. I was thankful they didn't voice their opinions on what they thought I should do.

Based on an online calculator, I was exactly seven weeks pregnant when I decided it was time to tell our parents.

My stomachs in knots and my hands are shaking. I'm thankful we're sitting on the couch because I don't know if my legs would hold me. My dad's in the recliner, sitting unnaturally still. My mom's standing off to the side, stepping back and forth from one foot to the other. Colleen and Heath are together on the love-seat, worry clearly written upon their face.

I open my mouth to speak, nothing comes out. I swallow and wet my dry lips. I feel like I'm in a desert with no water. I open my mouth again but Ryker speaks instead.

"We're pregnant." He glances at me and gives my hand a squeeze.

Immediately, my dad's on his feet. His legs planted wide, nostrils flared, his jaws tight, and his fists are clenched. This is the first time I've ever seen him look this way, with anger steaming off his skin. The man standing before us is not the fun-loving, everything's a joke dad I grew up with. Right now he's the man I've only ever heard stories about, his undercover days spent in a motorcycle gang. Right now he fits the image his body portrays, covered in tattoos and muscles for days.

The sound of my heartbeat thrashes in my ears as I give a quick glance around the room. My mom's hand covers her mouth, shock widens her eyes. Heath's arm is around Colleen. They're both watching and waiting to see what will pursue.

Before I know what's happening, Ryker stands as my dad storms to him until they're toe-to-toe. I stand, never letting go of Ryker's hand, and Heath comes up next to me. My dad is seething—his heavy breaths rippling the top of his shirt.

Ryker's back is straight and his shoulder's square. His gaze hasn't wavered from my dad's. He's not trying to challenge him. He also will not cower.

"I take full responsibility for what happened," Ryker says.

"You just couldn't keep your di-"

"Daddy, no!" I cut him off, "This is all my fault. I'm sorry." A sob breaks free from my chest. My dad glances at me briefly before Heath pulls me into his arms.

"Sir, the few times..." Ryker pauses to clear his throat, "I've always worn protection and been extremely careful. At least I thought I was. I'm not sure what happened this time."

He doesn't need to say the condom broke. By the softening of my father's features, I can tell he knows.

"Frank," my mom says. She's behind him with her hand on his shoulder. "Let's take a walk."

My dad doesn't give it a second thought as he turns around and stalks out the door. My mom hugs me tightly, reaching out her arm to pull Ryker in.

"I have to go after him," she says, "everything will be all right. We will all make this work and it will be all right."

"Kinsley Carmichael," The nurse calls my name, ready for us to come back.

I pull on Ryker's hand and follow the nurse down the hall. We stop for my routine vitals—weight, blood pressure, generic conversation—then move into the room.

Dr. Erbs rolls the ultrasound wand over my gel-covered belly. The black and white monitor shows us images of our sweet little baby, filling my heart with joy. Ryker is standing next to me holding my hand, a smile of pure bliss stretched across his face.

"Do you have any feelings on what the sex of your baby might be?" Dr. Erbs asks.

"I think she's a girl," Ryker states with pride.

When the Doctor looks at me expecting an answer, I glance back at Ryker before I tell her what I feel.

"I know we're having a boy."

Ryker's eyes widen in surprise. I haven't specifically voiced what I've thought. When his opinion would flip from one to the other he just always assumed I agreed.

The doctor rolls the wand back and forth over my belly attempting to get a better view when out of nowhere I see it. Or *them* is more accurate.

"Is that?" Ryker asks, "Are those his twig and berries?"

The gleam in Dr. Erbs' eyes confirms his question. "Looks like mom's right. You're growing a beautiful, healthy, baby boy. Congratulations, Mom and Dad!"

When she's done with the ultrasound she leaves the room giving us some time to gather our things. Ryker takes my hands and pulls me into a sitting position. I look at him and watch as a lone tear slides down his cheek, disappearing into the smile that's never left his face.

"We're having a boy!" His excitement is evident even though his words are a soft whisper, "You're creating me a son?"

His hands run through my hair until he's cupping the back of my neck. He kisses the top of my head then presses his forehead flush against mine. His eyes are metallic silver and they're showing me every ounce of love he possesses for me and our son.

"You make me so hap—" The words barely make it past my lips before his mouth crashes over mine.

His tongue slides over mine, hungry with need. There's so much passion floating around in the air that I know I need to stop this before he takes it to another level. This is neither the time nor the place.

I pull away from his lips. His eyes hold me captive. The same elated smile stretches across his face, and three beautiful words fall from his mouth. Words I've only dreamt of hearing again.

"I love you."

I want to tell him I didn't hear him that he has to say it over and over again. I want to ask him to repeat it into the voice memo on my phone so I can keep them forever, just in case he can never say them again.

His hand goes to my belly caressing the small protruding bump that remains bare and I realize I haven't said anything back to him. I don't know if I'm supposed to. Other people in this situation probably would, except this isn't any sort of typical for us.

"I love you," falls from his lips again as he stares at his hand moving on my stomach.

Oh no. What if he's saying it to our son? What if he can only say it to him and not to me? I've always been fine with him not saying those words. With Skittles being the way we express our love for each other, but I feel the hurt forming with the thought of him only being able to tell our son the three words I've always said don't mean anything to me.

Am I selfish? Is it selfish to want those words to be meant for me?

I stand up and pull my maternity jeans over my belly, smoothing my shirt down over the top. I grab my jacket and slip it on and try to keep the tears from forming. A war is raging internally about everything that just happened, about how I should feel. I breathe in deeply then slap a smile on my face so Ryker won't know.

We stop at the bakery to have them make us a cake with the center colored blue. Both of our parents are at my house, waiting to find out the gender.

As we pull into my driveway, I take in the number of cars lining the road. Apparently, our parents invited people over—Ryker's grandparents, Jenna, Liv, Mandy, and Logan.

Together, our mothers cut into the cake revealing the blue inside. The room erupts with happiness and joy, hugs and congratulations. It's only been a month since my parents have come to the acceptance of my pregnancy. With the way they are now one would never know they were ever mad.

Ryker's across the room talking to my father. Their conversation looks intense until my dad pulls Ryker in for an embrace. After my dad lets him go, Ryker makes his way to me and takes my hand. He clears his throat loudly. Everyone's attention turns to us.

"I could never express how much every one of you means to us," Ryker says, "The simple fact you're here, loving and supporting us, during an unconventional time, truly means the world to us." He glances at me as he brings my hand to his mouth and kisses my knuckles. "I've been thinking a lot lately about my first memory of Kit. I'm not sure how far back actual memories go. Whenever I ask others, they can barely remember anything from the age of five. I remember my fourth birthday." He pauses and looks around the room. He grabs his cup from the counter and takes a drink. "I believe everybody here knows about my history with my birth mom, so you all probably understand why I would remember those times, or maybe you'd think I'd want to forget them all together. The bruises and broken bones are not the prominent memories that flood me though. It's the days after. After I'd been to the hospital, was checked out, and bandaged up. After I was reunited with Heath and Colleen—my real mom and dad." His smile brightens as he looks over at them, "The day that's been playing in my mind is when I got to see Kit again, after what felt like ten years apart. Since obviously, six months feels like ten years to a four-year-old. I remember the car pulling into the driveway of our home, the Carmichael's awaiting our arrival at the front door, and before I could fully submerge from the backseat, Kit was running so fast toward me that I thought she would collide into me and topple us over. It wouldn't have bothered me though, not like how it might've bothered our parents. Somehow she was able to keep the speed and momentum, yet carefully and gracefully halt her legs while her arms wrapped around my chest tightly in one of the most memorable hugs ever." His face turns solemn so I give his hand a little squeeze. He looks at me and smiles. "We stood there in that embrace for probably five minutes."

"More like ten," Heath corrects him. Ryker chuckles.

"Yeah, you're probably right. Now, if we would've been older than four, I would've understood every ounce of emotion and every word she was giving me through that hug, and I would've kept all of it side-by-side with the knowledge I was going to marry this beautiful girl one day." He pulls me into his chest and kisses my forehead. I can feel how fast his heart is beating. "That day is also the day *Skittles* became our word. One word replaced the three my birth mother stole from me." He looks at everyone in the room and then looks at me. "I'm happy to say today I've taken them back."

Ryker takes a step back and turns to fully face me. He reaches out, skimming the back of his hand across my smiling cheek, and before I can absorb what he's doing, he's down on one knee before me. A gray velvet box sitting in the palm of his hand.

"Kinsley Mae Carmichael, I've loved you with my entire heart, ever since I can remember, but if you ask our parents, they'll say it was before you were even born. My life has always been spurts of chaos. As soon as you are near, it's serene. *You* create the calm within." He takes a moment and brushes the sweat off his forehead. "I prayed there would be a day I'd be able to reclaim those stolen words, and even though we're young, I need you to know I don't ever plan on going anywhere. I love you, Kinsley. I...love...you. I love our son. I love that you are so caringly creating him for me— for us. You're a stunning woman, my beautiful best friend, my confidant, and already the best mother. I'm excited to see what the future holds. The future I want nothing more than to conquer together, side-by-side." He opens the velvet box and presents it before me. "Kit, will you have me as your husband and do me the honor of becoming my wife?"

I'm nodding my head before I can even speak. Tears stream down my face as he slides the ring onto my finger. He stands and I jump into his arms, kissing him all over his face before landing on his lips, giving him everything I have in me.

This is really happening. I'm going to be his wife!

Chapter 11

Kinsley

"Dash, Dean, Diesel, Dwight," Ryker says.

Everyone left after the gender reveal, even our parents. They decided to have an evening out. Ryk and I are lounging on my bed searching through baby names. I'm propped against my headboard, Ryker's head's in my lap. He's holding the baby name book, reading the ones he likes while I write down the ones that pique my interest.

"Diesel, really? Who names their baby Diesel?" I'm a bit perplexed he even mentioned that one.

We've just finished through the D's and he's probably said a good thirty names already. I've only written down two. Hence the reason we're going about it this way.

Ryker just laughs at me. I know he's thrown in some different names to see my reaction. I normally just ignore them and let him move on.

"I think its badass. It's a big, strong, masculine name. Who wouldn't name their kid Diesel?"

Umm, Okay, he's serious about that one. I guess it's better than Caddock. I'll write it down as a maybe.

I set my pen and paper on the nightstand and grab my glass of water to take a drink. Ryker turns his head in my lap and presses a kiss to my belly. It's not hard yet like a pregnant belly and with the way I'm half laying it looks more like a food belly than a baby belly. It's still super cute when he gives our son attention.

With his mouth still on my stomach, he starts talking to our son, asking him his input on his name. He's been talking to him a lot since reading that your baby can hear you and get used to your voice.

"Hey little man, it's your daddy here. What do you think of these names I've been saying? Did you like Argon?" he puts his ear against my belly like he's going to hear a response.

"How about Beethoven?" pause for the ear again.

"Cleetus?" I'm trying so hard not to laugh right now since he seems to be saying ones I know he was kidding with.

"Diesel? You like Diesel don't you? It's a big, strong name like I know how you'll be."

He puts his ear back on my belly. His smile's as bright as the sun. I'm silently laughing when Ryker suddenly hops up in front of me onto his knees. There are shock and excitement flirting in his eyes.

"Did he just kick me, Kit? Did I just feel our son move for the first time?"

"Yes," I say, looking at him in awe.

He starts bouncing on the bed like a child excited for a new toy. I decide not to tell him how our sons pretty much been doing baby aerobics for the last twenty minutes, or how I'm shocked it's taken this long for him to feel them. Ryker knows I started feeling our baby kick a couple weeks ago and he's tried so hard to feel him too. Every time he'd place his hand on my belly our peanut would stop moving. I found it humorous—he did not.

"You know what this means, right?" he asks, catching me off-guard. He places his hands on my belly, probably hoping to feel another kick. "It means he wants us to name him Diesel."

"Does not," I say through laughter. *He can't be serious, can he?* My laughter quickly dies as his lips press against my neck, giving me feather-light kisses across my chest. When we first came in my room I changed into a jersey knit dress. It's the most comfortable piece of clothing I own and really great for sleep.

Ryker pushes off of me and stands next to the bed. I scoot forward and lay down, watching as he takes off his clothes, leaving his boxers intact.

He climbs on the bed, kneeling between my legs, and takes my left hand into his. He gazes at my engagement ring as his thumb skims over the top. The circle of love he's given me is gorgeous and fits perfectly with our story. In the center sits a round, clear diamond. Circling that diamond are ten smaller ones. Five are colored—red, orange, blue, purple, green—the other five are clear, resting in between each color.

He leans down and kisses my ring. "This ring is perfect on your finger. Made specifically for you, just like you were made specifically for me," he says. His words fill my heart while his love fills my soul. He places his hands on each side of my body as he leans over me, looking into my eyes.

"I'm going to make love to you," he says, "I know we've made love before. This time it will be different. This time it will be what you deserve." He kisses me fiercely, his arousal known. "I love you, Kit." He kisses my neck, right below my ear. "I love you, Kins." He trails kisses along my collarbone. "I...love...you...Kinsley." He kisses me between each word.

Thirteen years of 'I love you' is being spread across my body as he kisses away time lost. Every one of his kisses soaks the words into my skin.

He strips me of my underwear, his boxers come off next. He glides the tips of his fingers across every part of my skin.

"So beautiful," he tells me, "I'm the luckiest man alive."

My cheeks flush with his praise, and the words that have been locked away come spilling from my mouth.

"I love you, Ryker."

The smile he graces me with is exquisite. The most beautiful thing I have ever seen in my entire existence. He pushes into me, our breath is lost to the pleasure.

"Say it again," he demands in a whisper.

"I love...you...Ryker," His movements delay my words.

"Again."

I repeat the same words as he repeats the same movements, somehow filling me more and more each time. He doesn't fill just my body; he fills my senses, my mind, my heart, my soul.

Our gazes are locked together. Blinking is far from my mind. His irises are the clearest I've ever seen and I'm privy to the transformation happening inside. The damaged bits he's kept hidden from the world are mending themselves back together, piece-by-piece. Words that once broke him now make their way to his heart. They wrap around the broken pieces and create a bind that will never keep us apart.

Chapter 12

Kinsley

I wake, feeling amazing with last night's lovemaking still fresh in my mind. Our affirmations to one another have made me feel lighter. The weight which was holding us down is gone. The irony isn't lost on me with the whole situation. On how I've always told Ryker they're just words and don't have any meaning. The way we've been saying it has always been enough, yet somehow the simple fact he can freely say them now makes me happier than ever expected.

I head to the bathroom grabbing my black leggings in the process. This first week of November has been brutal with the cold and even though I'm inside I find it hard to stay warm.

I round the corner to the kitchen figuring I'd see Ryker behind a large bowl of frosted flakes. I'm slightly disappointed when I only find my dad. Ryker's been staying over here a lot lately, and the fact he isn't here now means he went home at some point through the night.

"Hi, Daddy," I smile at him while I make myself a bowl of cereal.

"Hi, Pumpkin." His smile is so big it looks like it should hurt his face.

"What has you so happy this morning?" I ask as I sit next to him at the counter.

"Oh, just you and life in general." he takes a deep breath, "I've been thinking a lot lately."

"You probably shouldn't do that, Dad. Your brain can't handle the torture." I laugh at my own joke as he shakes his head at me.

"You'll have to find better material if you want to thrive like I do with the jokes." He takes a sip of his coffee and stares at the cup as he continues. "I know it's taken me awhile to fully accept what's happening in your life." I stop eating and turn toward him. "It's just, as a parent you envision your child's future completely different."

"This isn't what I envisioned either," I say, trying to mask the hurt forming inside.

"I know. That's not what I'm trying to say. It was just hard at first. Hell, it's still hard when I sit and think about it too much. Your mother and I of all people know life sometimes throws watermelons in your way and you have to leap big or trip over them and smash your face." He always has the weirdest analogies—never taking anything seriously.

"I'm pretty sure it's something about lemons and making lemonade," I say.

He gives me a quizzical look. "Moot point. You say tomato, I say ketchup, and either way, it's one and the same." Reaching over, he takes my hand and gives it a gentle squeeze. "You know me and seriousness. I like to leave that crap at work. What I want to make perfectly clear is how incredibly proud I am of you. You put me in awe of how you've adapted to the watermelons life has thrown your way, facing everything head on and showing the world who's boss. I'm thankful for Ryker too with stepping up and being by your side. You guys make the best team, always have. I know you two have a pretty good handle on things right now, just know your mother and I are here for both of you whenever and however you need it."

He leans in and kisses my cheek, and I can see the tears gathering in the corner of his eye.

"Pregnancy looks beautiful on you, pumpkin. Reminds me of your mama when she was glowing pregnant with you," he says into my ear before I wrap my arms around his neck and squeeze tight.

I throw the covers off my bed in search of my phone. I know it has to be here somewhere. I had it last night. I find it stuck between my nightstand and bed frame. I slide my finger over the screen and call Ryker since I haven't heard from him, yet.

"Hey Babe," he greets.

"Hey. What are you doing?"

"Walking through the aisles of Wally World."

"That's fun," I laugh, "Ryk, why'd you go home in the middle of the night?"

"I didn't leave in the middle of the night. I did wake up at five though, and couldn't go back to sleep. I went home and took a shower and put some clothes in the wash. I just stopped here to grab a couple of things. I'll be there in twenty."

We say our goodbyes and I hang up the phone. My hair's still wet from the shower I took after breakfast so I gather it up and put it in a messy bun on top of my head, and then rummage through my closet for something to wear.

Once summer was over and the pool was closed I started working at a small diner, called Sunflower Diner, off Main Street. The interior transports you back into the seventies era—brown wood panel walls, yellow-gold linoleum, and big giant sunflowers everywhere.

I usually try to wear something to match the theme of the diner. Today I'm not finding anything I like. I look into the mirror hanging on the back of my closet door as my hands glide over my protruding belly, which seems to have grown overnight. Actually, everything looks to have grown overnight. My boobs barely fit into my bra and my underwear only half way cover my butt-cheeks.

I find a firm spot on my stomach, knowing that's where Baby Boy lays, and feel a rhythmic flutter against my palm. "Hi, Baby Boy," I say to my belly, "You must have the hiccups. That means you're growing. Mommy loves you so much." It's amazing how strong your love can be for such a tiny human you haven't even met.

I startle as the door behind me opens. The reflection of the mirror reveals Ryker holding a drink in one hand and a bag in the other. He scans my body, his eyes soaking up every inch before the most breathtaking smile spreads across his face. *I love this man so much.*

After setting the items down on the bedside table, he walks up behind me, his hands slip around my waist until they're settled on my belly. His mouth goes to my neck—kissing, caressing. He makes a path up to my ear and nibbles on the lobe. Everything he does ignites a fire between my thighs and I enjoy every second. *I wonder if we'll always feel this way.*

"I love you, Kit," his words are a violin, composing the sweetest music for my ears.

I pray this never goes away.

"God, you're beautiful. Every day you become more beautiful than the day before," he says.

I smile at him and then kiss him hard. His hands run down my back until they're resting on my butt. He squeezes right before he pulls away.

Ryker sits on the bed as I finally get dressed. Leggings and a flowered tunic will have to do for today. He grabs the bag he brought in and sets it in front of him.

"Did you buy me something?" I ask.

He bites his lip and smiles. "Close your eyes," he tells me.

I tilt my head and raise my brows before deciding to comply. I'm standing next to my bed with my hands on my hips waiting for him to tell me to open my eyes. The rustling of the plastic bag rings in my ears and it feels like he's taking his sweet time.

"Okay, you can open them."

I open my eyes and see the end of my bed covered with a variety of items. There's a large bag of Skittles, three bottles of Smartwater, two Hot Wheels, *one-two-three*-four onesies, and the cutest little boy outfit that has a tie and suspenders printed on the shirt with a fedora hat to match.

"I know it's a bit early for toys," he says, "I had to get these two cars for us. I can't wait to have daddy-son playtime." His face is glowing as he looks at the cars. "And look at this outfit. It's killer, right?" He puts the fedora on his head, "Our kid's going to be such a stud! I'm a tad jealous of how awesome he's going to look in this. I checked to see if they had a matching one for me. I didn't have much luck."

"I'm sure we can find something for you to match him. Then I'll have two studs to fight the girls off of." I step forward and hug him and he pulls me into his lap. He makes my heart melt with how amazing of a father he already is to our son.

"I'm not done showing you everything." He pulls the onesies closer for me to see. "Look at these. Aren't they fucking epic?"

His elation is intoxicating and makes my chest fill with happiness. *I love this man more than words could ever say.* He points to the onesies, one at a time, and reads them to me.

"Sorry Ladies, my daddy is definitely taken."

"50% Mommy, 50% Daddy = 100% cute."

"I only have eyes for Mommy just like my dad."

When he gets to the last onesie, he picks it up and holds it in front of me. The words on it bring tears to my eyes as we read them out loud together, "Every day is a Skittles day."

I turn in his arms and straddle his legs. My hands find their way into his hair. His back's against my headboard and he's holding my hips. His smile is pure and perfect.

"I love you, Ryker Elliot Pritt." I give his lips a peck. "You're an amazing human and already the best daddy to our son. I don't know how I got so lucky to have you by my side."

This time when I kiss him I ravish his mouth. He reciprocates adding sucks and nips to my lower lip, knowing it drives me crazy. His arousal bulges under his very light material pants. He lifts my hips and moves our bodies. I'm on my back now, laid across the items that are still strewn across my bed, he's between my thighs. His hips push into me one time, causing a moan to generate from my body. Abruptly, he stops and looks at me with regret-filled eyes. He scrubs a hand down his face.

"Fuck, we need our own place." He points over his shoulder to my open bedroom door. "Your dad was still here when I came in. As badly as I want to continue this, I won't disrespect him. Plus you have to be at work soon."

I sigh. "You're right." My hand goes to my forehead. "I don't know what's gotten into me. My lady-like actions have completely gone out the window since I became pregnant."

Ryker's chuckle vibrates my chest. He moves off my body and then straightens my shirt.

"Heh, your *lady-like* actions were gone way before you were pregnant." He smirks. I sit up and playfully smack his arm. "Hey, I'm not complaining." He laughs at me some more.

Ryker starts gathering the items he bought, putting them back into the bag. He hands me the Skittles and says, "for old time sakes." His eyebrows are drawn and he smiles at me but it's sad. I can tell there's something heavy weighing on his mind.

He sits on the edge of my bed and fidgets with his hands. "I think I'm going to go see my mom later." I look at him bemused. "Erin," he clarifies. A pit of dread forms in my stomach.

I sit in silence waiting for him to continue because I know he will. He likes to talk through his thoughts. To justify, to his self, his actions on still wanting his birth mothers approval and love. On still waiting for her to be a 'real mom' even though he's already an adult. I used to not understand it at all, part of me still doesn't. Heath and Colleen have never failed in making him their own. They love him unconditionally and provide for him in all the ways a parent should. It used to make me so mad that he would still want anything to do with Erin after every single thing she's done to him, physically and emotionally, but the more he's revealed to me on his thoughts and hopes, the more understanding I become.

"I want to check on her, see how she's doing and tell her in person that we're going to have a son."

Ryker keeps in touch with Erin, more on the phone than in person. He told her over the phone that I was pregnant and she took it surprisingly well, even seemed genuinely happy for us. I know he hasn't seen her in person for quite some time. It always makes me nervous when they do meet up since we never know beforehand how she'll actually be.

"I know she just moved again," he continues, "and I should probably check the place out. Maybe once she knows she's going to have a grandson she may be able to meet one day, it will help her stay clean for good."

His tone holds hope, but I know from all his let-downs it's not much and it's the one thing that stops my blood from running cold as I think about her with my child. I can tell he's been thinking about this for a while, the anxiety rolling off of him is tenfold. Probably one of the bigger reason's he couldn't sleep this morning, amongst all the excitement.

I often have to remind myself that he's still just a teenager, right alongside me. His life experiences have made him always seem older, more mature in a way, but there is a partially broken child still buried deep inside. One which still aches for the approval and unselfish love of the woman who gave him life. Sometimes I think things would be much easier if Erin would've been horrible one hundred percent of the time. If she never had her bouts of staying clean and was never strong enough to earn her custody over Ryker back during those periods, then he wouldn't know what a good mom she could be. The few times she did have him, things were good, so good between them, and even though she always ended up messing it up and hurting him more than she had before, it still gave him too much hope to hold onto.

I slip my hands between his and silently plea for his body to calm. I count to ten in my head, tapping his palm with each beat. It's a ritual we do when needed. On ten we take a deep breath—in through our nose, out through our mouth. I feel his body relax.

When I turned ten I joined Ryker in one of his therapy sessions. At that time in my life, I was just beginning to learn more and more about what truly happened during his stays with his birth mother—the good and the bad. I always knew he'd been hurt, even though things were never explained in detail. The reason I was asked to be a part of his therapy session was not to learn more truths, it was to learn how to manage my effect on him. His therapist realized early on how I was an 'extremely important aspect of his healing and well-being'. Those were her exact words.

She told me she always takes notes when Ryker talks during their sessions, even if it was about the small things like what he had for breakfast or his favorite game to play. After reading through her notes she discovered one common thread amongst them—his best friend. It wasn't even the fact that he talked about me a lot. Since I'm in his everyday life it's hard not to, but he would include me during his darkest moments of life. The ones I wasn't physically apart of. Her next words stuck with me ever since that session, engraving a tattoo onto my beating heart. *'Kinsley, when Ryker is around you or whenever he conjures you in his mind, his anxiety starts to disappear. You bring* the calm within.'

"Would you like me to come with you?" I ask, "I get off work at seven."

It's a rhetorical question since the answer is always the same, he surprises me by saying, "I do want you to go. I just need to check her place out first to make sure it's safe."

I nod my head and grab my bag. He walks me to my car and gives me and our son a kiss goodbye.

"I'll probably be home before you get off work, so I'll see you then, okay?"

"Okay. I love you, Ryk."

"I love you, Kit."

Chapter 13

Kinsley

I got stuck at work with a table for thirty minutes over my shift. They tipped really well which made it worth it. Ryker's not home yet and I haven't heard from him. I'm sure he's fine though. At least that's what I keep telling myself, hoping to ebb the queasiness in my stomach.

My parents made spaghetti for dinner and I was able to enjoy the meal with them. Between their work schedules and mine, I couldn't tell you the last time we sat down as a family to eat. Once my food was inhaled, worry started seeping into my brain and I decided to take a relaxing bath.

I pull on a pair of Ryker's basketball shorts and my precious cargo t-shirt and sit on my bed. I pick up my phone to call Ryker when a text comes through.

Ryker: It's getting late. I'm too tired to drive home. I'll stay here tonight.

What? His text does not make my worry go away, it actually makes it worse. He would never stay at her place. Even though he's eighteen now and can make his own choices, it's not one he would ever choose.

I begin texting out my reply when I decide to just call him. He doesn't answer. I call again. Another no answer. I wait five minutes, okay I barely made it two, and call again. This time his voicemail picks up after the third ring. *Why would he send me to voicemail?*

I text him and ask him to please call me back. No response and no call. My chest tightens. Panic bubbles below my sternum.

I call again...straight to voicemail.

I'm going to throw up. Fear gushes through my blood. Something's not right. I run down the hall to my parent's room, knowing if anyone can make sense of this it's my mom. The door is open and I hear the faint sounds of the television. I walk in and see my mom sitting on her bed watching CSI, one of her guilty pleasures. You'd think to be someone who's actually in the field she wouldn't enjoy watching these shows.

She looks at me and her face changes from amused to worry in an instant. "What's wrong, Kins?"

"Ryker went to see Erin and now isn't answering my calls." I sit on the end of the bed facing her and tell her about why he went to visit and the text he sent me.

"Oh Baby-Girl, I'm sure he's fine. If he was too tired to drive home safe then he made the right choice. I'm sure his phone just died and he probably doesn't have a charger." The confidence in her words should make me feel better, however, the slight crack in her expression tells me she's worried.

"Is there any way you can check on him or even find Erin's new address so we can go get him? Something doesn't feel right mom." She reaches for me and pulls me into her arms. I go willingly, needing the comfort of her embrace. Her hand smooths down my hair in an attempt to ease my fears.

"I'll make some calls. I'm certain he's fine though. You have to remember he's an adult now and will be able to take care of his self if something were to arise." I nod my head against her chest praying she's right.

11:46 pm shines brightly on my clock. The minutes have been slowly ticking by since I laid down at nine-thirty. My mom made a few calls to some friends hoping to get info on Erin's new place. Nothing turned up. The one person she thought for sure would know, Erin's parole officer, didn't answer her phone.

My mom told me she would come get me as soon as she heard anything and convinced me to try and get some sleep. If only it were that easy. Sleep evades me as my silent phone and beaming alarm clock taunt me to tears.

The sound of car doors shutting outside my house breaks me from a daze. Jolting from my bed, I look out the window to see who it could be. There are two men, one dressed nicely in a black button-up shirt and black pants, the other in a Nirvana shirt under a leather jacket, with faded jeans; his blond hair a stark contrast to the black of his shirt. The size of the second man makes me curious to know if he's really tall or if nice dressed guy is extremely short. The difference between the two is astounding.

The men come together and talk for a second before looking toward my house. The sound of my front door opening and closing ricochets through the walls like gunfire. Before I have much thought of anything, my feet are headed out of my room, down the hall and out the front door.

I focus on my mom and dad as they talk to the two men. I observe their postures. My dad is tense, rigid as he listens intently to what the tall man has to say. My mom's relaxed, but her heavily concentrated eyes are focused on tall man's mouth, as though she doesn't trust her ears to properly relay the words to her brain.

My heart is racing. The anticipation of wanting to know what's being said between them grows stronger.

My mother's hand covers her mouth, not before an audible gasp escaped her lips. A gasp that has caused my feet to falter below me.

She spots me as my knees hit the ground. Coarse grass pierces my skin. It doesn't compare to the pain in my chest. Everyone's attention snaps my way, their faces drawn with sadness, pity. My mother's sight connects with mine, and the look on her face has me frozen. Every part of my body is transfixed except for the erratically beating muscle trying to punch its way through the bone structured shield that's always been its protector.

I try to force my lungs to expand, to take in the air that's needed for my survival. They fail me.

My eyes feel like they're bleeding. The liquid seeping onto my cheeks is scorching in comparison to the chill taking over my body. I look at my mother again. Her mouth forms the words, "I'm sorry," and a sob claws its way up my throat.

No, no, no, no this can't be happening. Please God, don't take him from me.

My stomach churns, emptying the contents onto the cold dead grass.

Dry heaves rack my body. A hand touches my back. Distorted images surround me. I want to crawl out of my skin.

Someone helps me sit back on my legs. It's my dad I think, my brain is fuzzy. Hands grip my arms, as words leave their mouth. It's all gibberish to me.

My body rocks side-to-side. The noise is so loud...too loud, and I don't want to hear them. My hands seal tightly over my ears, muffling their sounds.

I won't hear what they're saying.

I don't want confirmation of what I already feel deep down inside.

I can't know what happened to the one person on this Earth who means more to me than anyone else ever could. The one person that I know is being ripped from my grasp before I fully have a hold of him.

My dad pulls my hands down and holds them in my lap.

"Breathe," he says, showing me with his chest how to do such a thing, and then his next words pull me from the agony I feel and start to rebuild the strength I need to carry on.

"Pumpkin, you have to calm down. You have to be strong, for yourself and for your son."

Chapter 14

Kinsley

Three Years Later

"Jenna, have you seen my keys?" I holler into the kitchen, "I think Elliot might have taken them from my purse to play with again. I can't find them anywhere."

I've managed to turn my house upside down in a matter of five minutes searching for my damn keys. I stick my hand into the corner of the couch, the last place I've yet to look, only to have orange sticky goo attached to my fingers when I pull them out. *Ugh!* On days when I have nowhere to go I can find my keys without looking, yet today when I have to get to the courthouse on time they've vanished.

I rush into the kitchen and turn on the sink, sticking my hands under the water. Jenna's sitting at the table drinking a dark green smoothie that looks about as appealing as the goo I'm washing from my hand. Elliot is sitting in his booster seat next to her, scooting his bacon around his plate.

"Yo, Eli," Jenna says, "you can play with your cars and trains, but don't forget to park some in your mouth."

"You silwy, my mouth's not a gwarage," Elliot says, filling the room full of giggles.

I finished my senior year of high school at home through tutors and online courses. I never even knew such things existed. When you have a baby on the way and your life gets flipped upside down your parents find any course of action to help get you through. I'd be lost without them. My friends all stuck by my side as well, but Jenna was there through everything. She is the rock of my new foundation, holding me up and helping me forge forward, and most of the time she doesn't even realize. When it came time for my friends to head off to college I made sure they knew I was alright. Jenna wanted to push everything back for me, I just couldn't let that happen. She went off to study at Mizzou to major in business and minor in personal training. Her dad bought a gym after they moved here and her goal is to be able to successfully run the business and take it over when that time comes. Jenna came home every chance she could get. She made it through one full semester before transferring her credits to the local college where she could still finish out her degrees. She works at a bar called Sage to help pay for college and her portion of the bills.

I landed a position within my mom's precinct when Elliot was four months old. I'm a Criminal Records Specialist, which just means I handle miscellaneous paperwork, clean up case files, input them into the system, and handle subpoenas for specific court proceedings. Tedious work really, however, I'm able to complete the work from home three days of the week, which I'm sure is something to thank my parents for. I've taken online classes to finish my basic courses for whatever degree I decide on pursuing, but I'm taking a semester off currently to try and enjoy life.

A little after Elliot's first birthday, I began looking into options for my own place. My parents were heartbroken by my decision, yet always supportive of me and my endeavors. They knew my decision had nothing to do with them. In reality, I wouldn't be where I am without them.

When I was searching for a place it felt like I was running into a never-ending wall—too small, no yard, wouldn't rent to a nineteen-year-old, too expensive. I was about to give up when a conversation with my dad gave me an opportunity I'll always be grateful for.

"Pumpkin, why don't you let me and your mother purchase a house with you?"

"Oh Daddy, I could never. You two do so much for me as it is."

"That's all part of being a parent, though. We can find you a reasonable house, not too far from here and the three of us can purchase it together."

I'm taken back by his offer. I don't know their finances by any means. I do know their own mortgage isn't paid off yet and they already pay for all of the college courses I've been taking. I'm sure they make a good living. This all seems too much. Plus, I don't know if I can even afford everything that goes into owning a house.

Before I even get a chance to respond, he places his hand on my own and continues in a low tone, "Pumpkin, stop overthinking every little detail." I give him a questioning look, wondering how he knows what I'm thinking. "Remember, Kins, you are a spitting image of your mama, and I know the workings of her brain. Don't worry yourself about everything. It will all work out."

It all worked out which is how I ended up here, owning my own three bedrooms, two baths, ranch style home. Which happens to be three streets from my parents' house. It's technically in a different neighborhood where the houses are much older, allowing it to be more attainable for my budget. Jenna didn't even hesitate when I asked her if she would move in with Elliot and me. In fact, she seemed relieved, since her dad had started dating, and things were getting awkward around their small apartment.

"You're really going to be late if you keep spacing out," Jenna states with amusement in her voice, pulling me to the present. I've been absentmindedly scrubbing my hands, which are now goo free, but raw. I guess I've been doing this for a few minutes too long. Turning off the water, I grab the bright red, sunflower printed dish towel to dry my hands with.

"Your keys are on the new key holder I hung right by the front door," she says, "Remember me telling you about it when I hung it?"

She has a look on her face that might be questioning my sanity...or memory. Maybe it's questioning if I ever listen to her when she talks. In high school, I used to swear Jenna could read my mind. Then I discovered I could read hers too so we came to the conclusion we just might share a brain. Although, after having pregnancy brain, baby brain, and now toddler brain, my thoughts and memory are all over the place. I guess my hearing is too.

"Oh shit! I totally forgot. Sorry J." I walk over to Elliot, giving him a kiss goodbye. "Wait, you knew they were there this whole time as I was tearing this place apart?" Jenna smirks at me.

"Yep, I thought it was funny and it kicked up your heart rate a bit. You can thank me later. Oh and you'll have to clean up when you get home since we're having company," she says nonchalantly.

"Who's coming over?" I ask, my eyebrows drawing together.

"We'll talk about it later. Your moms picking Eli up from preschool today and is going to keep him for a few hours so we can discuss some things over dinner."

Whoa, Jenna never makes babysitting plans for Elliot, not that it bothers me at all it's just something she doesn't do. Whatever she has to discuss must be really important. *God, I hope she's not moving out.*

Jenna gets up and walks to the sink to rinse out her empty smoothie cup. "Kins, don't overthink things. It's nothing bad and I'm not moving out. Now get your ass to work so you're not later than you'll already be."

She doesn't ease my worry much. At least I know our brain connections still work.

Chapter 15

Kinsley

I've made my way through security at the front door of the courthouse and now I'm running, all too slowly, towards the elevator that's about to close. I shout ahead for someone to please hold it, praying whoever's in there has enough common courtesy to press the door open button.

As I watch the doors connect in the middle, creating a barrier of dull metal right as I reach them, I know this is not going to be one of my best days. Usually, I just work at my little makeshift desk at the precinct when I have to report to work, but days such as today, I have to bring a case file to the courtroom for a proceeding that will take place, and right now I'm needing about five more minutes of leeway to get to where I'm going. I would take the stairs, except the navy blue, knee length pencil skirt I chose to wear won't allow my legs to come apart enough to run up the two flights.

While hastily pressing the up button for the elevator, my ears hear the distinct gruff baritone of Lieutenant Jake Grand.

"You know once the button is lit, pushing it more times is not going to speed up the process," he says with amusement in his tone.

Lieutenant Grand works under my dad and if I had to guess his age, I would say late twenties or very early thirties. He has bleach blond hair he keeps closely buzzed and sparkling blue eyes that can light up any room. I've often wondered how he looks when being stern with someone since he could totally pull off the surfer boy image if we lived anywhere near an ocean.

"Yes, I know. It makes me feel better though and anything that can make me feel better right now is a plus."

"Ah. I take it hasn't been a good morning so far?"

The doors to the elevator finally open and I move to the side, impatiently waiting for the current on-goers to file out. I make my way into the four by six tin box as my nose is assaulted by an incredibly bad mixture of old socks and too much aftershave that hasn't had enough time to clear out.

Lieutenant Grand slides in after me, asking if I'm going up to floor three as well. I nod my head and smile as he presses his thumb to the button until it lights up allowing the doors to shut for our ascent.

"How's Elliot? He has to be getting big now," he asks.

"He's really good and yes getting too big. Gosh, he's going to be three soon." Tingles form in my chest at the thought of my baby boy growing up.

"Wow! Three already? Time sure does fly."

The metal box jerks to a halt, the heavy doors taking a second to slide open and then we make our way into the hall. My feet keep moving, knowing I don't have another moment to spare.

"Have a great day, Lieutenant Grand," I say over my shoulder. Before I can round the corner to begin my trek down the long hall to room 305, I hear him call out for me to wait. *Ugh, I don't have time for this.*

I plaster a smile on my face to mask my annoyance before turning to him. "I'm sorry for running off so fast. Its just...I'm really late."

An amused smile touches his lips. His face now looks like it's been kissed by the sun.

"I, uh... well I was going to ask if Elliot likes Paw Patrol as a joke, to lighten the situation, but I don't want to hold you up any longer then needed." He hesitates as I look at him with polite impatience, trying to figure out what my son's interest in cartoons has to do with anything when I've already let him know I'm late.

And then the most embarrassing, horrifying thing that could happen on my already shitty day happens.

He reaches around me, catching me off guard, and grabs my butt. Not in the meathead that just wants to cop a feel kind of way. No, this was more purposeful. His fingers lightly graze a large portion of my rear, yet try not to touch it at all.

Heat surfaces to my face. Everything's moving in slow motion as his hand starts at the crease where my butt and thigh connect then gradually moves up until he reaches right below my lower back.

He stands up straight and holds his hand out before me. My jaw falls slack, my eyes are as wide as saucers, and my heart is racing. *Please floor, open up and swallow me whole.*

Jake is holding a rather large Paw Patrol window cling. The one I put on Elliot's bed after fighting with it to go on straight to his window. I must have sat on it when I was searching for my keys and the static this time of year caused it to stick. *Oh God! I've walked through this entire building and not one person said anything to me.*

"Oh yeah...I knew that was there." I know my face is beet red. I'm going to play this off though as if it's an everyday occurrence, "It's my reminder to go to the party store later for Elliot's birthday supplies." I pray for confidence to fill me to make this believable.

I take a step forward to snatch the window cling from his hand when my foot catches on a rip in the carpet, sending me straight into Jake's chest.

His. Very. Hard. Chest.

Jake's strong arms hold me a moment too long. Somehow, I'm able to control my unease. Gently pushing myself away, I look down and notice the case file, that I so desperately need to get to the end of the hall, is now scattered around our feet.

A deep chuckle rumbles through Jake's chest, followed by the warmest smile I've seen in a while.

"Let me help you get all that up, even if you *meant* to do that too," he says with a wink.

Man, I haven't had a day this rough in a long time.

Chapter 16

Kinsley

I had to circle the parking lot of Sushi Tank two times before I found a place to park. I texted Jenna when I was finally done with work, forty-five minutes later than I should've been, and she told me to meet her here. I sure hope she already has a table for us though, because I'm starving and don't really want to wait in this crowd.

I walk in through the signature neon green double doors and scan the large room, hoping to discover Jenna. As my sight comes across the left side of the room, I spot her waving from a corner booth. I make my way to her and notice an assortment of sushi rolls as well as a salmon salad on the table.

"Oh thank God you've ordered. I'm starved," I say around the Shinko roll I've stuffed into my mouth.

"I see that. You know you can actually bite into the sushi roll? You don't have to shove the whole thing into your mouth all at once," Jenna teases. "How was work?"

"The morning was shit. You'll never guess what happened to me."

I tell her about my embarrassing encounter with Lieutenant Jake Grand and before I can even finish the story she's in a fit of laughter, tears pooling in the corners of her eyes. *Oh no, she better not have.*

"Jenna Marie Tierney, did you know I had that damn window cling stuck to my ass when I left for work this morning?"

She's laughing so hard it's silent, her head bobbing up and down is clear as day.

"Ugh, you bitch!" I say as the sushi roll I was about to put into my mouth busts apart on her head.

Jenna yelps caught off guard and gives me an incredulous stare. As funny as it was to watch rice explode across her forehead, I kind of wish I hadn't wasted a perfectly good California roll.

I dig into my salmon salad as Jenna picks out the few rice bits from her hair. My knee bounces under the table. I'm beginning to become anxious wanting to know what she needs to talk to me about.

"We need to talk about my brother," she says as if on cue with my thoughts.

Jenna has an older brother, whom I've never met before. His name is Caleb and he's four years older than us. I don't know much about him, except he took their mother's death extremely hard. Their dad had to make the tough decision to send him to live with their grandparents when he was nine. That happened right before Jenna and her dad moved here to have a fresh start in life.

"My grandparents are getting up there in age," she says, "They've been in the process of selling off acreage of their farm, but are still keeping enough to have a continuous cash flow. They have a few farm hands that take care of everything. They've been with them so long, they're practically family." She's absentmindedly shredding her napkin into pieces on the table. "To be honest, they could really sell everything and be set for ten generations to come, but the farm is their life. It's where my gramps was raised and where he fell head over heels for my grams. Where they raised my mom and my brother, so I understand the history and attachment to the place." A small smile appears on her face, her gaze unfocused with the memories playing in her mind.

I love these rare moments when she gives me a glimpse into her family life. She's very tight-lipped about so much, the best secret keeper I've ever known. If it's not her story to tell she doesn't feel she has a right to tell it.

"That's good for them, right? It's about time they semi-retired and relax." I know nothing of the farm life, except the tidbits Jenna's shared with me. It seems to be extremely hard work and takes so much discipline to take care of the animals and the crops on a daily basis.

"Yeah, it'll be good for them, except I don't think they'll actually retire though." She picks up her glass and takes a sip of her water.

"What's Caleb going to do now they don't need him? Has he only worked on the farm?"

I'm not sure if she actually talks to her brother still or if she gets her information from her grandparents. The last I'd heard he was shutting her out.

"Actually, if you can believe this, he became a police officer two years ago. Gramps recently told him it's time to move on and create his own life, so he accepted a promotion." She looks at me from the corner of her eye as she takes another sip of her water. "The promotion is transferring him here to your parent's precinct."

"Wow, that's awesome! I'm super happy for him. Do you think with him being close you'll be able to work on your relationship?"

I would love to see Jenna have a good relationship with her brother. Even though I know their mother's death tore them apart, I believe it's never too late to try and mend things.

She smiles at me brightly, with pride in her eyes. "I'm happy for him too!" Her expression changes as she looks at her hands. "We can hope for the best on the relationship part, but I have no expectations, really. I'm just happy he's found his way and has something that seems to make him happy."

"Is he going to stay with your dad?" I ask.

Jenna clears her throat and her focus lands on me. "That's what we need to talk about. You know their relationship is...well, strained." Strained is an understatement. "Which means Caleb will need a place to stay. Just until he can find one of his own." She said the last sentence in such a rush it came out mumbled, yet I still understood what she said and what she's implying.

Her eyes dart around the restaurant then down to the smartwatch that's always around her wrist. She clicks the side, lighting up the screen, then looks around the room again.

"Okay, where do you propose he stay? All of our rooms are full and the couch wouldn't be the best place with Elliot running around."

Elliot's not much of a morning sleeper, and by that I mean I'm lucky when he sleeps in until six in the morning. We have a basement. It's very unfinished with its concrete walls and open rafter ceiling. There's a rough in setting in one of the corners for another bathroom to be added, and a small room with shelving units for storage.

"I was kind of thinking he could stay in the basement. He's really handy and offered to finish out the bathroom and maybe build some rooms instead of paying any kind of rent. I don't think he will be here too long. Either way, it would be a great thing for the house."

She does make a good point. Having my basement somewhat finished only adds value to my home. Regardless if he fixes up some of the basement or not, I could never say no to Jenna, especially when it comes to family.

"Jenna, of course, he can stay with us." I place my hand on top of hers. "Why do you seem so nervous about all this?"

She gives me a bright-eyed look. "Because he's coming tonight."

"Oh! Well...I guess he'll learn what kind of slob he's living with," I say as I think about the disastrous shape I left the house in this morning.

"Nah, I cleaned it up. There will be plenty of days to break him into your hot mess." I roll my eyes at her devious smile.

She clicks the side button on her smartwatch again, illuminating the screen, and then scans the room again. I give a quick glance around the room as well, wondering what she's looking for, but find nothing.

Before I can ask if Caleb's meeting us here she says, "since your parents are keeping Eli tonight, we," she motions her finger between us, "are going out."

"Nope, not going to happen," I say as I shake my head back and forth. I turned twenty-one yesterday and already spent the evening with the people I love. I don't go out. I have no desire to, which she knows. But, how did she know my parents are keeping Elliot? They just asked me over the phone on my way here.

A hand runs over my shoulder catching me off guard. I turn and find Mandy, Liv, and Trex standing next to me.

"No way!" I exclaim, "What are you guys doing here?" I jump up and hug each one of my friends.

Mandy and Liv are finishing up their third year of college, and Trexton is working on his Masters. I don't get to see them very often, but I'm their biggest cheerleaders. When I do get to see them I try to soak in as much as I can.

"Our baby's twenty-one!" Mandy says as she claps her hands together.

"It's about fucking time," Liv adds loudly, generating enormous amounts of unwanted attention.

I used to think the attention was a big reason Liv spoke the way she does when in reality, she could care less if people are watching or listening, and what they think of her never crosses her mind. I'm sure growing up with four much older brothers doesn't help, it's just the way she is, which is also why she's going to make one badass lawyer.

Nervously, I look down at my wringing hands and decide to embrace the argument I'm about to ensue.

"I can't go out," I say, barely above a whisper.

"It'll be okay, Kins," Jenna says, trying to reassure me.

Glancing at each one of my friends, I try to communicate with my eyes what my mouth won't open to say. Unshed tears build up in the corners. I look at the ceiling to keep them at bay.

Jenna wraps her arms around me and rests her head on my shoulder. "One night of fun isn't something to feel guilty about. All Ryker ever wanted was for you to live life to its fullest and be happy while doing so. Plus, you know if he could, he would be with us making sure we had the best party of our lives, especially for your birthday."

Jenna's voice is soft yet firm. She has a way of making me feel wrapped in velvet and kicking me in the ass at the same time. I look between the beautiful faces of my best friends and smile as Jenna convinces me to go.

Chapter 17

Kinsley

I'm standing at the foot of my bed, staring at the outfit Jenna picked out for me to wear. It's a stunning black dress, however, almost looks too small for my curvy motherly figure. Studying it, I figure my only realistic option of getting this scrap of fabric on my body is to step into the top and slide up.

The majority of the fabric is made of spandex, allowing it to slide up my body effortlessly. The hem lands just above the middle of my thighs. The neckline is low and wraps into small lacy sleeves that sit off my shoulders. It has a built-in bra encompassing my breasts giving the best illusion of nice, full, plump cleavage.

On the floor are red stilettos which I would normally protest against since I don't wear heels very often, however, she made sure they have straps. The straps crisscross over the top of my foot and circles around my ankle before securing in a clasp. I always feel better when heels have some type of strap keeping them connected to my feet so they're not slipping off and tripping me up.

As I'm securing my first heel in place a knock on the door sounds, followed by Trexton's husky voice.

"You decent?" His question floats through the air as he pushes himself through the door, obviously not waiting for an answer.

"Geeze Trex. It's a damn good thing I wasn't naked...for your sake." I look up from my shoe and see him just standing there, still in my doorway, gawking at me.

"Fuck, Red. I was going to say that I was hoping to catch you indecent, however, the sight before me just might be better."

His words cause heat to rise to my face. Trexton is such a tease, always making me blush.

"So this club we're going to, Sage, am I dressed up enough for it cause this dress you're wearing makes me feel very casual."

I laugh as I look him over because as long as I've known Trexton, I've never seen him in anything other than Gucci or Louis Vuitton tailored suits unless he was working out or in his football gear. His father believes in dressing for success and to him that even meant during school, however today, Charles Trexton Newton IV is not dressed in a suit at all. He's wearing a black t-shirt fitted to his lean muscular body with a black jean jacket that has different zippers and buckles all over. He's paired it with tight-fitting dark jeans that end into black combat boots.

Trexton looks good...okay, okay, I may be downplaying how he looks right now so let me rephrase. Trexton looks hot; scorching, on fire, burning me from standing too close to him...hot. All the black he's wearing makes his crystal blues shine brightly and gives you a very delectable Trexton ready to be served on a platter.

Mr. Newton's been grooming Trex to follow in his footsteps since birth, and although Trex has done everything his dad's asked of him, most people always knew there was something more, something *edgier*.

When I kissed him on my seventeenth birthday he had a tongue ring. Now he's added diamond earrings in both ears, and a silver hoop lip ring smack dab in the middle of his plump lower lip. Definitely not the look you imagine when thinking of someone on the brink of their masters in finance and business.

"No, I'm probably way overdressed. Jenna work's there and it's owned by hipsters who opened it a couple of years ago. They do a lot of theme nights and even opened a store next to the club where you can buy or rent outfits for the theme. You don't have to participate in the theme nights. They do give a discount on drinks if you do though," I ramble off while looking at myself in the mirror, wondering if I should change.

"Hmm, that's actually interesting and a really good business plan," he responds as he walks up behind me.

Placing his soft hands on my shoulders, he turns me around to face him. "Red, stop worrying about things. Ryker would agree with me that you look painstakingly beautiful and he as well as the rest of us just want you to truly enjoy yourself for one night. That's all we ask."

I look down at my hands and take a deep breath. All of my energy goes into raising Elliot and working hard to provide a great future. I guess one night of being selfish won't hurt. Plus, he's spending quality time with my parents.

"Hey," Trex says as he puts a finger under my chin and pulls my face up to look at him, "You good?" I nod my head. "Cool. Want to see my new ink?"

I nod my head again as he slips off his jacket. Intricately detailed lines of a full sleeve tattoo start on his right shoulder down to his wrist and there are beginnings of one on his left.

I knew he had a couple of tattoos before he left for college. They were very concealed so his parents wouldn't know, well mainly his dad. Now he's showcasing them as if he's part of an art exhibit and with how beautifully done these look, they should be a part of one.

"Wow, Trexton! I'm speechless. The work on you is exquisite," I say as I admire everything, "Now I understand why you seem so different today. You seem more relaxed and not just with the clothes you're wearing," I pause as I'm met with a quizzical look. "Trexton, you're finally able to wear your own skin."

His megawatt smile appears, letting me know I'm indeed correct.

Chapter 18

I scan the open floorplan of the bar I was told to come to when my focus is intercepted by the stunning woman moving in the middle of the dance floor. Many people surround her, yet I can tell she's alone—at least for the moment.

My stomach hardens and my chest constricts. I'm well aware that I'm starting to feel jealous...irritatingly jealous of the music coming from the speakers. The way the rhythm flows through her effortlessly, sensually, as though it's a soft wave caressing the shore.

I've never been jealous of an inanimate object before. Hell, I don't recall being jealous of anything, not since I was a boy. It's a weird feeling for me, foreign even and very unwelcome. I want to be the music. I want to be the song, the rhythm, the beat, the melody. I want to be the lyrics pouring into her ears, whispering sweet promises into her soul.

Want doesn't satisfy the description of what I'm feeling right now, it's more of a need. I *need* to be those things.

The tight black dress she wears showcases her curves perfectly and those fuck me red heels make my jeans feel a bit tighter as I think about doing just that.

My feet move me until my body is pressed against the beautiful stranger that has captivated my attention; my front flush to her back. She doesn't flinch, or jump, in the slightest like I thought she would. Instead, her body molds into mine almost as if we're two halves of one whole.

The thought of her having someone she might be waiting for crosses my mind. It's gone before my hands have time to hesitate on their path to her hips. Hips which are perfect and comfortable for my hands to hold onto. Her brown hair wisps just above her shoulders with what looks to be a natural wave running through the strands.

The back of her head connects softly with my shoulder and I can see her mouth move with a few words that are drowned out by the music. The way her head lays exposes just enough skin on her neck making my mouth ache to have a taste. I wet my lips.

The song has switched to the next. The tempo much faster than the last, but our ears haven't relayed the information to our brain. Our bodies continue the slow grind they're currently in, lost in the melody of their own tempo.

Not that I'm complaining at all.

She holds a tall skinny glass in her left hand with about a third of the reddish tint liquid left. I put my hand on her shoulder, skimming my fingertips down the length of her arm until I reach her hand. I pull the glass from her grip. She willingly lets it go. I touch the cool glass to my lower lip and tip my head back emptying the last bit of the contents down my throat.

It's sweet and has a cherry flavor. It's exactly how I imagine she'd taste.

Bringing my head back down, my eyes land on someone standing in front of us. She's pissed, fuming, as she shoots daggers at my head.

Before I have a moment to think, I feel the beauty I'm pressed against completely freeze. I don't even think air is moving into her lungs.

The woman shooting daggers at me has moved her focus to the frozen statue in my arms. Her expression instantly softens. She looks to be speaking to her with her eyes and I'm unsure of what she's saying.

The next ten seconds happen quickly as the front of my body feels cool from the lack of her warmth pressed against me. I watch the beautiful stranger, which feels weird to call her now I've gotten to know her body, throw a hand over her mouth like she's going to be sick. She hasn't looked at me and I'm uncertain if she will.

Not sure why I want her to look at me anyway, I doubt it would stop her from running away as she's doing now.

Two girls run off after her. Before I can move to follow suit a guy with an evil smirk on his face appears out of nowhere. He looks like it would be the highlight of his night to throw a few punches my way.

I straighten my stance causing my chest to puff out and acknowledge his glare. *If this mother fucker is ready to take me on, I'm game.* I've got a good couple of inches on him. Even though his body's leaner than mine, I can tell he's got muscles hiding under his shirt. It would probably be a good, fair fight between the two of us, but judging by the fancy names embroidered on his tailored clothes, he doesn't have the history using his hands the way I do.

I'm actually hoping this douchebag is the beautiful stranger's boyfriend so I can pound him a couple extra times for leaving his girl alone. When you're lucky enough to have a woman that looks and feels like her, you don't leave her to the wolves of a dance club. Not even for a second and I had her a good five minutes.

Chapter 19

Kinsley

I can't believe I let some guy put his hands on me, let alone dance up against me. What the hell was I thinking or better yet why wasn't I thinking?

I knew coming out and drinking wouldn't be a good idea. I honestly can't even say the alcohol I've consumed is what fogged up my ability to brush off the last guy. There've been a handful of other men who have hit on me and even came up and attempted to dance with me, however, every time I had no issue telling them to get lost. After like the fifth guy who tried, Trex came to my rescue *claiming* me as his.

Trexton became my knight without shining armor and we danced for a few songs. I had a blast laughing at his attempts to not step on my toes, but I didn't want to get in the way for him. You know, in case he was looking for a hookup and by hookup, I mean time alone with Liv. Trex and Liv have a history together, not a dating history. A history nonetheless and even though they like to pretend no one knows about it...we all know.

Mandy and Liv were off dancing with some really good-looking identical twins, while Jenna was behind the bar talking to her boss, Thor. As our drinks became low, Trex offered to hit the bar to grab us another. I was feeling good, the alcohol in my veins making me feel weightless and sexy. Two things I haven't felt in a very long time, so I decided to continue dancing by myself.

I don't believe it'd been a full minute of Trex being gone before I felt the man's body flush against mine, his large hands expanding over my hips. He didn't startle me in the slightest and deep down I knew it couldn't have been Trex. It's like I felt the man's presence near me before ever feeling his touch. *Ugh*, that's stupid to even think, because how do you feel someone's presence when you don't even know who they are?

I'm at a loss for an explanation as to why I felt so comfortable with him, in his arms. Why was I drawn to him, molding our bodies into one? And why did I dance with him for so long?

I'm nauseous and regret fills my insides to the brim. I close my eyes and silently count to ten, inhaling deeply.

I'm just going to blame the buzz of the alcohol for the response of my traitorous body.

When I noticed Mandy glaring at the man behind me, I sobered up in an instant. I ran to the bathroom hoping to chase away the last five minutes only to have panic induced dry heaves set in.

Liv was at my side within seconds pinning my hair away from my face. She began reassuring me everything would be okay, "Don't beat yourself up over this. It's natural for our bodies to have cravings, to give into the want and need of another's touch, especially if you've lacked it for years."

I know she was trying to make me feel better, except all it did was make me feel sad and lost and ashamed. Once Trexton came barging into the packed-full women's restroom, I knew it was time to suck it up and head back out there.

It was just one innocent dance with some guy, some stranger I don't even know and will never see again. The best thing I can do now is to ignore it ever happened.

Chapter 20

Kinsley

Ignore. Seems like such a simple word—refuse to take notice of or acknowledge: disregard intentionally. Sounds easy enough, except it's not. Ignoring is not easy in any way, shape, or form. Especially when your best friend walks over to the booth you've decided to sit in, to do the said ignore, with the man that was a part of the situation you're attempting to ignore.

What. The. Actual. Fuck.

My back tenses as my mind searches for all the reasons she'd bring him over here to our table. I shouldn't know what he looks like, but of course, it wasn't just my body who betrayed me out on the dance floor, my curiosity became the best of me as I was running to the restroom, creating the urge to turn my head to catch a glimpse of the man I left behind.

The man who is now standing before me.

If I were a different woman I could explain to you how incredibly attractive he is. How the way the lights of the club make his eyes look as black as the hair on his head. His attention is bouncing around to each person sitting near me, but never actually landing on me.

If I were a different person I could describe to you how his thick eyebrows arch in the best way over his deep penetrating eyes. How his nose is straight, encased by cheekbones that are not too high, not too low, but overall perfect.

If I were anyone else I would tell you how the sharp, angled edges of his jawline reveal strength and masculinity. How his mouth is almost crimson in color with a sinuous upper lip that rests over a generous lower one.

I glance at him, taking him in some more. He has large, broad shoulders, and although the white dress shirt he's wearing doesn't quite reveal what's hiding underneath, I can feel the hard, contoured lines of his body as if they were still pressed up against me.

The contrast of his height next to Jenna's petite five-foot frame makes him look like a giant. If guessing on his height by where my head laid on his shoulder when we were dancing, I would say he's probably six foot two.

This man has a smoldering presence, and as I move my focus to the people surrounding him, I realize I'm not the only one who notices.

Men want to be him. Women want to be with him.

I pin my gaze on Jenna, questioning without words why on earth she would bring him here. Her look is deeply apologetic.

"Hey guys," she says, and then bites her lower lip. Her eyes dart around the entire table before landing back on me. "*This* is my brother, Caleb."

Chapter 21

Caleb

Kinsley's eyes close tightly for a few seconds as she takes in a deep breath. Her hand goes to her chest, fingering the lace at the top of her dress. She's biting the insides of her cheeks, her mouth a perfect pout, as she looks at Jenna. When she finally looks at me she forces a smile on her face. I told myself I wouldn't look at her when I came over here, which was working out at first. As soon as my sister told everyone who I am, I couldn't stop myself from wanting to catch her reaction.

I break my gaze from her by downing the rest of my beer and then decide to use my empty bottle as an excuse to get away. The tension surrounding me feels like a vice grip on my neck.

"I'll be right behind you," Jenna says, never taking her attention off Kinsley. *Fuck! I can't believe that's her.*

It wouldn't bother me at all if Jenna just stayed here with her friends. I feel like I need to re-balance myself after being thrown off kilter and I'm sure there are plenty of women here who would love to help me do just that.

As I'm ordering a Jack and Coke, Jenna steps up beside me and orders two shots of Patron. I squint at her, she just laughs.

"This is your welcome-to-your-new-home shot," she says.

Yeah, my new home. A change I'm so far regretting.

The bartender places my drink and our shots in front of us and I lay a twenty down on the counter.

"Hey Thor," Jenna says to the man behind the bar, "this is my brother, Caleb. Thor is the owner of this fine establishment here."

"Owner and Jenna's boss," Thor says, reaching his hand to me and winking at my sister. "It's nice to meet you." I grab Thor's hand, giving it a brisk shake.

"Don't let him fool you," Jenna says, "I'm the only boss around here." The smirk she gives Thor makes me wonder if there's more between the two. As Thor walks away I don't give it a second thought.

Jenna throws back her tequila, no salt, no lime, and not even the slightest grimace comes across her face, which both makes me proud and concerned.

After she sets the glass down she looks at me from the corner of her eye and says, "Wipe that overprotective brother glare off your face." She faces me, giving me her own glare. "You haven't been around long enough to earn that role." The sharp edges of her words stab into my chest even though they are very much deserved.

I throw back my own shot and down the glass of Jack and Coke. I order another round and a beer hoping it will help me forget this unfortunate night.

I only lived with my sister for the first five years of her life. I'm almost four years older than her, three years and nine months to be exact, and I moved in with my grandparents' right after I turned nine. She was a cool little sister from what I remember; only annoying some of the time. I don't know if our age difference or just her being a girl made any sibling rivalry obsolete. We didn't fight like what I assume normal siblings would.

When my parents told me they were having a baby, I remember being so excited to be a big brother and didn't care if it was a boy or a girl. I was ready to have a live-in best friend and someone to protect.

After the accident happened, I went a little...crazy, to say the least. The feeling of being able to protect anyone vanished with my mother that night out on old Highway 23.

I couldn't keep my shit together. I was hurt, angry, enraged, destroyed. I lashed out any way I could. I needed an outlet I didn't have. In reality, I may have had access to whatever outlet I needed, I wasn't sure of what it was to know. I was only nine for fuck's sake and a nine-year-old doesn't know what to do when death slaps him in his face.

My dad tried so hard to help me, pushing his grief and mourning aside to allow me time to get through mine, only nothing worked for me. I was sinking quickly into the depths of the darkness I had never experienced before.

After starting a fight every day for a full week, the last day I started two fights within an hour, the school didn't know what to do with me, so they threatened expulsion. I was only in the fourth grade and pissed they hadn't threatened expulsion with the first fight. My school didn't take any type of fighting lightly, but when the death of the crazy kid's mother was looming over everyone's head, they tend to let some things slide, until it couldn't anymore. What they hadn't realized was expulsion was what I wanted, or maybe they had realized it and that's why it took five days of fighting for them to react. On my last fight, they finally took action, only it wasn't with expulsion. I wish they would have expelled me. They did something worse, in school suspension.

Isolation in a classroom with only me and a teacher spells out disaster.

Even though I was in a regular size classroom, it might as well have been solitary confinement in a six by two jail cell. It was a living hell, one that, if I would have been in any sort of right mind, would have actually made me never fight again. Except I wasn't in the right state of mind and this wasn't a jail cell. Fortunately for me, unfortunately for Mr. Riggs, the Fox Elementary art teacher as well as the high school's head football coach.

Kind of a contradiction, I know, and by the mere size of him, you would've never guessed art as his major, but instead an NFL linebacker.

What he wasn't, though, was not a guard manning my jail cell to keep me in and he wasn't a presumptuous person either. He didn't presume I would attempt to take my built up anger out on him. In reality, he was right to think I wouldn't. What thirtysomething man would ever think a prepubescent scrawny, short nine year old boy, even one full of complete rage would catch him off guard by picking up my entire school desk—the heavy, old, industrial ones where the desk portion has a compartment to house all your belongings and is attached to the chair by a metal bar—and chuck it at him.

It hit him, not the way I'd imagined it to, which was over the head knocking him out. That shit was heavy, it hit him regardless. I wasn't successful at hurting him or the chair, my success was where I wanted it the most...expulsion.

My dad was at a loss and couldn't handle me anymore, or he wised up. He sent me to live with my Gramps and Gram about one hundred miles west from here. It was only about sixty miles from where we used to live.

My dad and Jenna moved six months after he sent me away. It was as though he had to escape from the things which reminded him of my mother and put even more distance between us.

I was already a little nervous about living with Jenna, even if it's temporary. I might have just made things awkward for all of us.

I hate myself for trying to claim Kinsley for the night. The only thing I can do now is to play it cool as if nothing ever happened. When Jenna told me I'd been dancing with 'my new landlord,' as she put it, I felt kind of relieved and a lot pissed. Relieved that my sister isn't actually the nagging cockblock I was beginning to tell myself she was but pissed I'd ever promised to keep my hands off her best friend. Technically, I already broke my promise, except she can't be mad at me since I didn't know it was her.

I know very little about Kinsley. I know she befriended my sister when they were little and they've been close ever since. I know her last name is Carmichael since her parents are detectives around town and I know she has a son, which is one of the main reasons Jenna moved in with Kinsley, so she could help with the boy when needed. Other than that I know nothing more. I've never even seen a picture of Kinsley to know she was the drop dead gorgeous woman who was in my arms. I wonder if I would have known it was her out there dancing if it would've stopped me from moving in on her.

Jenna throws back the shot I ordered and then puts her hand on my shoulder. "I'm going back to the table. You good?" I nod once before she gives me a hug. "Welcome to your new home, Big Brother. Let's just forget what happened earlier and enjoy the rest of the night."

"Yeah, sorry about all that. Obviously, I didn't know who she was, otherwise I wouldn't have touched her at all."

The words taste like a lie as they leave my mouth and I know things are *not* going to go as I'd originally planned.

Chapter 22

Kinsley

This last week has been interesting, or maybe not interesting at all depending on who you ask.

I drank only water after I had the mishap of dancing with Jenna's brother. I was actually able to enjoy the rest of the night with my friends.

I'm not sure where Caleb ended up running off to, nor do I care. He never did re-join us after his trip to the bar. In fact, I haven't seen him since that night.

When I went to pick up Elliot on Saturday morning, I noticed the truck which had been parked in my driveway the night before was no longer there. Elliot and I hung out with my parents all day, and on Sunday I took him to the zoo since it ended up being a really nice day.

Part of me wonders if Caleb decided to move elsewhere. The few male items I've noticed in the hall bathroom, and the fact his truck is always parked here when I get home from work, has let me know he's still here. Even though we work opposite shifts, it seems odd to me that two people can live under the same roof, yet somehow our paths never cross.

My work's been pulling me in between my office and the courthouse the last three days due to an increase of caseloads, and it's been wearing me thin.

This morning I dropped Elliot off at the parent's day out program he attends twice a week and now I'm sitting at my kitchen table finishing some items up on my laptop which need to be turned in today.

As I finish typing the last page I'm working on, I pick up my coffee cup that's sitting next to my laptop screaming my name. I put the edge of the cup to my lips and take a moment to admire the bouquet of flowers sitting in the middle of the table. I saw them when I first came in but didn't take much notice. They are fresh and vibrant. There are a few tiger lilies amongst a beautiful mixture of wildflowers which look like they came straight from an open field somewhere. The bright colors make a smile involuntarily spread across my face as I scan through them all...blues, oranges, whites, yellows, purples, and reds. Reminds me of when Ryker would pull some out of the common grounds behind my parent's house, handing them to me with a bag of Skittles and his signature smile.

Before my thoughts get carried away they're interrupted by Caleb entering the room. He's only wearing basketball shorts. The sweat dripping from his neck seems to contour every muscle in his back.

He heads straight to the counter holding the coffee pot and opens the cabinet directly above to pull out a cup. He pours his coffee into the cup then adds a pinch of sugar before taking a drink.

As he stands there, with his back to me, looking out the window sitting over the sink, I wonder if he didn't actually notice me sitting over here or if he's a master of avoidance.

He begins to move his body, turning himself around, so I take this moment to put my coffee cup back to my lips and take a really long sip, even though the contents are nearly gone.

I don't want to be the first one to say something, because I don't know what I should say.

"Good morning," he says as he leans against the counter.

I stutter over my words as I try to give him back the ones he just gave to me. Placing my cup down on the table next to my computer I clear my throat before I proceed to speak again, "You work the night shift?"

I cringe at the words falling from my mouth since he's aware I already know the answer.

"Yeah, I get off at six thirty. I like to go for a run as soon as I get home, to get it out of the way."

That explains the lack of shirt and the sweat which is still taunting me as it moves down his chest.

"Are you off to bed now?"

The smirk playing on his lips makes my brain replay how my question may have sounded. I don't want him to think I'm being a bitch who's implying he needs to go to bed, but I definitely don't want him thinking I was insinuating anything either.

"S-sorry," I stutter, "I'm just not sure how your schedule works with your hours."

"You're fine, Kinsley. I stay up till about one thirty then sleep until eightish when I have to get ready to do it all over again."

My mouth morphs into an Oh, "I don't think I could stay awake that long if I worked nights."

"What's the difference between nights and days? Regardless if the sun is out or not, there's not much difference when it involves a work, eat, sleep schedule. You don't go to bed right after you get off work, right?"

I nod as the blood rushes to my face. *I'm such a dumbass!*

"Makes complete sense," I tell him as I wonder why I never thought of it that way. "I guess I always think about how I wouldn't be able to stay awake my entire shift, let alone hours after. Hell, some days I would love to go straight to bed after my work is over."

"Who says you can't? It's your life. Don't you get to make the rules?" Caleb says, as though it's that easy.

The smirk is back on his face before it disappears behind the coffee mug. After he drinks at least half or more of the contents inside, he nods his head toward the table I'm sitting at and says, "flowers, for you."

"Oh, nah. Jenna probably brought them home. I'm not actually sure where they came from." My hand reaches out and touches the petal of the blue daisy sitting in front. *They are really beautiful.*

"It wasn't a question," he says.

"Huh?"

"The flowers are for you. It wasn't a question. I was informing you."

"Oh." My vocabulary seems to lack immensely with him around.

I wonder how Caleb knows these flowers are for me and who they could possibly be from.

"I stopped by the store to grab some milk on my way home," he says, "and these beauties were sitting there calling out for someone to take them home. They reminded me of you, and Jenna told me your birthday was the day before I showed up last week." He explains as he stares at the arrangement in the center of the table.

Pulling my cup to my mouth, I notice there's barely even a sip left. *Dammit, I'm already out of the one cup of coffee I allow myself to have.* I go through the motions of taking a drink, acting like I have more than the sip left, before giving him an awkward thanks.

"It's also an apology for what happened Friday night." His words bring forth the pressure in my chest I don't want to feel.

My head turns towards him, my eyes meeting his for a very brief second. Before I can get out any words to let him know he should forget it ever happened, he continues, "If I'd known you were my sister's roommate, I would've never come near you."

His words are a confession I should be happy to hear. Instead, they toy with my emotions. I should feel relieved by them, so why do they make my chest ache instead?

Chapter 23

Caleb

I didn't show up to Kinsley's house until Saturday afternoon and thankfully only my sister was home. I only had an hour before I had to leave for work and I wasn't ready to face Kinsley.

After everything happened at the bar I found myself a cute little honey who ended up being a nice distraction. We headed over to a hotel room she'd rented for the weekend which gave me high hopes she doesn't actually live here. I don't need to begin anything when I came here for a fresh start.

I'm happy to say nothing even happened between us since somewhere in between leaving the bar and arriving at the swanky hotel, she became obliterated. That's not my kind of show. I helped her into her bed just in time for her to pass out. I used her bathroom to take a quick shower and opted to sleep on the turn-out couch. I didn't want her to wake up next to a complete stranger in her bed and freaking out.

I thought about calling an Uber to take me to my sister's place. I'd forgotten to get my key from her and it was already two in the morning. I didn't want to wake anyone. Plus, I really needed the distance to try and figure out a how to clear my mind of the way Kinsley felt in my arms.

It's been seven days now since I moved into this house, my temporary landing spot, and I've only seen Kinsley twice. The morning I brought her flowers and last night as I was leaving for work.

I got to meet Elliot Monday morning after I got home from the hardware store. Kinsley had to work so Jenna had him for the day. Elliot is probably the cutest damn thing I've ever seen in my life, with his sandy brown hair, and chubby cheeks.

I'd gone to the hardware store as soon as they opened for some two by fours and six by eights to build some walls in the basement. I stayed up all night Sunday night so my body would become acclimated to my new schedule and I spent the entire night mapping out different things I could do in this basement.

I told Jenna I would work on it and make it less unfinished as my thanks for their hospitality. What she doesn't realize is I have a need for this kind of thing. I need to be working and utilizing my hands and brain or I sometimes fall back into the past and become trapped in the darkness that lives there.

When I walked in the front door, on Monday, with some of the pieces of the wood I bought, Elliot came bounding up to me like he'd known me since the day he was born, even though it was our first time meeting.

"Hi, Caweb. You have big wood!"

That was the first sentence to come from the tiny human's mouth, and I damn near choked on my spit. He's been by my side ever since, at least when he's home and I'm awake. For some reason, he likes to hang out with me. He's helped me build some walls, we eat lunch together, and he asks me every question his learning brain can come up with. For not even being three yet the kid can sure talk your ear off, and he doesn't hold anything back. I'm finding I enjoy his company.

It's seven fifteen in the morning and I just stepped out of the shower. It's the weekend so I don't have to work, but I don't know what anyone else around this house has planned.

As I pull my clothes on I hear the pitter-patter of tiny feet running down the hall. Three small knocks sound on the bathroom door.

"Caweb! Is that you? Are you naky?" Elliot asks through the door.

This kid cracks me up. As I'm getting ready to answer, I hear another set of footsteps come down the hall joining him.

"Elliot Ryker," its Kinsley and she's using what I assume would be her 'mom voice'. "We don't ask people if they're naked. And didn't we talk about not bothering someone when they're in the bathroom?"

I suppress my laughter as I tug my jeans up my damp legs, forgoing a shirt since I didn't bring one in here anyway. Turning the lock, I grab the handle and open the door right as Elliot responds to his mother, "Mommy, I didn't bover Caweb, I asked a question."

I decide to chime in before the little booger gets himself in trouble. "Hey, Buddy. As you can see, I'm not naky." I crouch down to his level and notice his mother staring at my bare chest.

"Do you wear pants in shower?" Elliot asks

"No. Do you?" I respond.

"No way! I wouldn't be able to pway with my wight saber."

Kinsley covers her face with her hand as she shakes her head back and forth. Her reaction confirms that I already know what he's talking about, but why not play dumb.

"You have a lightsaber? So cool! Does it actually light up?"

"No siwly," he giggles through his words, "it does someting better...it grows super big when I pway with it." The biggest smile moves across his face like it's the best toy ever.

Kinsley's hand is now over her mouth. "Oh my gosh," she whispers with wide eyes.

"That's pretty cool Elliot. Can I tell you a secret?" He nods his head enthusiastically. "That's *your* special sword, and you want to make sure you keep it all to yourself. Don't tell anyone about it and never, ever show anyone or it will lose its special power."

Elliot soaks up every word I say and then he starts to look a little worried. Figuring he's worried about telling me, I assure him it was alright to tell me this one time, "but you shouldn't ever talk about it again."

"Otay," he says as he runs off to his room— probably to check if his lightsaber still works.

"Oh my," Kinsley says, "I'm so sorry about...all that. Thank you for handling it the way you did. I don't know if he would've listened to me on why he shouldn't talk about his lightsaber'."

"It's not a big deal at all, you know since I have one of my own," I say with a wink.

She rolls her eyes at my lame joke and I don't blame her for it.

As I make my way down the hall, I turn and walk backward. "Hey, Kinsley? You're raising one hell of a smart, witty, cute kid."

Her cheeks turn pink as Elliot comes racing out of his room, back down the hallway.

"Caweb, Caweb! Will you come to the party store and to my soccer game with us today?"

"Oh honey, I'm sure Caleb has to sleep, he worked all through the night," Kinsley attempts to explain to him.

"Is that true Caweb?" he asks me with sad drawn eyes.

"It's true. I did work through the night, except I don't plan on going to sleep until later so I can do all those things with you. Well, only if it's alright with your mama."

We both look to Kinsley with puppy dog eyes. She looks between the two of us before spouting out, "Oh, alright. We have to go now or we won't have time to get everything done."

So off we went.

Chapter 24

Kinsley

I wasn't expecting to have company with me today. It's always just been me and Elliot when going to the party store to pick out his decorations, even though the last two years he wasn't old enough to understand, it was still just the two of us. Yet, Caleb's made the journey fun and interesting, to say the least.

Elliot ended up picking Rusty Rivets for his party theme. It's a new kid show where they fix and build things. I didn't even know he liked that show since he doesn't watch it much. He told me Caleb's been teaching him how to use tools and showing him how to build things, which is probably the real reason for his choosing.

Elliot's seemed to really take a liking to Caleb, which I'm not quite sure I'm completely comfortable with. I just don't want him to get so attached and used to having Caleb around our house since his stay is only temporary. I know he'll still be around town, but he won't be seeing him every day or even multiple times a week like he does now. I think I'll have to have a talk with him about our living situation later.

Elliot's soccer game went about as well as a bunch of two and three-year-olds running around a field kicking a ball is supposed to go. They don't actually have winners at this age. It's more to learn the fundamentals of it all. Caleb was amused watching him run around the makeshift field. My mom, dad, Colleen, Heath, and Jenna were all there to cheer on my little man as well.

The parents all got along with Caleb really well. My dad's met him once at the precinct. My mom works in the city now so this was her first time. My dad, Heath, and Caleb stood next to each other on the sidelines carrying on a conversation practically the whole time.

After the game ended, Colleen suggested we all go over to the local pizza buffet for dinner which worked out great since it's Elliot's favorite—and secretly mine.

My mom and dad took Elliot for the night after he begged and pleaded for them to. He said, "I miss you soooo much and Caweb works me wike a dog." An expression I had to laugh at coming from my child, which in reality is nothing new. The shocked look on Caleb's face made it even better.

"So am I going to have to call child labor law enforcement on you for working my minor son like a dog?" I ask Caleb, humor lacing my voice.

He's sitting in Jenna's recliner, while I sit on my tan leather couch. The television's on but there's nothing good to watch on a Saturday night while the rest of the world is out enjoying the weekend.

"I can't believe he said that," Caleb responds, "Where does he come up with half the shit that comes out of his brilliant little mouth? He's the one who wouldn't stop pestering me until I showed, named, and explained every tool I've been using to him and how to use it."

"Apparently I missed some fun times while I was stuck working at the office. What on earth have you been building and where?" I inquire.

"Well, I told y'all I would work on the basement and try to finish it out for letting me stay here for a bit."

"Oh yeah, I completely forgot. You really don't have to do that. It's no biggie that you're staying here and it's not like you're in the way or anything," I tell him so he doesn't feel obligated to continue working on my basement.

"I've only thrown up a couple walls. I mapped out some rooms Y'all can turn into a playroom or more storage after I leave. I figure I'll try to finish the bathroom also."

"Oh crap. Speaking of building things, I just remembered I have some of Elliot's birthday stuff I need to work on." I get up and head to the kitchen closet where I stored the bag of supplies.

Caleb makes his way into the kitchen and grabs himself a beer from the fridge. "Do you want one?" he asks, holding up the bottle so I can see the kind he has.

"No thanks. I don't care much for beer. I'll just pour myself a glass of wine in a minute."

Opening the bags, I start taking all of the items out and lay them across the table for easier access.

"What are you making?" Caleb asks.

"When Elliot picked out Rusty Rivets I started looking through Pinterest for some cute decoration ideas. I found these cute little fleece tool belts I'm going to make. I also want to make a birthday sign to hang."

Caleb's leaning against the counter eyeing all the stuff I just set out. Leaving him there, I run down the hall to my room and retrieve my container of craft supplies which holds my good fabric scissors, glue gun, and other items I've picked up at the stores when I feel a need to be crafty.

I make my way back into the kitchen where Caleb is now sitting at the table. He's working on cutting out the stencil for the tool belt I printed, and there's a full glass of wine sitting on the table in front of where I was sitting.

I set the container down and take a seat. I place my hand on the stem of the glass and bring it to my lips, as I watch Caleb continue to cut on the paper. His eyes catch mine for a split second right as the cool liquid begins to pour into my mouth and down my throat.

I set the glass back on the table and take a second before looking back to Caleb. His usually dark brown eyes are almost black, just like the first night we met. His gaze falls to my mouth as my tongue darts out and moves across my bottom lip, retrieving the moisture which was left behind from the wine. His stare turns heated creating flames which lick across my skin.

What the hell is happening? I can't let this happen.

Diverting my eyes quickly, I begin to fiddle with the construction paper I'm going to use to create the birthday sign for Elliot's party. Caleb reaches his hand out and touches my cheek, his thumb runs along the corner of my mouth. His movement causes me to startle and flinch away from his caress.

When I look back at him trying to figure out what he's doing, there's regret and apologies written within the lines drawn across his forehead.

"I'm sorry Kinsley. I didn't mean to scare you. It's just... you do this thing...with your mouth," he pauses, taking a moment to determine his words and stare at my mouth some more. "I think you're biting the inside corners of your lips."

Another pause, maybe for confirmation from me. I know I do this. I didn't realize other people could tell, and I don't understand what he's getting at now. I barely nod my head, just enough for him to continue.

"I'm sure you do it more subconsciously than not, however, when you do it, your lips form into a pout." I watch as his Adam's apple moves down and back up when he swallows before the next sentence spills from his mouth. "I'm having a hard enough time convincing myself I don't want to kiss you, but then to see you...with those lips, pursed and ready to be pursued, it makes me question why the hell I'm convincing myself to begin with."

His unforeseen words paint an expression of surprise across my features yet send sorrow coursing through my veins.

Chapter 25

Caleb

We've had a great day today and it scares me a bit how my thoughts are contemplating different ways to be able to have more days like this, more days spending time with Kinsley and Elliot.

She'd started avoiding me after the shit I spouted off last Saturday night, and it made me think I would never be able to have her friendship again if I ever had it to begin with.

I knew I made her uncomfortable, so I feigned exhaustion and went down to my bed for the rest of the night. In actuality, I really was exhausted from being up a solid twenty-four hours, but there was no way in hell I was going to fall asleep after everything.

I gave her the space she seemed to need, at least until I couldn't handle not being around her anymore. Or maybe it was until I worked up the courage to say something to her, which lasted until Tuesday.

She was coming out of the laundry room with a basket of clothes in her hands. I was standing in the wide doorway leading from the kitchen to the living room. She looked like she wanted to bolt as soon as she saw me, so I knew I had to be quick with what I wanted to say.

"So, can we just pretend I didn't say anything Saturday night and go back to how things were before?" I ask her, praying she'll give me an answer.

She hesitates. "How were things before?"

"Friendly, non-awkward, less avoiding."

"Well, then it's a good thing all I remember from Saturday was some delirious rambling from the exhausted state you were in," she responds with a cocky grin, and things have been perfect ever since.

Now we're at the start of Elliot's birthday weekend and I'm looking forward to enjoying it in its entirety since I took tonight off work. I skipped my run this morning. It tends to amp me up so I opted for six hours of early sleep instead.

Kinsley took Elliot to his school for a few hours so he could share some birthday treats with his friends. I figured waking up at one o'clock would be a good time so I could get ready for the day and go with her to pick him up. Unfortunately, though, I never relayed my plan to Kinsley and wasn't aware she was going to pick him up early, so to say opening my eyes and seeing Elliot, standing at the edge of my bed, scared the absolute shit out of me is putting it lightly.

He was standing there being eerily calm and quiet, just staring at me, even after I jumped a bit and a gruff sound came from my throat. Definitely not one of my finer moments.

After Kinsley put Elliot to bed for the night, she asked me if I would want to watch a movie with her. Of course, I said yes. To be honest, though I haven't watched the movie at all. Hell, I don't even know what movie she chose to put on.

I'm sitting in the recliner rather than the couch. I didn't want there to be any possibility of our bodies coming into any kind of contact, even if it was just our toes.

She's sprawled out on the couch, legs crossed at the ankles, and one arm placed behind her head, causing her shirt to rise up just enough to tease me with a glimpse of the soft skin of her stomach. Her breathing has evened out, and I know she's succumbed to the pulling of slumber.

I like being here while she's asleep. It gives me the opportunity to take her in, to completely absorb her features.

Her sandy brown hair is splayed across her arm and the pillow beneath her head. Her long lashes are resting on her cheeks, her lids hiding the fact that the shape of her eyes are like a full moon and the color is from an artist's masterpiece, as if he started with a golden brown then splattered different hues of green across them. She has a small round-button nose and a perfect set of pink pouty lips.

Who wouldn't want to have more with this stunning woman? I don't know how she doesn't have every guy in this neighborhood, in this town, knocking down her door for a chance, an opportunity, to be amongst her presence.

I see the way other men look at her. It's not always just with lust filled eyes, wanting to sack her in bed. Majority of them look adoringly at her like they just need the right opportunity, the perfect place and time to make their unforgettable move causing her to envision them as a potential suitor worthy enough to give them her time of day.

It's the same way I look at her, I'm sure of it.

Kinsley is a force of nature. A beautiful, uninhibited force created by Mother Nature herself. I've seen her at all hours of the day and into the night. With makeup and without, in hole worn pajamas as well as dressed to impress, with food on her face or shirt or both, and right after a shower—always dressed, unfortunately for me.

It doesn't matter how she looks or what she's wearing, she can make a grown man cry with her beauty alone. Then you add in her sweet, soft, tender voice which caresses you like a thousand count satin thread sheet on your body, the determination and confidence always coursing through her veins to take on the world, while also reaching her arms around the globe to hold onto it in the mothering way she does.

Certain aspects of Kinsley remind me of my mother; at least the parts of my mother I still remember. I remember looking at some of my friends' moms, and always wondering if mine was truly as beautiful as my eyes lead me to believe or if everyone saw their parents in a certain way.

My mother's personality was loud and vibrant, full of laughter and love. She could walk into a room full of grumpy, hating life, old people and within minutes have each and every one of them smiling, laughing, and praying for more time on this earth, or maybe just more time with her. I think it's one of the main reasons her death was so hard on me. I knew I would never get that back. There could not possibly be another person out there like the one who was taken too quickly from me.

Man oh man, how wrong could I be, because she happens to be lying less than two feet from me.

As I sit here, continuing to study every detail of what creates Kinsley. Studying her like I'm studying for a big exam I'm about to take, the sound of footsteps nearing me catches me off guard; my body stiffening in response.

"Jesus, Jenna! You scared the fucking crap out of me." I whisper-yell as I try to calm my heart. I look back over to where Kinsley lays to make sure she didn't wake.

"Why aren't you at work?" Jenna asks while she takes in Kinsley's relaxed, sleeping form.

"I took off to help with Elliot's birthday party tomorrow. I didn't want to be overtired since Fridays can get a little hectic at night. What about you? Last call isn't for another four hours."

"Same. Well, I went in early then convinced Thor to cover the rest of my shift for tonight and Tanya is taking my shift for tomorrow."

I don't know why it didn't dawn on me that my sister would take the weekend off from the bar since she's practically helped raise Elliot. My eyes follow Jenna as she moves over to the couch where Kinsley lays, and takes the blanket off the back, laying it over her body.

Why didn't I think to do that?

Kinsley begins to stir and I watch her as she shifts her body from the supine position, turning to where she's facing the back of the couch, her right hand underneath her face, her left hand coming out of the blanket to rest on her hip.

Oh. what I would give to be either of those hands. I mentally kick myself for not sitting my ass on the couch when she was putting Elliot to bed. She could be using my body as a pillow right now.

A throat clears beside me, making me realize Jenna's sitting next to me in the other recliner.

"I hope you're not doing what I think you're doing," she states, flatly.

"I guess it depends on what you think I'm doing," I throw back her way in the same tone she gave me.

"Well let's see, from the doorway where I stood for a solid two minutes *after* I opened and closed the garage door, open and closed the door leading into the house, and walked through the kitchen, none of which you heard, I watched you," Jenna pauses before her gaze locks onto mine. "You never once moved your attention away from her."

Leaning forward, I place my elbows on my knees and take an interest in my hands as they clasp together. I don't have a response for my sister, or at least one she would want to hear. I don't know what I'm doing. It's only been two weeks since I officially met Kinsley, and even though we've hung out quite a bit this past week, I still don't know anything about her, yet somehow I feel as if I've known her my whole life.

Jenna lets out an exasperated breath. "Has she told you anything?" I give her a blank stare. "Anything about her past or anything about herself at all?" she clarifies.

I don't even have to think about this one because even though we've spent a good amount of time together, neither of us has talked about ourselves. Our conversations tend to revolve around Elliot and occasionally our work.

"What is there to know, Jenna? We all have pasts." She knows what I'm getting at. She was there when our mother died, except she was five and barely conscious. There's one part of that dreadful night which her and our father don't know about. One part which still haunts me in my sleep at night.

"I don't know if you've learned this about me yet. I'm not one to share other people's stories, so I'll just say this..." Her eyelids close as she breathes in deeply, holding it for a few seconds before allowing the oxygen to expunge from her lungs. When her eyes reopen they're filled with sadness and what looks to be regret. I don't know what she's about to say and she's kind of making me nervous.

"That woman right there is *the* strongest, bravest woman you'll ever meet in your life, only that will not always be the case. There will come a time where she's going to shatter before our very eyes. Shatter into a million or more pieces—heart, mind, and soul. When the time arrives she will need someone patient, determined, and stronger than she is to slowly and meticulously put all those pieces back together, and I'm sorry to say this, Caleb, I just don't see it being you."

Jenna's words slice through me, opening me bare to the elements surrounding me. I will not show her how they affect me.

My body's decided that sitting here, between them, is too painful anymore, so I stand up abruptly and cross the room toward the front door.

"Wow, Jenna. Thank you so much for telling me how you truly fucking feel about me." She mumbles my name to try and stop my words. Her attempt falls on deaf ears as I continue, "You know, there are things about the past—the part we lived in together—you don't know about. I've kept it to myself to protect you and even dad. You've always thought I just couldn't deal with our mother's death. There's more to it, yet you always think you know everything. Just because you don't share other people's stories doesn't mean you have them all. You sit here and basically tell me I'm impatient and weak? Don't act like you know who I am for a fucking second. You don't know me at all and your words mean nothing to me. I don't need your approval, or your fucking opinion for that matter, to be me."

My voice has become loud and I can tell the venom I've spat at Jenna has made my point clear. She doesn't move, not even a blink as she stands there looking at me like I've grown another head, or lost my own.

I need to get the fuck out of this place before I blow the roof off. I haven't had an angry outburst like this since I was thirteen and it's pissing me off even more how I let her get to me, even though I told her she didn't. I'm shocked she hasn't called me out on my bullshit. I'm also thankful for it because I feel like I'm going to explode.

Checking my pockets for my wallet and keys, I walk the few steps to the front door and slip my feet into my boots. I unlock the deadbolt and then grab the handle. Before I turn the knob I make the mistake of looking back to the couch.

It's a mistake because Kinsley is now awake and sitting up. Her tired eyes are wide and *dammit*, she's biting the inside corners of her mouth, causing her lips to push out into the pout I love to hate. She hasn't taken her gaze from me but hasn't said a word either.

I briefly wonder how much she's heard before I rip the door open to make my exit. I want to slam the damn thing shut. I think better of it since I don't want to take any more chances of waking Elliot up.

Fuck! I need to find my own place fast.

Chapter 26

Kinsley

Elliot's party, to celebrate his third year of life, was an absolute success. It always amazes me how everyone in my life pretty much drops whatever they have going on in their own to celebrate my little man. Along with my mom, dad, Colleen, Heath, and Jenna; Liv, Mandy, and Trexton, seem to make sure their weekend revolves around him and his party. Even when it means flying In or driving hundreds of miles from college or wherever they may be at the time.

I had it here at the house and rented a bounce house with an attached slide. I set it up in the backyard for the kids to play on. My dad and Heath maned the grill, while my mom and Colleen took care of the sides. I wanted to help. They wouldn't let me, telling me I need to mingle with my friends and play with my son.

I made sure to invite some of my friends from the precinct who have kids so Elliot would have someone to play with and he wanted to invite a couple kids from his preschool as well. It ended up being a very nice turnout, except there was one distinct presence missing. It created an ache in my chest whenever I would hear the question of where he was or if he was going to make it, come from my sweet Elliot's mouth.

When Caleb did finally show up, late Saturday night, Elliot was already long asleep in bed. I wanted to ignore him and act like he didn't exist. After he kicked his boots off at the door, he went straight to the bathroom. I was almost finished with cleaning up the boxes, which were left out from opening all of Elliot's gifts when I could feel myself moving faster. I needed to make my way to my room without running into him. After all, the toys were neatly placed in the toy box and the trash tucked away within a bag ready to be taken to the bin, I headed to the hall. My feet were kicking up swiftly as my nerves carried me forward. I was trying my hardest not to seem rushed to get behind the confines of my bedroom door.

I barely made it to Jenna's door, whose is the first one on the left, before I was halted in place. Caleb was standing in Elliot's doorway gazing upon his sleeping form. With the way his shoulders were slumped over I could tell sadness seemed to be his companion. I couldn't bear to talk to him and we've been in an avoiding dance ever since. That was two days ago and I've still been raging a war within myself, wanting to be pissed from his lack of consideration, yet knowing I have no right to be since he has no obligation to me or Elliot.

Or maybe I'm just pissed at myself for allowing this man to make such an impression on my son's life after only a short two weeks.

I know Caleb and Jenna had a falling out the night before the party. I woke up at the tail end of what Caleb was saying. Literally, I only heard the last sentence about him not needing her approval or opinion, and as expected, Jenna won't tell me anything.

There could honestly be a lot of things they were arguing over, deep down I know it had something to do with me. I knew I should've kept my distance from Caleb, especially after the first night we met. I should've been straightforward and told him about me. About Ryker. About my past. About my present. The last thing I expected was to easily fall into a mutual friendship with him.

Caleb's a really cool guy. It feels strange to me when people say he's intimidating. Sure, there's no arguing the vast largeness which creates him. Not only is he tall, his broad shoulders and muscular physique play a visual trick on your mind making him appear even bigger. Somehow my mind forgets his size when he's around me and especially when he's around Elliot, which you would think would make him look like a true giant.

Then there's his personality. His persona has a binding grip and once you've been entrapped by it, it's hard to stay away from and even harder to avoid. He's funny, charming, polite—most of the time. Add on his carefree confidence coupled with his ability to demand dominance in a way that doesn't seem demanding or dominant. Contradicting, I know, I don't know how else to explain him.

It's been a long time since I've had such an active male presence in my life who's a peer and not a father figure, I find myself looking forward to Caleb's company. It's nice having a handyman around the house to fix the broken shit I don't feel like fixing or asking my dad to fix. I'm not saying it's the only reason I like having Caleb around, he's also funny. In fact, I'm not sure I remember the last time I truly enjoyed laughing like I do now when he's around.

He also makes me feel safe. I wasn't aware I had a want or need to feel safe. With him around, that's how I feel. I also know Elliot absolutely adores him, sometimes a little too much.

These things are the very reason why I need to have this talk with Caleb today, about my life, about everything. Then I will encourage him to find a place of his own a little faster to put distance between us because I start to get these deep feelings of remorse when enjoying too much of life while Ryker's not.

Bringing my cup of coffee to the kitchen table, I sit down and open my laptop. Caleb appears from the laundry room scaring the bejesus out of me, causing me to scream and jump from my seat.

Thank God I didn't have my coffee cup in my hands still or I would be scalded right now.

"Holy shit, Caleb! I didn't know you were in there."

He looks a little sheepish, but still manages to crack a smile as he mumbles out a, "sorry." The basket he has in his hands is full of, what smells to be, clean clothes, and he takes them down the stairs to his room.

I settle back in my chair, pulling out the first file I need to work on. Today is one of Elliot's preschool days which mean I usually have about six hours of alone time to catch up on my work before I have to pick him back up. However, today doesn't feel like a day it will happen.

I tuck the file I just retrieved back into my briefcase and put my laptop back into sleep mood. I need to have a conversation with Caleb and get past this awkward avoidance stage we're in once again.

As I'm getting up from my chair to head to the stairs, I'm caught off guard as he emerges from the darkened basement.

"Fuck!" My hand clasps my shirt over my racing heart. *How in the hell has he scared me twice now?*

Caleb's laughter fills the space between us as a scowl develops across my face.

"What's so funny, *Caleb*?"

It takes him a couple seconds to calm himself down before he responds.

"What's funny, *Kinsley* is the simple fact I've managed to scare you not once but twice within a span of five minutes. And an added bonus is hearing that pretty mouth of yours say the word Fuck."

I guess it's kind of funny after I think about it. I don't know why I'm so jumpy this morning, or why my cussing amuses him so much.

"So what? You've never heard a grown woman curse before?"

"Oh, I've heard plenty of grown women cuss before. The thing is, I've never heard *you* use those words. It sounds *nice* coming from you."

"*Nice?* That's a...different way to describe it. They're just words, Caleb. Don't get used to them though. I'm a mom who needs to watch her mouth around her three-year-old parrot mimicking son."

No further words are exchanged between us, and the quiet now in place is making me uneasy. I take a deep breath, knowing I need to move this conversation to the one I was headed for when he caught me off guard.

"Hey," Caleb speaks before I get to, his focus remaining locked on the ground. "I wanted to tell you how truly sorry I am for not showing up to the party Saturday." His hand is on the back of his neck and he's still staring at the floor.

I personally didn't want to mention anything about Elliot's party and a big part of me wants to brush off his words now. I don't want him to know how many times

Elliot asked where he was or how his smile would dim a bit with each time we couldn't give him a good answer. I have no clue how much longer he'll be living here. Since he's my best friends' brother I know he'll continue to be in our lives.

Caleb straightens his stance and finally looks at me. My eyes divert to the window over the sink behind him, I can still see him in my peripheral. His stare is scrutinizing. Probably trying to decipher if I'm angry or upset, I won't let him know how I truly feel.

"Caleb, you don't have any obligations here. There's no need for an apology." I pause trying to think of how to convey what I need to say nicely. "I'm not sure of your history with being around kids if you've been around any at all. I feel the need to make you aware of how most kids, especially Elliot, tend to become attached pretty fast to people who are in their life. They notice way more than we realize and they tend to always remember if you told them you would be a part of something with them. And then they notice when you're not. So I just wanted to throw that out there for you."

A simple quick nod tells me he's heard and understands my words, and for now, it's all I need.

I retrieve a cup from the cabinet and fill it with water from the tap. I take a sip, or maybe it's more of a gulp. I don't really know. I do know how my mouth is extremely dry now, as I work up the courage to speak my next words.

"If you don't have anything exciting planned for today, I would like you to come with me." He looks to me with a question on his face. I go to open my mouth to give him more of an explanation, nothing comes out.

I close it and clear my throat, then try again.

Chapter 27

Caleb

As we drive along the I-60 I study the buildings passing by. I've lived in this town nearly three weeks now and I've started to get a feel for my surroundings. It does help being an officer since I ride around in my car roaming the streets when there's nothing else to do. I know if we were to take the next exit, it would bring us to Turnpike Road where there's this octagon shape building full of stores. It's called Combining Eras and it houses stores with a variety of items—from current and trendy to nostalgic and antique. One day, I wandered into one of the stores and everything in it reminded me of Kinsley. It was full of flowers and vibrant colors and the scent of vanilla wafted through the air. Everywhere I looked, every item I saw made me want to buy it for the woman sitting next to me, just to see her smile.

I glance over at Kinsley, noticing the way she worries her bottom lip and how white her knuckles are from clenching the steering wheel. The ring on her finger catches the sun just right, sending tiny shimmers throughout the car.

She takes the exit marked Clovers Grove and I begin to wonder if I've ever been in this area before. We're only ten minutes from her house, but this area is out of my jurisdiction.

I still have no clue where she's taking me and she's been completely silent since she sat behind the steering wheel of her car. I'm trying not to think too much about the words she said or how going anywhere will make me learn new things about her. Or why she couldn't just tell me at home.

She turns right onto a street which looks like it would lead us to nowhere. The road consists of three lanes, the middle lane designated for turning. On the left is a vast space of nothingness. Just, what looks to be, miles of the untouched earth with a few trees sporadically placed. Then out of nowhere headstones begin to appear—a cemetery.

She turns into the entrance of the cemetery and my mind begins to race. *Why are we here?* I don't care for cemeteries. I understand people have a need for something tangible to grieve near after loved ones have passed. To me, it's just a body rotting in the ground. Your loved one is no longer present.

Immediately, she takes another right turn onto a narrow road. It feels more like a path we should be walking on, not driving. We stay on this road for about a mile, twisting and turning, until the cemetery I thought we were going to, is left in the gravel dust behind us.

We head over a small hill and I spot a building at the end of the road. Kinsley turns into the parking lot and pulls into the first available spot. She puts the car in park and turns off the ignition.

As I look at the name on the front of the brick building, I find myself more anxious now than ever before to learn about the inner workings of her world.

Chapter 28

Kinsley

Pulling the keys from the ignition, I put my index finger through the key ring and grasp them with my sweaty palm. I tend to do this when I need something to fiddle with, and right now I need it more than ever. My nerves are working my insides to a pulp and I don't know how long I'll be able to keep the nausea from coming up. I haven't been this nervous in a very long time.

The car is filled with complete silence and I'm curious to hear the thoughts floating through Caleb's head. I work up the courage to look at him. His eyes are slightly tightened and his eyebrows are squished together as he observes the building before us. The name Charleston Manor doesn't give much away.

I open my door and step out of my car. I head toward the entrance of the building. I don't have to check to see if Caleb's following, I can feel him behind me. He still hasn't said a word or even asked what we're doing here, and I'm okay with it because I'm not ready to tell him just yet.

We make our way through the small lobby and past the receptionist desk. I give my greetings to the staff as I walk by. I'm thankful I decided to come here during the day with Caleb because even though the day staff knows me they are nothing like the evening ones who can talk my ears off for hours. I love everyone here. A few of them have even become like family.

When we reach our destination—room 209—I stop right outside the door and turn to face Caleb. I'm still messing with my key ring and finding it difficult to look him in the eyes, or even look above his chest for that matter. He must sense my unease for he reaches out and stills my hand holding the keys.

I quickly remove my hand from his and look at his face. I can tell he's caught off-guard by my curt reaction, and it makes me regretful. Place that on top of the guilt I already feel, for him being able to calm me here, in a place I shouldn't need to be calmed, and it makes me a pile of mess.

I need to get this done with.

"There's someone I need you to meet," I say as I turn around and open the door. I head straight to the side of the bed which is closest to me and carefully grab onto the railing, hoping it will help keep me grounded.

"Caleb, this is my fiancé and Elliot's dad, Ryker." I lean over the railing, softly kissing Ryker's head and then stroke his cheek with my hand. The stubble on his face is thicker and I love the way it feels.

The steady beep of the machine which monitors his heart is always a sound I'm thankful to hear. He must've received a bath recently since the wires to his brain activity monitor are not in place.

Righting myself, I keep my eyes trained on Ryker as if waiting for him to say hello. Something I've craved for so long. I'm not ready to face Caleb and see the pity his eyes are sure to hold. I didn't even look at him when I introduced Ryker and although I feel like my voice was strong and loud, it may not have been loud enough to hear from wherever he stands. Honestly, I don't even know if he followed me into the room.

I glance quickly over my shoulder just to make sure Caleb's indeed inside of Ryker's room. He's only one step from the open door. It's a small enough room to assume he most likely heard what I said.

"The day after Ryker and I found out we were having a boy, he went to see his birth mother. I didn't go. We were unsure of her housing situation. To make a long story short, his birth mother didn't raise him and she never told him who his father is. She probably didn't even know. Heath and Colleen, whom you met at Elliot's soccer game, raised him. They're his foster parents who have raised him all his life as their own," I pause, take a deep breath and release it. "His relationship with his birth mother was rocky, to say the least. I'll save most of the details for another time. She had a drug addiction. A couple of times she cleaned herself up and gained custody rights over Ryker. She always screwed it up."

I take another deep breath and squeeze Ryker's hand gently. I've never had to tell his story before. I tend to not let new people into my life and the ones closest to me already know it. It's different for Caleb though. As far as I understand, he didn't even know a Ryker existed. "His birth mother abused him, emotionally and physically. She held a deep jealousy of me. Of the love Ryker gave to me, even when we were kids."

My throat is dry, I force a swallow down. I thought I was prepared for this, dredging up the past is never an easy thing. Especially when it's the worst parts. Caleb needs to know some of it to understand how Ryk got here.

I look over my shoulder at Caleb again. At some point, he must have taken a step toward me for he's no longer within the door frame. His stance is wide, his broad shoulders squared, and his hands are tucked away in his pockets. He almost looks tense, except when I look at his face, he's relaxed. There isn't a part of his body moving, except for his eyes. When I first looked at him they were staring at my hand lying on top of Ryker's, specifically at my ring. Then they moved to Ryker's face, and now they're on me. I started wearing my engagement ring on my right hand two years ago. My intent wasn't to look available, only not to have to explain my situation when people asked if I was engaged.

Caleb has a great poker face leaving him expressionless, which oddly relieves me. I don't know if I can handle his emotions on top of mine. I look back to Ryker before closing my eyes.

"It'd been a good six months since he'd seen her last. He told her over the phone we were pregnant, but wanted to tell her in person she was going to have a grandson. He was always so optimistic. He held hope she would be joyful about being a grandma. That maybe it would give her the strength and willpower to stay clean forever. A second chance, of sorts, for her to make amends."

The blood pressure cuff on Ryker's forearm begins to inflate. His heart monitor continues to beep steadily. I concentrate on the sound, letting it soothe my rapid thoughts.

"He went to her place. She was living with some friends in not the best part of town. He told her the news and she was happy. She gave him a beer to celebrate. Told him, 'if you're old enough to be a father, you're old enough to have a drink.' So, he drank the beer. Maybe he did it to please her, I'll never know."

I let go of Ryker and grip onto the bed's railing to try and steady my trembling hands. *Deep breath, Kinsley. Deep breath.*

"I received a text from him telling me he was too tired and going to stay the night. Everything about it was wrong. It felt wrong like it wasn't actually him at all. So, when two cars came to my house in the middle of the night, I knew something had gone wrong. I could feel he was gone." I squeeze my eyes closed tightly. I want to block out the memories of that night. "Technically, I was right. He'd been dead for four minutes."

Caleb places his hand on my shoulder. "You don't have to tell me any more," he says.

I look at him, "I do, though. I want you to know and I should be the one to tell you."

He nods his head slightly and uses his knuckle to wipe away the tear falling from my eye. His hand remains on my cheek for a brief moment, before dropping to his side. He's so close to me now.

I look back at Ryker and scan over his beautifully peaceful face. I stare at his chest and wait for the rise and fall.

"You see, the beer his birth mother gave him...she put a strong sedative in it. Which is why he was tired and he soon passed out. Then, Erin, his birth mother, she..." *breathe,* "she put," I run my shaky hand across my forehead and close my eyes, "she put heroin into his veins."

Caleb wraps his arms around me, pulling me to his chest as I continue, "She gave him so much and then just left him there. Left him to die, to make it look like he overdosed on his own." My tears flow freely down my cheeks, soaking into Caleb's shirt, yet my voice is calm and collected. "How does someone do such a thing? How does a mother murder the child she brought into this world?"

Caleb remains holding me as I think about the night I so desperately want to forget. After I calmed down, out in my front yard, my parents told me everything they'd learned. Ryker overdosed. He was found in time to be brought back to life. Only, it was a life of machines breathing for him and feeding him. His body went into a coma due to the amount of heroin forced into his system and the loss of oxygen to his brain.

"Lieutenant Grand was undercover and living at the house Erin was staying in for about a month. He was there that night, in and out the whole time Ryker was there. He's the one who discovered Ryker's lifeless body and he's the one who saved him. The next day when the detectives went to question Erin, they found her dead from her own overdose. In her hand was a written confession."

I move to the nightstand and grab a couple tissues. It was nice to have Caleb's comfort, only I can't handle his embrace any longer. I need some space.

"For months, Ryker endured so many tests from so many doctors. His brain scans showed no movement, no life, and then one day they pronounced him brain-dead."

I didn't want to believe them. I wasn't in denial, it was straight up refusal. I refused to believe my Ryker would be taken from me so soon. We were too young for this to happen, we had so much more life to live. And the fact he would never meet our son, and our son would never know his father, was beyond my comprehension, my understanding.

"There was so much paperwork and different options to go through, but never the option of him waking up. Once you're pronounced brain-dead, they say there's nothing more. Brain-dead is dead to doctors. I wouldn't believe them. I wanted them to prove he couldn't breathe on his own and since the Brownlees are his decision makers, I'm thankful they agreed.

"It wasn't supposed to be possible. There are less than twenty documented instances where people woke up or breathed on their own after the diagnosis, I never gave up hope. Miracles do happen. He's proof. Even though he hasn't woke up when they turned off his ventilator he began to breathe...on his own."

I grab my bottle of water from my purse and take a drink. I'm exhausted and don't want to talk anymore.

Caleb clears his throat, bringing my attention to him. "Kinsley, I know this might be an odd request. Would you mind if I had a moment with Ryker...alone?"

He seems a tad ashamed that he's asked, but truly sincere. I look over to Ryker lying in his bed so peacefully, too peacefully. I've been praying for a long time for him to move some part of his body on his own.

I'm not really sure why Caleb's requested time alone with Ryker but who am I to deny him? Maybe he just needs time to process everything he's just learned.

I look at the clock hanging on the wall near the television. He'll only have ten minutes. "His physical therapist will be here at ten. There's a small cafeteria to the left, at the end of the hall. I'll be there when you're done."

Leaning down, I kiss Ryker on the forehead then head out the door.

Chapter 29

Kinsley

Caleb found an apartment and he's moving in today. After I introduced him to Ryker on Monday he apparently started actively searching. I hadn't even encouraged him. I wasn't going to begin doing that for at least another week. When he told me on Thursday he'd found a place, paid a down payment and would move in Saturday, I'm certain the shock was evident on my face.

"You're going to wash the paint right off that cup if you continue scrubbing it so hard." I startle as Caleb's voice meets my ears.

I'm washing the last cup from the sink, unaware of how hard I've been scrubbing it. I rinse it, place it on the drying rack then pull the plug to drain the sudsy water.

When I asked Caleb if he wanted my old mismatched dishes, I wasn't expecting them to be this musty. I never got rid of them after I received a new set. I shoved them into a box and set them aside. I'd planned on handing Caleb the box and sending him on his way. Unfortunately for me, Elliot decided to open the box and pull everything out. It's unbelievable how stuff gets so dirty even when stowed away.

"Oh well. They're *your* dishes now. Who cares what they look like?"

He sticks his tongue out at me then sets the box in his hands on top of the table. I throw my wet dish towel at his face, only he catches it before it hits him.

"Ha, Ha! Victory for me," he cheers, throwing the towel over my head onto the counter.

I reach behind me, grabbing the towel and throw it again before he catches onto what I'm doing. It hits him right in the middle of his face.

I throw my hands in the air and scream, "touchdown!" while running around him in a circle.

He shakes his head, laughing, as he watches me. "You're such a goof," he says.

"Am not," I retorted, crossing my eyes.

"Mommy!" Elliot hollers, running into the room. He's dressed as his own version of a superhero. A sheet around his neck for a cape, fireman's hat on his head, foam hand with a pointing finger as his sword, and Caleb's large Aviator sunglasses as his mask.

Elliot sees Caleb and takes a fighting stance. "Stop right there, Mister. Wet me see your hands."

Caleb puts his hands up slowly before taking off in a sprint. He moves around Elliot and runs to the living room. Elliot chases him, screaming like a warrior.

I grab my dish towel and start drying the dishes before packing them back in the box they were in. Once the last dish is safely packed away I fold the flaps on the box and grab the packing tape. As I slide the tape across the top my chest becomes weighted. *Why do I feel this way over him leaving? I thought I'd be relieved.*

They make their way back into the kitchen. Caleb's running slowly, almost prancing, and Elliot close behind. Caleb gets behind me and holds onto my shoulders, using me as a shield.

"You'll never catch me now," Caleb boasts, "I have my magnificent shield." He maneuvers my body to thwart Elliot's advances.

"You can't do that. Mommy's not magmifitent," Elliot whines.

"You have no idea how magnificent she is," Caleb says, too low for Elliot to hear. My body stiffens. Caleb's hands drop from my shoulders.

My son's attention has moved on already as he spots the two boxes on the table. "What's these?" he asks.

I look back at Caleb and slightly widen my eyes. "I haven't told him yet," I whisper.

His mouth pulls up to one side as he makes his way to Elliot. He drops to one knee when he gets to him, bringing himself to Elliot's level.

"These are boxes I'm using to carry my stuff in," he says.

"Carwy where?"

"Remember when I told you I'd have my own place to live in one day?"

Elliot gives him two big nods, not understanding where this is headed.

"I found a place and I'm moving there to—"

Elliot's whines drown out the last of Caleb's words as his little body melts to the floor.

I figured he'd have this reaction which is why I hadn't told him. Caleb looks at me with his mouth agape and his eyebrows almost touching his hairline.

My shoulders rise as I mouth, "Sorry."

Caleb grabs at his chest as though I've wounded him and then dramatically falls to the floor next to Elliot. He begins flailing his limbs and crying out just like my child. There's no stopping the laughter from escaping me as I watch.

Elliot suddenly stops. He turns his head to the side with his cute nose wrinkled as he stares in wonderment at Caleb. His little hand reaches out and pats Caleb on the shoulder.

"Why you crying?" Elliot asks.

"Why are *you* crying?" Caleb says back.

Elliot looks at Caleb confused, before looking around the kitchen as if trying to remember the reason why. Caleb takes the opportunity to sit up and tickle Elliot on his belly.

This is what I'm going to miss.

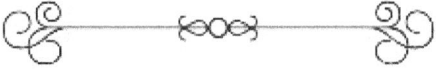

"I can't believe you only had four boxes and one suitcase to move," Jenna says to Caleb, "and one of those boxes only held cowboy boots."

"Hey, don't knock my boots. Cause once you try 'em you'll only buy 'em." Caleb says in the most southern drawn accent I've ever heard.

Jenna rolls her eyes and chucks the boot she has in her hand at him.

"Oh, now you're gonna get it. How dare you treat genuine leather that way!" Caleb playfully hollers, "Elliot, attack." He points to Jenna as he says attack. Jenna runs down the short hall with Caleb and Elliot chasing after her.

I laugh to myself at their antics as I grab the last picture frame from the only box I had to empty. Looking around his apartment, I try to find a place to put it. It's a picture of Caleb with his grandparents and it appears to be fairly recent by the walker his Grams is holding on to. The three of them are standing in the middle of a front porch, which looks as though it wraps completely around the beautiful white farmhouse it's on, and Caleb's arms are around both of his grandparent's shoulders. The smiles on each of their faces are pure happiness and full of bliss, almost as though they were caught in the middle of laughter.

I place the picture on the kitchen counter. It's really one that should be hung, but Caleb's tools are in his truck and he doesn't have any end tables or furniture in here to put it on instead.

The sound of my phone ringing interrupts the craziness happening in this tiny apartment. I reach into my back pocket and retrieve my phone, placing it to my ear.

"Hello?" I say.

"Hi, am I speaking with Kinsley?"

I pull my phone away from my ear to look at the screen. The number is one I don't recognize, however, the soft-spoken voice is one I'd know anywhere.

"Dr. Rose? Yes, how are you?"

Dr. Rose is Ryker's primary care physician at Charleston Manor. Although she's only been with him for the past year she's the most amazingly sweet, loving, and caring person I've ever met.

The clearing of her throat booms through the speaker. Her hesitation to answer my simple question causes my insides to drop. "Could you come by today...soon?" Her words are a dance—quick, quick, slow—trampling over my emotions.

"What's going on?" I ask, "I was just there yesterday."

Silence is all I receive.

"Dr. Rose, please tell me. You're making me worry." My trembling hand brushes across my forehead.

Her heavy sigh feels as though it reaches through the phone and runs along my neck. My skin rises with the chill surging my bones.

"Ryker...he," she pauses. My heart throbs in my chest. The noise it makes echoes in my ears breaking apart her next words.

"Sometimes...coma...long...body...motionless...

Heart...can't handle...stopped...gone...I'm sorry."

My phone slips from my grip making the same sound as my heart shattering on the tile floor.

Heart...stopped...gone.

I grip the counter as the air gets stuck in my throat. My knees buckle. Strong arms wrap around my waist, sinking with me into the floor. I choke on my sobs. My fist pounds into the chest I'm being held to. I'm pulled in tighter as a hand smooths down my hair.

I don't understand why this is happening to me. Haven't I lived through enough heartache in one lifetime? None of this makes sense. He was supposed to wake up. I prayed for him to breathe on his own and he did. I've been praying for him to wake up, but now he's gone.

Oh God! Whhhhyyyyyy? Why? Why is this happening?

Crystal A. Blanton

Chapter 30

Kinsley

The funeral came and went. I don't know how I was able to stay composed throughout the proceedings. At times I question if I was truly even there at all, at least until the very end. A panic attack is not how I imagined concluding my time with the physical being of my best friend, my fiancé. Just knowing he was inside of a metal box was enough to create claustrophobia within me for the rest of my life. I know the box doesn't hold my actual Ryker. It's now just a body, a vessel, one which was given to us by God to navigate through this life we have here on earth. Even faith doesn't make the mourning easier.

Time stands still now. Minutes tick by and they feel like hours, hours feel like days. Maybe days have passed, this I'm unsure of. They all feel the same. A repeat of the last once I submerged myself under this comforter. After we put my Ryker six feet into the ground.

I know I haven't moved much, my despair tethering me to my sleep, keeping me trapped within its reins. From time to time I hear Jenna make her way into my room. She never says anything, or maybe I'm never conscious enough when she does.

After they lowered the casket into the ground, my parents left taking Elliot with them, and my friends stood back allowing me to have some space—my time to say my final goodbye. I just stood there staring down into the hole, watching, waiting, for movement, for a sign, for something to wake me from this nightmare.

This is not the way it's supposed to be.

When they started covering the casket with dirt, things became hazy. A fog swept around me until everything went black.

That's when my chest began to constrict.

On the outside it felt like a thousand pounds sitting on me, restricting the little movement I had over my lungs. On the inside, it felt as though my heart couldn't handle being a part of me anymore. Its beat so fast and too hard, pushing up and out to break free.

It succeeded—that heart of mine. It cracked right through my sternum and split open my skin, jumping straight from my chest into the dirt hole in the Earth.

And it's still there, with the other half of my soul, where it belongs.

At some point, I changed out of the clothes I wore to the funeral and into one of Ryker's shirts. I've kept them all, waiting for him to wake up and come home. I've gone through his belongings so many times over the course of these last three years, typically after some deep mourning of the potential loss of him.

The first time was the night before we took him off the ventilator. I donated quite a bit of his clothes. I couldn't fathom ever getting rid of any of his shirts, or my favorite pair of his holey jeans—the ones he wore on my seventeenth birthday. The day we finally became more than friends.

His shirts have their own drawer in my dresser. About once a week I open the drawer and spray them with his cologne he always wore. When I take one out to wear at night, I'm able to feel his arms wrapped around me.

I honestly thought I'd prepared myself for when the time came where Ryker would no longer be here with me anymore. It's amazing how my mind was able to trick me into truly believing I had a handle on things. How it made me believe I could move through this part of my life easily and sanely since I felt I'd already done this more times than one should have to.

I was a fool to trust this part would be even a fraction easier than the ones before.

I've even made sure to talk to Elliot about everything when it comes to his father. Even though he just turned three I try to explain everything in ways he might understand. And to be honest, he seems to have a better understanding than most people I know.

To think the only father he's ever known has been lying lifeless in a hospital bed. Elliot knew his dad's heartbeat. I always laid him on Ryker's chest. He knew he breathed. The movement small but there. He also knew his daddy loved him. My endless reminders now ingrained in his heart.

Yet, there are so many things he doesn't know or has never seen. He will never see his daddy's eyes. He will never observe his smile. He will never listen to his daddy's voice. He will never hear his laugh...he never will.

Although, Elliot doesn't notice these things. He never asks why his daddy doesn't move or open his eyes, or why he doesn't talk when they 'play' together. He just plays with him. He plays and talks to his daddy as if he's playing along and talking back. Maybe it's because it's all Elliot's ever known. He loves his dad to the core and knows his dad loves him.

Elliot's simply amazing.

Thoughts like these are the ones bringing forth the searing pain. The pain which makes its way through my entire body, holding me captive within the confines of my room, trapped beneath this cover. The pain which, somehow, I don't feel today. In fact, I don't feel anything at this moment, and it scares me more than the pain. With the pain, I at least knew I was still alive.

I would check for a pulse, except when one's heart is buried six feet under, even that won't confirm life.

I focus on my breathing, my mind playing images of my lungs expanding to accept the intake of air and contracting to expel it.

My bedroom door opens. Heavy footsteps move past my bed and into the bathroom. It sounds as though they're gathering or moving things around. Water begins to flow and it takes me a moment to figure out the water's not coming out of the bathroom sink. It's coming from my shower.

Why is my shower running?

My comforter lifts slowly, the edges having to be tugged from the grip of my fingers. I'm taken from the blanket cocoon I'd made as my safe haven. My eyes remain closed, sealed shut like they've been all along.

Arms scoop my body up and off the bed, one under my neck, the other under my knees. The muscles constrict and I can feel just how strong they are as they pull me against a bare, firm chest—coddling me the same as a small child.

I scroll through the possibilities of whose arms and this chest belongs to. Part of me thinks I know who it is, the other part knows I don't, at least not in the physical aspect.

It isn't until he takes a step and I breathe in, which is so damn hard to do. I know exactly who's holding me, as his distinct scent penetrates my nose—*Caleb.*

If there was any life left in me, I'd probably freak out right now, because he's taking me to the running shower. For a moment I think he'll just dump me under the faucet to hose me off. When I feel his weight shift from one foot to the other, smoothly maneuvering both our bodies through the small glass door, I know I'm wrong.

Caleb gently places me on my feet, my back toward the water. I'm not directly under the head, but the mist from the spray kisses the back of my legs. I hear the door to the shower close. I'm unsure if I'm alone. I'm not ready to open my eyes yet. I'm not ready to face any part of reality.

My legs tremble. The lack of use they've received recently taking its toll. Before I can sink myself into the floor, the soft graze of fingertips at my thighs gives me the strength needed to remain standing.

Caleb grips the hem of Ryker's shirt I'm wearing, and tenderly pulls upward until it's completely off of my body.

His inhale is sudden, stifled. My flesh tingled, raised.

Images of what he's seeing conjure in my mind, wanting a reason for such a response. Bones protruding all over my body; the remembrance of eating substance gone. The stench of my skin; imprisoned days seeping from my pores. Or the simple fact the shirt which clothed me was the only piece I had on at all.

I believe I'm supposed to feel self-conscious, embarrassed, or even ashamed. I'm none of these things. I guess this is what happens when you have no heart and your soul has been ripped to shreds, you stop feeling at all. My arms haven't even moved to conceal the parts of me I know Caleb can see. They're just hanging limply at my sides, as forlorn as the rest of me.

The heat from his body sears the front of mine. His fingertips brush against my forehead, slide into my hair. Cupping my ears, he slowly tilts my head back, the stream pouring over the strands. I remain in the same spot he set me in, not quite beneath the spout. He tenderly touches my hip, guiding me until I feel the sting of hot liquid cascade down my skin.

His hands leave me, his presence moves away. Curiosity opens my eyes to a slit revealing Caleb's taught, muscular back and tattoos I didn't know exist.

I close my eyes before he turns, basking in the water pouring over my aching soul. The aroma of sweet vanilla permeates the shower, mixing with the steam in the air.

With deft hands, he creates a frothy by-product in my hair; the excess washing away my self-imposed burial. He rinses the suds away while holding me steady. His hands are gentle, contradicting his solid frame. For the first time in years, I feel safe, protected. For the first time in days, I...feel.

None of this is real though. The heat of the shower, the smell of my favorite shampoo. Everything's a fallacy, a momentary reprieve, nothing more than a lie. I open my eyes and stare at the ceiling. The steam collects, forming back into water, waiting for its chance to plummet back down...plummet to where I belong.

My lids pierce shut as my chest pulses. I'm trapped in my head with these unforgiving thoughts. I'm not sure how I've been standing here this long or standing at all, in this world, when part of me is gone.

Thumbs swipe softly across my cheeks, pulling me from my sudden despair. His hands remain on the sides of my face, his fingers touching my neck. I feel his gaze upon me, watching the tears I was sure I had no more of, pour from my eyes. We stay this way for a lifetime before he ultimately withdraws.

Coarse fibers press against my skin. *My loofah*. With secure, sturdy hands, Caleb takes care to wash away my stench with soapy suds left in the wake of the loofah. He leaves no part of my body left unwashed. If only my emotions and memories could be wiped clean just as easily, the hurt would be gone.

His care for me has an intimate feel. Not one of sexual need or desire. One drawn from a natural instinct to protect and care for another.

Thoughts and images bombard my mind...Ryker, our childhood, friendship, stolen words, skittles, wildflowers, sunsets, rainstorms, birthdays, holding hands, kisses, finding love, making love, smiles, happiness, dreams, goals, pregnancy tests, ultrasounds, picking names, baby boy, baby, Elliot, Elliot...

Elliot. I'm a mother who's failed.

I feel it again. I feel it all. It hurts. It's too much. The weight of my body is breaking my legs. They feel weak. They are weak. I don't want to stand. It's too hard to stand. I can't stand anymore...

So I don't.

Chapter 31

Caleb

As I walk out of Kinsley's room I about damn near run smack dab into Jenna.

"Jesus H. Christ, Jenna! Why are you out here lurking in the dark?" I slip my shirt over my arms and pull it over my head and down my chest. I feel my shorts to see how wet they got—*they're soaked*. I didn't bring any clothes with me so I'll just have to deal.

"What the hell, Caleb? I didn't know calling you over here to help me meant you were going to take a long ass shower with her."

"You've got to be fucking kidding me right now." I pinch the bridge of my nose. "You called me as soon as I got home from work this morning, begging me to get over here so I could help you. I didn't know what I was walking into in there. You have been keeping how bad off she really is away from all of us, saying you have everything under control, that she just needs time. It's been twelve fucking days, Jenna. Twelve days she hasn't eaten or moved out of her bed, and don't try and lie to me saying she has, because if you would've seen the shutdown, thin, shell of a woman I just took care of, then you wouldn't have let it get this far."

I'm pissed and having to whisper-yell since we're still standing outside of Kinsley's door isn't helping release the anger boiling inside.

I understand how Jenna thought she had things under control. I understand she wanted to be the one to take care of her best friend during the most difficult time of her life, but the woman I just left in that room is not being taken care of. When she collapsed in the shower, I wanted to scream to the sky. All I could do was hold her. Thankfully, I was close enough to prevent her from hitting the ground.

Moving past Jenna, I make my way down the hall and into the living room. I can hear her footsteps on my tail. Before she says anymore, I'm going to finish what I have to say.

"How dare you get onto me about giving her a shower! She needed it. I also hoped it would help waken her some." *How was I supposed to know she was only wearing a t-shirt?* "She's not mourning or working through her emotions and I get it, I'm the last one to say she needs to do things a certain way, but hell, she's practically lifeless herself. "

"Oh my God, Caleb, was she naked? Did you have *your* clothes on?"

"Fuck you, Jenna. Out of everything I've just told you, you're obsessing over if we were clothed in the shower? Really says a lot of what you think of me. Especially, if you think seeing her like she is right now is a turn on for me. She just lost her fiancé, her son's father for Christ sakes!"

I'm in her face which is hard for me since I'm over a foot taller than her. It's fucking ridiculous I even have to have this conversation. She should be less concerned about me trying to get with her friend and more concerned about taking care of her and helping her get through this shit storm.

I walk away and grab my shoes, slipping my feet inside them. As I grab for my car keys on the small table near the door I feel Jenna's hand touch my arm stopping me in my tracks. I'm tired and don't want to keep going around with her over something so minuscule.

"I'm sorry, Caleb. You're right. I shouldn't have even questioned anything you've done. You're just here to help and I appreciate it more than words can say. I know she needed a shower, badly, and there's no way I could've got her in there, so thank you." The air she pushes from her lungs sounds broken making me turn to face her. Her eyes are full of tears threatening to take a leap off the ledge they're poised upon.

"I thought I knew what I was doing," she says, "I thought letting her grieve in her own way, on her own terms is what she needed. I thought I was strong enough for her, strong enough for myself. I thought Ryker's death wouldn't hurt as much as it does." The agony in Jenna's words hit me hard, reminding me of the only significant pain I've ever felt—the loss of a woman I never imagined could be gone, especially so early in my life.

A chill runs through me as her emotions surround my body, threatening to suffocate. I roll my shoulders, I'm ready to bolt from this house so I don't have to deal with any of this. I've perfected my game of hide and don't seek when it comes to my own feelings. I wouldn't know the first thing to do with someone else's. My therapist would tell me, 'it's time to break the cycle and learn how.'

Looking at Jenna now, I watch another tear take its course down her cheek to its imminent death. I picture my five-year-old sister I left standing in front of our mother's casket, tears streaming down her face as they are now. I know I have to make this scenario different.

My hand goes to her shoulder, pulling her to my chest. I hold her tight, letting her release the anguish she's built up inside. Her arms go around me as her body trembles, except no sound escapes.

I feel the need to apologize for not taking care of her in the past. For not holding her like this while she stood over our mother's body crying out for her to wake up. And then while she stood over her open grave wondering why the men were throwing dirt on the woman we love.

"I'm sorry," I whisper...*for not being the big brother, the protector I always thought I would be.*

"I'm sorry," I repeat...*for leaving you behind. Making you the one to take care of our dad when you weren't even old enough to take care of yourself.*

"I'm sorry," comes out once more...*for ignoring your requests to come home to try and be a family, even though our family would never again be whole.*

I don't voice the reasons for my apologies and she doesn't ask me what they're for.

Jenna dries her eyes with her hands and takes a step away from me. I jiggle my keys in my pocket, stepping back and forth on my feet. I've had enough emotional outpouring today to last me a year and it's making me anxious to leave.

"I gotta go so I can get a few hours of sleep before I pick Elliot up from school." I've been helping the Carmichaels' and Brownlees' with Elliot whenever needed.

"How's he doing?" she asks. I can tell she misses him, misses his presence around this house.

"Honestly, he's good, really good. In fact, he has such an amazing grip on death, and life, I often forget he's only three." Everything I just said is a complete truth. Whenever I talk to Elliot I feel like I'm talking to someone much older.

"Good to hear." A sad smile forms on her lips. "Well, tell him I miss him bunches and I'm going to do everything in my power to get his mommy back to him as soon as possible," she says, and with that, I nod and head out the door.

"Caweb! Caweb! Caweb!" Elliot comes barreling into my thighs. He was too fast for me to get down and pick him up.

He hugs my leg then jumps backward showing me the big paper in his hands.

"Wook what I made for you today."

He opens it up. It's a drawing of...well, I'm not really sure yet, but I'm going to act like I know exactly what it's all about.

"Wow! It's amazing, Elliot. You're a very talented artist. You made this for me?" I'm down on my knee next to him, holding the drawing out in front of both of us, hoping he will explain what I'm supposed to be seeing.

The paper is full of colors and squiggly lines, and colorful squiggly lines. After looking at it completely there appear to be a few circles drawn among the colorful chaos.

Pointing to one of the circles, Elliot says, "this is Mommy."

He moves his finger to the next circle and says, "this one is Aunt Jenna."

I find the smallest of the circles and ask, "is this one you?"

His smile is so big it takes up his entire face. "How'd you know?"

"I'm a great guesser."

I begin to roll the paper back up when he tells me to stop, "I'm not done." His little finger brings my attention to a circle close to the top. "This is my dad, and this one here is you."

The one of me is an oval shape directly next to the circle he said was his mom and behind the tiny one of him.

"Oh wow, Buddy! You did a really great job with this drawing. It's very nice of you to include me in your picture, but you didn't have to." I say.

"Mmhmm. You'll take care of Mommy and me and Jenna."

His words catch me off guard. I don't know how to respond, or if I should. I snatch Elliot up, giving him a big hug before rolling up the picture.

"I will keep this forever and ever," I say. It's a promise I know I can keep.

Chapter 32

Kinsley

Time eludes me again. I should feel saddened by how I don't even care to know what day it is, yet I'm not.

My door opens. Faint footsteps make their way to me, my cover lifts and a body moves in next to mine. I open my lids partially and see Jenna lying beside me.

"Hi," she says, a tentative smile on her face.

I open my eyes wider, allowing them to adjust to the light seeping through the thin sheet lying over us. She must've taken my big fluffy blanket off or I wouldn't have been able to see her at all.

"Kins? It's time you get out of this bed and start living your life like Ryker would want you to."

Her words are soft and sincere, yet still hurt when I hear his name.

"How long's it been?" I'm not sure why this is what I chose to use my first words on or why I even asked. It doesn't matter. It could be years and I'm sure I'd feel the same.

"Fourteen days."

How did I let two weeks escape me? Why does it only feel like one day?

"Elliot?" *I've failed him.*

"He's really good, Kins. Your parents have everything under control and between them, Colleen, Heath, and my brother they've all been able to keep a normal schedule."

I nod my head as a tear rolls down my cheek. I've never liked to be a burden to anyone and hearing how everyone else has been doing my job makes me more aware of the mess I am.

"He knows you're mourning. How you miss his daddy so much it hurts. He truly understands it all." She takes my hands in hers and squeezes. "You have one hell of an amazing son there. I'm so happy to be a part of your life."

"He *is* pretty amazing. A duplicate of his dad," I say, as more tears stream down my face.

"A duplicate of his mama, too. He's the best of both of you."

"Thank you for everything you've done for me."

"Don't thank me yet. I haven't been living up to my duties of taking care of you, so I'm coming in full force. It's time to get up, get showered, and brush your damn teeth cause your breath is rancid." She pauses a moment to laugh as I cover my mouth so I don't breathe on her. "Most of all it's time to pick up your pieces and start living your life again."

"I don't know if I can," I say from under my hand. It's not a whine or a protest, just a fact. I truly don't know if I can.

"Kinsley, look at me. Yes, you can. I know how strong you are. I've witnessed it myself and know without a doubt the strength is still inside you. It's not going to be easy by any means and unfortunately, there will be lots of days which are just as bad as now. Days you'll pray for the earth to open up and swallow you whole so you'll have a little reprieve from the despair you feel. There will also be better days. Days which feel new and breathe life back into your soul. Those are the days' worth fighting for."

Her words hit me with such conviction it's hard to do anything but believe them. Plus, I have a son I need to raise, who needs me more than anyone or anything on this planet. He's the reason I've been able to exist so far, and he's the reason I will continue to go on.

I don't know who stands in front of me. The reflection an image, a stranger, I've never seen before. Pale skin. Dark, sunken eyes. Fifteen pounds gone.

I put on makeup, fix my hair. I go with curls to make my face seem fuller then chastise myself for giving it too much thought. A low bun now sits at the nape of my neck. I put on a pair of jeans and have to rummage through my closet for a belt. I slide on a pink shirt and a light jacket, then head to the living room to put on my shoes. Jenna awaits me, keys in her hand.

I blink and we're at my parents. My heart pounds, my breathing accelerates. I pray seeing them will help me more than hurt.

Before I fully emerge from the car, the best sound a mother could hear flitters to my ears. Joyful squeals of my baby boy.

He runs into my open arms, squeezing my neck tight.

"I missed you, Mommy!" he says, his arms becoming tighter.

"I've missed you too, Baby. So much."

As we head into the house I greet my parents each with hugs, never once setting Elliot down. Worry floats in their eyes briefly before relief moves in.

"I'm going to be okay, Mama. I promise," I say.

The kitchen smells like bar-b-que. My stomach growls. Caleb stands at the far end of the counter. I'm thrown back by him being here. Even though Jenna told me he's been helping with Elliot, I wasn't aware he'd made himself comfortable at my parent's house.

Dinner is ready, only, two people are missing. I pick up my phone and press call.

"Hello?" Colleen answers.

"Hi," I breathe out, "We have a lot of food here. Where are you?"

She sighs. It's a happy sigh. "Kinsley, are you sure?"

"Never been surer in my life!"

In less than five minutes they walk through the door. Their embraces are welcomed. I hold on to Colleen until it feels right to let go. Tears line her eyes and for once I don't cry. Today I can be strong for others. I may have lost my fiancé, however, they lost their son.

The familiarity and chatter amongst the table provides comfort, a distraction from my mind. Love and laughter from family and friends help fill the hollow parts deep inside.

Jenna washes the dishes, I dry. Elliot plays with his papa and grandpa on the living room floor. My mom and Colleen watch from the couch. Caleb's still at the table seemingly lost in his head.

"Hey," I say to Caleb as I sit next to him. He glances at me, then looks back out the window. "I wanted to say thank you for everything you've done. For Elliot...for me."

He takes a moment, lightly tapping his fingers on the table. When he finally looks at me his eyes hold sadness even though he puts on a tight-lipped smile.

"Anytime." He looks back and forth between both of my eyes. "I mean that with everything in me. You need help in any way, with anything, you call me. Anytime." Elliot's belly laughter catches our attention. Caleb sighs. "He sure is something special."

I nod in agreement even though he's no longer looking my way. My son is so much like his father, knowing how to make every person in a room fall in love with him.

As we head out the door, Elliot and his bag in tow, he takes off running to Caleb's truck. Stopping him from getting inside.

"Caweb, can you come over to my mommy's house now?" Caleb lifts Elliot into his arms.

"No, not tonight, Buddy. I think you should spend your time with Mommy and Jenna. Give them lots of snuggles since they've been missing you bunches."

Elliot's laughter fills the air as Caleb gets him in his tickle spots. Before he sets him down, Elliot hugs him tightly. The amount of affection he has for Caleb makes me ache, yet creates a small glimmer of happiness all at the same time. I hate how Elliot will never have his daddy here to do those things with, however, I'm thankful for the male influences who are already a part of his life.

Chapter 33

Caleb

As I drive to Kinsley's house, I'm excited to surprise Elliot. It's been over a month since I've seen him last and it's slowly starting to kill me inside. Who knew the little booger would make me like him so much, so fast.

We lost two officers due to transfers a month ago, which created a need for the rest of us to take on more shifts. Their spots finally filled a week ago giving me much relief and freeing up some of my time. I was offered a change in my shift if I want it, moving me to days instead of nights. I declined. I joined the police force for a reason and nights are where I belong for now.

About two and a half weeks ago, Gramps called me up to let me know Grams fell in the shower. She broke her hip. I raced to the hospital that day ready to quit my job and move back to help take care of Grams and the farm. I was ready to help where-ever Gramps needed me, only he wouldn't allow it. Now I travel every free day I have to the farm and give him no choice except to let me help, even if it's just being by my Grams side as someone for her to chat with.

I'm off work today and tomorrow and planned on going back out to the farm. When Gramps called me and said, "your Grams is recovering really well over here. I could do without seeing your ugly mug for a while. I suggest you go on over to your sister's house and chat it up with that pretty Kinsley Mae and play with the strapping young man of hers," I knew right where I should be.

My Gramps is a good ole southern man always thinking I need to be fixed up with someone. Wanting to make sure I'll have a woman to make an honest man out of me before I become 'too old'.

When my dad and Jenna visited the farm when we were younger she'd talk a lot about Kinsley. I typically tuned her out. What I hadn't realized was how she talked about Ryker too. Gramps has known all about Ryker and what happened to him. Over the years I've learned how easy it is to talk to Gramps about anything. He's someone you can trust with your secrets. I'm sure he's the one Jenna inherited such a quality from. I'm just happy she has him to talk to, a confidant when other's secrets become too heavy to hold.

Two days ago, when I was there last, my Gramps wanted to see a picture of Kinsley and Elliot. *He said, "well you talk about them so damn much I figure I ought to put a face to their names."*

I wanted to argue with him to make him aware it was only Elliot I talked a lot about only I knew it would be a waste of breath.

I have quite a few pictures of Elliot on my phone and absolutely zero of Kinsley. I had to finagle my way through Facebook to find one of her.

The minute I handed Gramps my phone with her picture plastered across the screen, a smile lit up his entire face. After I was in my truck, ready to make the trip home, Gramps stuck his head in my open window and left me with words to ponder.

"Caleb, my boy, I've always thought of you as a bright young man, however, you may change my perception if you don't heed my words of wisdom," he pauses, making sure I'm paying attention. "Kinsley Mae is a beautiful woman. She's evidently made a fast impact on you since you moved to her town."

I open my mouth in protest, only to shut it when he raises his brow.

"No, no, don't you interrupt me, boy. I need you to hear my words. Let them sink into that thick skull of yours. I say this because every day you've shown up here since your Grams had her fall, you've filled us to the brim

with stories of her and her boy." He looks at me, pointedly. "You may be oblivious to it right now and even after I tell you, you most likely won't believe me. You're falling for her, Boy. If you haven't already." His hand taps the side of my truck; his eyes glaze over as he looks beyond me to the pasture.

"I know she just went through a crapshoot time in her life and things might still get worse before they get better for her. This is where you come in. You need to be there. Be by her side so you can catch her pieces as they fall and put those strong hands of yours to good use helping mend them back together." He focuses back on me, his gaze never wavering. I shift uncomfortably in my seat. "Always keep your patience, for it may take a long time before she's healed enough to stare love in the face again. Just make sure you're the one she's staring at when she discovers she's ready."

The whole way home I felt jittery. My leg bounced and my palms were sweaty. I couldn't believe Gramps tried telling me I'm falling in love.

Sure, I've had a lot to say about my new town and the people in it. Which, of course, includes Kins and Elliot. It doesn't help that Elliot's the coolest kid I've ever met. Anyone with sight can see how beautiful his mother is, even in her darkest moments, however, love and fallen in love are strong words to throw around on just an assumption.

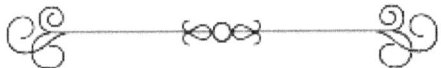

My knuckles rap against the wooden door. It's unfamiliar to knock, waiting for someone to answer. I've always just come and gone as I pleased. I still have my door key, but it feels a little weird today to just barge in unannounced, unexpected.

As Jenna opens the door I feel an unexpected release of tension.

"Hey bro, why didn't you just come in?" She turns on her heel, and I follow her to the living room.

"I wasn't sure if I should."

As the word 'should' comes out of my mouth, Kinsley appears from the hall wearing tight, flower-covered leggings with only a bra on top. A very sexy, satin, teal color bra which holds her breasts up quite nicely.

"Oh hey, Caleb," she says, "I didn't know you were coming by. Did you come for Elliot's last soccer game?"

She's just standing there, in her bra, making casual conversation as though this is an everyday occurrence. Her body is back to the way it was before Ryker's passing—her skin soft, hips ample. My hands itch to touch her. I'm chanting a mantra of sorts in my head to stop my focus from drifting...*look at her eyes, look at her eyes, look at her eyes.*

She's never made looking into her eyes easy though, at least for me. She's never held my gaze for more than a second, and I've never understood why.

"Yeah, sorry for just showing up unannounced like this. I finally had some free time and wanted to come by and surprise Elliot. I thought his final game was last week?"

Kinsley holds up her index finger, informing me she'll be back in a minute as she goes through the kitchen into the laundry room. I follow her until I reach the kitchen table, that way if she ends up responding I'll be able to hear her clearly.

She comes out of the laundry room fully clothed and only a small part of me is thankful she put something on. The other part makes me realize it doesn't matter that she put a shirt on since the one she picked is also teal and has a deep V-neck displaying her cleavage nicely.

"His last game was supposed to be last week. They still had to make one up because of that crazy storm we had."

"Nice! This works out perfectly then. I was so bummed about being so busy and missing the last two games, especially thinking last week was his last one. Now I get to be there for it."

As if on cue Elliot comes barreling into the kitchen with Jenna following behind.

"Mommy, is it time to go to my game?" he questions. He hasn't noticed me standing near the table yet.

"Not quite. We'll leave in about ten minutes," she tells him.

"Hey E," Jenna grabs his attention, "someone came to see you." She looks my direction.

Elliot follows her gaze. When he sees me his eyes become the size of saucers.

"Caweb!" he shouts. The excitement his face holds lights up my heart.

Man, this kid makes me happy.

He runs into my arms and holds onto my neck as I give his little body a squeeze.

"Looks like someone might have missed you," Jenna states with a giant smile on her face. I'm not sure if she's referring to me missing him or him missing me.

I glance over to where Kinsley stands. She's leaned up against the counter looking at us, yet her eyes are glossed over as if she's not seeing us at all. Her lips showcase a hint of a smile, however, she doesn't completely look happy. She looks as though she's unsure if she should even be smiling at all.

Chapter 34

Kinsley

"Great job Elliot!" Caleb says as he walks next to Elliot, guiding him on the field. "Your coach says to keep doing little kicks, stay close to the ball. You're doing great!" I laugh as Elliot picks up the ball and places it in the direction he wants it to go. "No hands, no hands!" Caleb exclaims, "Remember you don't use your hands in this game."

Caleb ended up riding here with us after Elliot begged him. Then the little stinkpot made him squeeze in next to his car seat in the back so he could sit by him. Jenna was perfectly fine riding in front, but I know it couldn't have been real comfortable for Caleb. His size alone makes my car seem like a play toy.

I know Elliot's missed Caleb. I hadn't realized the extent until we arrived here though when he had a full out meltdown wanting Caleb to run the field with him.

I used to walk next to him, reminding and guiding him of how to play the game. Elliot caught on so quickly, I only did it for a few weeks. This is the last game of his second six-week session, so I was shocked by his outburst. I'm grateful Caleb didn't mind. He was able to calm Elliot down within seconds and seems to enjoy being on the field with him.

In fact, Caleb seems to be favored by most of the kids on the field, and some of their mothers. I watch as their heads move back and forth, their focus glued to Caleb. They're taking every part of him in, like a bunch of wild hyenas in heat.

Okay, maybe I'm exaggerating a bit. It's just crazy how they all become helpless and pretty much brainless in his presence.

"Oh Caleb, you're the only man I've ever seen my daughter completely listen to. You should think about becoming a coach. I know we would sign up for your team for sure." The bleached out blonde with clothes looking like they were made for her daughter says to him as she throws back her head and laughs at nothing.

Another mom just walked over and agreed with blondie, then rests her hand on his bicep. "Oh my word!

Your muscles are *so* big; you must work out all the time," she says.

"Get off the field. Coach Oscar is trying to finish the game." I shout, trying to get the flock of women, who now swarm Caleb, away from him."

Jenna chuckles next to me, most likely at my random outburst. My mom's standing on the other side of me and I feel her bump my shoulder with her own.

"Is it bothering you how those women are throwing themselves at Caleb?" my mom asks.

"Ugh no, it's *bothering* me how they're interrupting the end of the final game with their blatant hoochyness. They can do whatever they want with Caleb, just move it to the sidelines." I tear my gaze from the fiasco remaining in front of me and pin it on my mother. Her eyes twinkle, her brows are raised. Her expression informs me of the lies my tongue created. The lies I may try to fool myself with but won't get past her wisdom.

"Mmhmm," she says, "and calling them hoochies obviously proves the statement you just made."

I'm not even going to bother responding to her absurd ideas. Rolling my eyes will do that for me.

All the kids received a little trophy at the end of the game for doing such a great job during the learning process. Elliot's little face beams with so much pride. He's holding his gold plated stand with a miniature soccer ball on top for everyone to see.

We're all taking turns having our picture taken with Elliot and his trophy. My mom, dad, and him. Colleen and Heath with him. Jenna, Caleb, and him. Myself and him.

Thinking we're finished, everyone begins to say their goodbyes when there's a tug on my hand.

"Mommy, one more, pwease," Elliot says with excitement.

"One more what honey? A picture?" He nods his head, "Okay, are you wanting one with all of us?" It's the only one we haven't done.

"Nooo, with you," he pauses for a split second as his eyes search in front of him, "and Caweb."

Caleb's currently having his ear talked off by yet another soccer mom. When Elliot says his name loud enough for him to hear he turns to us and smiles wide.

Elliot's request tilts me slightly. I'm trying my hardest to ignore the reasons for his request. *A picture with* only *the three of us?* Instead, I focus on the satisfaction I feel over him interrupting Caleb's conversation.

My hand goes out in front of me waving him in our direction right as the soccer mom asks to exchange numbers. Without a moment of hesitation or another word, Caleb walks toward me. The woman looks flustered as she stands there waiting, assuming he'll come back to her, he doesn't.

"Sorry," I say to Caleb, receiving a perplexed expression, "for interrupting your conversation."

"What conversation?" he says, allowing his smirk to say the rest.

"Caweb, pick me up," Elliot says, tugging on Caleb's hand.

Caleb picks him up and tickles him. "Didn't we just take a picture? You already want another one with me?" he says.

Elliot's laughter is infectious. He's trying his hardest to tell Caleb he wants it with the three of us. When his words finally come out in bits in pieces through his laughter, Caleb ends the tickles. His gaze connects with mine for confirmation.

A nod of my head and a small smile is all I manage to give him.

He adjusts Elliot in his arms holding him more to the side. I hand my phone to Jenna, then stand next to Elliot. When I hear my son, not so quietly, tell Caleb he's supposed to put his arm around me, I'm filled with dismay.

I don't move. And, when Caleb switches Elliot to his other arm, I don't stop his free arm from going around my waist.

I pull into the gas station and find a place to park. I'm dying for a soda.

Caleb unbuckles Elliot from his car-seat, pulling him out of the car. He squeezed himself next to Elliot again so Jenna could have the front.

"Can I hab a Sprite Mommy?" Elliot asks.

"Sure. Can you grab the small cup?"

I fill his cup and one for me. Put lids on and grab straws for both.

"Elliot, can you carry your cup without dropping it?"

"Yes, Mommy," he says.

I hand him his cup and pick mine up off the counter. Scanning the store, I look to find where Caleb and Jenna have gone. Jenna's coming out of the restroom. Caleb's nowhere to be found.

"Skittles?" a familiar voice says next to me.

The beautiful word assaults my ears. Emotions turn into waves, crashing through my body. My grip loosens, the cup falls.

I'm standing in shock and covered in soda as *our* word runs circles through my mind. His voice taunts me clear as day.

How?

Why?

It's not him. It can't be. He's gone, dead.

Ryker's dead.

Thoughts gnaw my insides.

Why must he be engraved into so much of the world around me?

Nausea flows like a dirty river. Regret becomes my friend. A world devoid of the man I love is not a place I want to be a part of.

Chapter 35

Caleb

"Kinsley?" I give her a small shake. "Kinsley, What happened? Can you hear me? Please say something."

What just happened? I don't understand what's going on with her.

I adjust my hands on her biceps. Her legs seem to be regaining strength even though I'm not ready to let go. After watching her cup disintegrate all over the floor, I saw her knees buckle. I grabbed her, preventing her fall.

"Caweb, what's wrong with my mommy?" Elliot asks.

"I'm not sure Buddy. I'm going to make sure she's okay though."

Jenna finally makes her way over to us, which I'm extremely thankful for. I was about to scream her name across this entire store.

"Oh, my God Caleb. What happened?" she asks, taking in the mess and frozen appearance of her best friend.

"I'm hoping you can tell me. She was standing here with her soda until it came crashing to the floor. I thought she'd lost her grip. She's completely zoned."

Jenna says her name in a low, soft tone—nothing happens. My heart's heavily beating against my chest.

"What do we do?" I ask Jenna, "Is she having a nervous breakdown?"

My sister remains calm, looking around, trying to fit the pieces together.

"Are these yours?" she asks, holding up the bag of skittles I set on the counter.

"Seriously? Now is not the time to talk candy. We have a situation on our hands."

"This can clear up everything for me. Did you ask Kinsley if she wanted skittles?"

I'm so confused. How does knowing if I asked about skittles help?

"Yes. I thought she might like them."

"Shit, okay," Jenna says, as she quickly looks around. "Can you get Kinsley to the car?"

I nod.

"Good. I'll take Elliot to pay for his drink and let them know about the spill. I'll be out as soon as I can."

I watch Jenna take Elliot by the hand and lead him to the counter. Looking back to Kinsley, I briefly wonder if she could walk if I were to guide her. She's obviously not hearing things, or at least not registering what's going on.

I decide not to chance it and do the only rational thing I think of. I swiftly pick her up, with one arm under her knees and the other behind her back, and hold her against my chest.

The way I'm holding her, the way she's not rejecting me or fighting to stand brings me Déjà vu. I hope this doesn't mean she's falling back into the black hole we worked so hard to pull her from.

My feet have created an indentation on the living room floor. As soon as we got Kinsley home and in her room, Jenna told me everything. Just thinking about all of the details she gave me only ensures how extremely worried she is about Kinsley.

I rub my hand down my face. "Fuck! I wish you would've told me earlier to never say skittles," I say to Jenna who's on the couch, her legs tucked under her.

"Caleb, it's not your fault. You could've never known how a certain candy was symbolic to them."

The sound of footsteps advancing down the hall holds me in place. Jenna laid Elliot down for a nap after we got here and I'm hoping I wasn't too loud to wake him.

I'm pleasantly surprised when I see Kinsley making her way to the couch. She sits down and brings her knees to her chest, circling her arms around them. Her focus remains on the floor and I wonder if she'll find the strength to scold me about the spot I've worn thin.

"How are you, Kins?" Jenna questions, rubbing her hand on Kinsley's back.

Her shoulders barely move up in a shrug. "I want," she begins, only stopping to clear her throat. "I need to apologize."

"What?" I say, "There's nothing you need to be sorry for. I said something which threw you off balance and it's completely acceptable." Conviction is wrapped around my words.

Her head comes up and she looks at me barely before turning to Jenna. Her chin trembles, fresh tears stain a path down her cheeks. My sister wraps her closely in her arms.

The carvings of her heart seeping from her eyes might be the death of me as I fight myself to stand here and not be by her side.

"It was Ryker," Kinsley speaks, "I heard him. His voice was so clear."

Kinsley sits up causing Jenna's arms to release her. I can't stand here anymore so I move to the recliner beside them.

"I know it sounds crazy," Kinsley continues as she wipes her flooding eyes. "I know the difference between their voices." She speaks to Jenna as if I'm not even in the room. "Caleb's tone is deeper than Ryker's, and has a sexy rasp to it."

She says *sexy* so casually as though it's always how she explains my voice. I wonder if she realizes she said it at all.

Jenna holds her hand, coaxing her to continue.

"I swear I heard Ryker, though. He said it just like he used to." A small whimper comes from Kinsley's chest as Jenna pulls her close.

Everything I've learned about Ryker and Kinsley, their relationship and the love they shared, makes me long for something of my own. Which is something I've never wanted before.

Chapter 36

Kinsley

"Hey Jenna, is there any chance you can pick Elliot up from school today?"

Sometimes I'm such a procrastinator. Which is not a good thing seeing as I have four files waiting to be finished and a meeting with the justice division at two. Although, I can't completely blame procrastination for my error this time since I actually forgot they moved the meeting to the tenth of July, which is today. *Ugh!*

"I can't today Kins. My dad asked me to be at the gym for some inspections that are scheduled and then I'm headed to Sage to help Thor with the books before my shift."

Jenna's always so busy. Between classes, helping her dad with the gym and the bar, the only time I get to see her lately is early in the mornings. She likes staying busy though. It's a rare moment when she even sits. She has copious amounts of energy which never stop running through her body.

"Oh okay, no biggie, I'll just see if my mom can do it."

Jenna just stands there looking at me like I've lost my mind. "Uh no you won't, they all left for their cruise at four this morning."

Shit, shit, shit, shit, shit. How did I forget that my mom, dad, Colleen, and Heath left for vacation? It's a seven-day cruise. *Where the hell has my brain been lately?*

I grab my phone and start going through my calendar. I need to see if I'm able to move anything around or have someone cover for me.

"Ask Caleb to get him," Jenna suggests.

That could work. He is on the list for pickups at Elliot's school and I know he would do it in a heartbeat. I just feel bad asking.

"I don't want to bother him. It'd be right in the middle of his sleep. Plus there's having to move the car-seat and all that...I'll just tell them I have to leave early."

Jenna tilts her head to the side as she looks at me. Her lips are pursed and eyes slightly narrowed.

"Moving the car-seat isn't needed. Caleb has his own, and it's early enough for him to sleep now and be refreshed by the time he'd have to get him." She takes my phone from my hands and presses a few buttons.

Caleb has his own car-seat?

Jenna hands me back my phone with the screen lit up on an outgoing call to Caleb. "He bought one when he was helping out a lot," she says shrugging her shoulders like it's no big deal. "He keeps it installed for if he's ever needed on a whim."

"Kinsley?" Caleb's throaty voice reverberates from the phone in my hand.

I press the receiver to my ear and hesitate. He repeats himself. My name on his tongue blazes a trail across my skin. Little bumps rise in its path.

"Hey, Caleb. Sorry to bother you." I pause, forcing a swallow down my throat. "I'm in a bit of a predicament and was wondering if there was any chance you could pick Elliot up from school today? I totally understand if you can't." I throw in the last part to make sure he knows he's not obligated.

"Absolutely I'll pick him up! I've been dying for some time with my little buddy." His voice is laced with excitement and I feel my insides warm at the thought of him looking forward to hanging out with my son.

"Are you sure it's okay? I don't want to deprive you of your sleep." I ask tentatively.

"Kinsley, listen to me...I look forward to the days which are filled with you and Elliot. I'll always do everything in my power to fulfill the needs you ask of me. Don't ever hesitate to ask me for something. No matter when or what time, I'm only a phone call away." His tone's assertive, yet light, making sure I understand he means what he says.

My hand moves to my chest as I nod my head. He's probably unaware how he included me on the days he looks forward to, it doesn't keep my heart from pounding a little bit harder.

His amused chuckle makes me realize I haven't responded. I've been nodding my head.

"Thank you," I tell him, then end the call and finish getting ready for work.

I hurry through the stop light only to be slowed down by the car in front of me waiting to make a left-hand turn. *Come on, come on. Go already!*

I can't believe my meeting ran over so late. I hate taking up Caleb's time when he still has work to get to tonight. Even though he told me he doesn't mind, I'm sure he'd rather be relaxing than taking care of a three-year-old.

I walk in the front door of my house, slipping my shoes off and tossing my bag on the small table, the aroma of bacon and eggs greets me. *Mmm...there's something about breakfast for dinner which brings happiness to my soul.*

I head to the kitchen, finding it empty. Retracing my steps back through the living room, I head for the hall in search of Caleb and Elliot.

As soon as I step into the hallway I'm assaulted by a smell so foul my hand automatically moves to cover my nose along with my mouth.

Oh, my! What is that?

I hear water swishing around in the tub as I near the bathroom. The sound of Caleb's voice carries through the door as he says, "Hey Buddy, what's the sad face for?"

"I sorry I messed in my pwants." Elliot's sadness seeps through his words and it makes me want to sweep in and take care of him. I don't, mainly because the poop smell is still so strong I'd most likely have my head in the toilet rather than comforting anyone.

I started potty training Elliot right after he turned three. He was a very early talker and the rest he's just done on his own time. Potty training has been one of them because, before three, he just wouldn't have it. I am a little shocked to hear he had an accident since he's been doing so well.

I hear the tub start to drain and it sounds like Caleb's helping Elliot get out of the bath. There's movement and rustling. I assume he's trying to dry him off.

"Elliot, can you look at me please?" There's a pause. "Thank you for saying sorry, even though you didn't need to. It was an accident. Sometimes things are out of our control...even poop." Elliot giggles before Caleb continues. "Plus we took care of it. We hosed you off and nobody other than us even has to know. Okay?" Caleb is so caring and gentle with Elliot. It makes my heart happy he came into our lives.

The bathroom door opens before I can move out of the way. Caleb's completely relaxed even though his eyes widen a little. *I guess he wasn't expecting me to be standing here.*

"Hi, Mommy!" Elliot exclaims as he clutches his towel around him. "I had an apcident. Caweb heped me cwean up."

It humors me to hear Elliot tell me about his accident since he doesn't seem the least bit phased by it now. And I also guess he didn't care to keep it to himself.

"That was very nice of Caleb. I hope you thanked him.

Elliot looks at me blankly before he turns around and says, "Thank you."

Caleb ruffles Elliot's hair with his hand. "No problem, Buddy."

I watch Elliot as he stares up at Caleb and smiles. "Why don't you head into your room. I'll be right in to help you get dressed." I tell him.

Elliot's little feet shuffle him down the hallway and into his room. I turn to Caleb with my brows raised and controlled breathing through only my mouth.

"What did you feed him?" I ask, "That's the foulest shit I've ever smelled and it's still so strong. How are you breathing?"

Caleb's chuckle rumbles through his chest. His eyes hold a small glimmer.

"I think he might have a little stomach bug or something. It was a little liquidy." I pinch my nose with my fingers, creating another chuckle from Caleb. "Oh come on Kins. It's not that bad."

I quirk an eyebrow at him. "It's so bad," I say.

"This is nothing. You have to remember I was raised on a farm. I've dealt with many harsh smells and loads of shit on the daily."

I playfully smack him on the arm. "Are you comparing my son to farm animals?" I ask, feigning offense.

A smirk forms on his face.

"Actually yes, it's the perfect comparison for this," he says.

I retrieve a plastic bag from the hall closet and hand it to him.

"Please, just get rid of the evidence. I'm praying I still have an appetite after being assaulted by that."

His laughter fills the air as I head to Elliot's room to get him dressed.

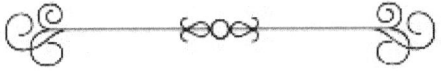

"Thanks for making dinner tonight. You really didn't have to," I say to Caleb.

I'm sitting on the couch drinking a glass of wine while Elliot's playing on the floor with his toys. Caleb has a couple hours before he has to leave for work, so he's propped back relaxing in the recliner.

"Did you like it?" he asks.

"Um yes, I loved it. Breakfast for dinner is the best meal ever."

"Duly noted. It was my pleasure."

He puts his hands behind his head causing his shirt to move up a sliver. I'm transfixed by the image before me, thankful he decided to close his eyes.

"Were you able to get enough sleep today?" I ask, hoping to divert my attention from abs. It works since he opens his eyes and pins his gaze on me. I briefly stare back at him then move my focus to the wall behind him.

"Actually I did. It worked out really well for me today."

Dammit, why did I ask him? He probably wanted a little more sleep before he has to go in.

We sit in silence, watching the television for a while. As it gets closer to Elliot's bedtime he grabs his blanket and climbs on to my lap. I twist and lie back, moving Elliot until his head's up on my chest. Caleb's foot moving catches my attention and I look to him. He's looking at Elliot, deep in thought as a small smile rests on his face.

"What time do you have to leave?" I ask, pulling him from his thoughts.

He glances at the clock and then sits up, pushing the footrest of the recliner closed. "About thirty minutes." Getting up, he heads for the front door. "I'm gonna go get my uniform out of my truck so I can get ready."

"Okay," I say as I rub Elliot's back. I can tell he's already fallen asleep. His light snore gives it away.

After Caleb has his uniform on I accept his offer to carry Elliot to bed.

"Why'd you decide to become a police officer?" I ask while he sits on the couch next to me.

I once had a dream to become a detective, follow in the footsteps of my parents. Ryker was going to as well. Following his coma, my dream was placed on hold. After his death, our dreams were buried with him, together. Now I plan to work on a degree in social work.

Caleb slips on his boots. "To make the nights safer," he says. He leans forward, resting his elbows on his knees. "A drunk driver took my mother's life. It's the reason I choose to stay on the night shift. At least for now." He runs his hand over his head, his hair sticking up in the perfect places as though he's spent time styling it. "I figure if I get as many impaired people off the roads as I can, it will help even out the karma of my wrong-doings from my younger days."

I smile and think of his words a moment before I respond, "I'm sure any karma you had is well taken care of. You're a great man, Caleb. You may not think it yet, but I see it in everything you do. You're a giver. Always caring for others without expectations in return. It's an amazing quality to have, and I hope Elliot grows up to be that way."

He moves back slightly as though my words were too much for him to hear even though it's nothing but the truth. He rests his hands on my shoulder and says, "thank you."

He stands to leave for work and continues talking, "I wasn't always this way though. There were many years when I was a taker, and times I felt I could never keep anyone safe." He gives me a small smile and then opens the front door.

"Caleb." He looks back at me, "You make me feel safe."

His smile is small yet lights up his whole face.

"Night, Kinsley."

"Have a great night at work."

I wave goodbye as he closes the door behind him.

Chapter 37

Caleb

I decided to take a drive and ended up in my old town. This morning after my shift I went on my usual run. When I came home and took a shower I felt jittery, anxious, and knew I needed something more to clear my thoughts.

I honestly was just going to drive around the city. Apparently, my subconscious had other plans since I'm now an hour and a half away from my place.

I'm sitting here in my car, parked in this empty parking lot, staring at the white brick building before me. The bricks used to be a dirty red, worn and old. It's amazing how a fresh coat of paint can make such a change.

Tim finally upgraded from a dilapidated worn down sign to the nice vinyl imprinted one sprawled across his double-paned glass doors. It's nice to see how it actually reads The Office of Dr. Timothy Greivens, MD, instead of the partial lettering sign before. People had to guess what this place was.

Although, it's not like many people have to guess what any place is in this small little town of Quatin, Missouri. When a town barely has two thousand residents, there tend to be only one of many places— grocery store, gas station, auto shop, doctor and the farm animals overpopulate the people ten to one.

When I was ten, I started going to Tim's dad, Dr. Gerald Greivens. My Gramps is a man who can admit when someone, even himself, needs more help than the hard, therapeutic labor of farm life can give. Dr. Greivens is the town's very own family physician. My gramps learned he'd studied psychiatry in his University days as well, which is what led him to take me to him for therapy.

It took the doctor a long time to break through my façade. I was thirteen when he truly began to reach me. Three years of me putting up a fight to keep my tragedy captive, and then when he finally got through he went and had a massive heart attack on me.

Thankfully, he didn't die. He's alive, strong and very healthy. After the heart attack happened he shut down his practice for a while until his son came in to run it.

When I started having my sessions with Dr. Tim, Dr. Greivens son, it was extremely hard for me. I shut down even more than I was before. Going from the doctor I'd barely begun to trust, then moving to one who was a measly twelve years older than me, was something my mind couldn't wrap around. Doctors are supposed to be old, gray-haired, and wise. Dr. Tim was barely a man. He couldn't grow a beard and didn't look a day older than fifteen. I remember thinking how is this twenty-five year old already a doctor of medicine and psychiatry and running the family practice on his own.

Intelligence. Tim is beyond smart. He knows how to connect with people on a deeper, more personal level. Except, it backfired on him when he had to deal with me—the angry, brooding, pubescent kid who was now pissed about another person being taken from him.

When he would try talking to me as though he was my friend, my buddy, it would irritate me beyond belief. There's an irony here, though, since now he's my closest friend.

When he'd push, I pulled. When I pushed he moved with me. He never backed down, however, he found a way to turn things around and make it seem like I wanted to talk, it was my idea. It's what makes him the best damn doctor, and as I started getting older I figured out I could trust him with all my secrets.

I called him fifteen minutes ago and woke his ass up. I was shocked to find out he was still sleeping being its Friday and almost nine in the morning. He said he's not due in until ten and I thought about just heading over to his house. Except I have a need to get things off my chest and his office is the only place I feel comfortable enough to let all my walls down. I think it helps to keep the doctor part of his life separate from the friendship portion we've created.

His faded red 1974 Chevy pickup pulls into the spot next to me. I have to laugh at the huge smile sprawled across his face. I get out of my car and greet him, slapping my open hand into his, pulling him in for a quick hug.

"Well, well, well. The doctor was able to have his large cup of coffee already or is just really happy to see me." Tim's not a morning person at all, and coffee is his weakness. Although it usually takes two large cups before he looks this chipper.

"Shit Leb, can't you just call me Tim since the office isn't even open for business?" He shakes his head with disapproval. I never call him by his first name when we're at his office. I just can't. "Oh, and I quit coffee about a month ago so this smile is *all* for you."

He unlocks the front door and re-locks it after we're both inside the building.

"Did the town of Quatin run out of coffee beans and put a ban on shipping it in or something?" I ask, wondering how on earth it's possible for this man to quit the love of his life.

"Nah man, you know how Kimber's been getting onto me for years about the amount I drink. She kept beggin' me to cut back. I figured if I'm going to give some of it up I might as well do it all." We make our way to his office in the back. "It was hard at first, with the withdrawals and headaches. Somewhere along the line, it started to get better, easier, and now I feel really good."

"Great job, Man. I'm proud of you." I clap him on the back.

I opt to make myself comfortable in the comfy brown leather chair opposed to the couch sitting alongside it as Tim takes a minute to clear off his desk. He pulls a fresh notepad out of his top drawer, placing it on top then grabs his good pen and sets it beside the notepad. I doubt he'll take notes today. He's turned on professional doctor mode and likes to have it handy just in case.

Leaning back in his chair, he looks the epitome of relaxed. He's waiting for me to talk, to spill my reasons for being here unexpectedly. There was a time when he had to ask questions and goad me into the conversation. Now he just chills until I'm ready to tell all.

"Man, when was the last time I was here for an actual visit?" I ask as regret sweeps through me questioning the reasons I've come here.

"In ten days it will be exactly two years ago since you sat here in my office for an actual visit." He says without looking at a calendar or my file for reference.

The lines in his forehead reveal he's on to me. He knows I'm deflecting, especially since I already know the answer to my own question.

In ten days it will be August 12th. Sixteen years since my mother's death. Two years ago, on my last visit, I worked up the courage to tell him *everything* from the night she died. I was finally starting to heal. It felt as though I could stand taller, most of the weight I carried had been lifted from my shoulders. It's also how I discovered my need to pursue a career in the police force.

Then five months ago I walked into a bar to meet up with my sister and ended up wrapping my eyes and my arms unknowingly around her best friend.

"Leb?" Tim says my name, pulling me from my thoughts. He's the only person who calls me by that ridiculous nickname.

On my twenty-first birthday, he and a couple of buddies of mine took me out to some bars a few towns over. Of course, I had way too many drinks and don't remember much of the night. After a few days, it dawned on me how Tim kept calling me Leb. He told me every time I introduced myself to a lady that night, I would pronounce my name as two separate ones—Ca Leb.

"Dude, where's your head at? I know ya didn't drive all this way and make me come into the office early just to stare off into space. If that was the case you could've come to my house and chilled. So spill."

I rub my sweaty hands across my shorts, taking in a deep breath. I'm a little uncertain myself on why I made the trip out here.

"Honestly Tim, I'm not sure what to say. I've been feeling antsy for a couple days and my run this morning didn't help at all. I got in my car and went for a drive. Ended up here." I shrug my shoulders.

Tim leans forward, his hands clasp together and sit on top of his desk. There's not an ounce of emotion moving across his face. He's perfected this portion of his job.

"Antsy because of Kinsley?" he asks.

My head nods instinctively. I didn't even have to think about the answer to his question. I guess I just wasn't ready to admit it to myself.

"Do you think the attachment you've formed with Elliot is driving your feelings for Kinsley?" he questions.

I laugh just a little, thinking about how it could be so true in some people's scenarios. Not in mine.

"Nah man, my attachment to Elliot is what propels me to try and remain only friends with her." His eyes widen a fraction as he waits for me to continue. "If I dated Kinsley and shit failed since it always does, I ultimately lose getting to be around Elliot." I rub the back of my neck at the thought. "You know the one commitment I've been in was with Abby."

Having the same fuck buddy for eighteen months wasn't much of a commitment. It was enough for me. I'm extremely thankful Abby reciprocated my feelings for a sex only relationship until she found Brendan. I don't deal well with feelings.

"Yet you put yourself around Kinsley even though she makes you have all the feelings."

I shake my head trying to deny his words even though I know they're true. I take a moment to think about what he just said. Tim knows just about everything of Kinsley's and my encounters. Somehow through our calls and texts, he's able to pull information from me without me realizing it for the most part. I try to tell myself he isn't always analyzing me, and he's been a great friend by never talking to me as my psychiatrist unless it's in this office. I'm sure it's pretty hard for him to shut that part of his brain off though even when he's in friendship mode.

"I can't stay away from her. I'm a bee in search of the copious amounts of pollen she provides."

He tries to hide his smirk as his shoulders shake in silent laughter. "That was the stupidest fucking analogy I've ever heard."

"You understand where I'm going, so mission accomplished." I swipe my palms back and forth against each other as if I'm dusting them off.

"Yup, the understanding is loud and clear," he gives me an all-knowing look, "I need to focus more on the fears you're harboring which are keeping you from leaping into the unknown." Getting up from his chair, he comes around to the front of the desk and leans back against the edge with his arms folded across his chest.

And this is how I know shit's about to get real.

"Caleb, since we have about five minutes left until my doors have to open to the world, I'm going to stop beating around the bush and give it to you straight." He pauses a short second waiting for a protest, yet not actually giving me enough time to do so.

"I know your commitment issues stem from the loss of your mother. You've made a lot of progress over the years, which I'm proud of, however, you haven't tied all the loose ends together. You have to be able to completely heal to move on. You need to talk to your father *and* your sister. Tell them everything. Let the burden drop from you entirely. Trust me when I say you'll feel like a new man."

He makes his way over to the chair next to me and sits, relaxed. "When it comes to Kinsley, I will say, in my *friend* voice, to get the fuck over yourself. I say this with much love. Things don't always work out, life continuously changes, and every one of us is going to die at some point. Stop letting those fears hold you back from a woman who could possibly be your soulmate."

My chest tightens and my mouth is dry. *Soulmate? Why would he say such a thing?*

"I know she just went through a huge loss," he continues, "She most likely fights even wanting to look at another man in the same light she held her fiancé in. From everything you've told me, she seems to have as much interest as you do. It's as though her subconscious is aware of how she's your pollen and keeps creating more."

He laughs at his own attempt at a joke, but I'm feeling a little too queasy to join him.

"All I'm saying is let yourself enjoy her company fully. Don't be afraid to soak up all she can give. You two can essentially help rebuild each other and come out the other side stronger than ever, and hopefully together."

My response is silenced by the thundering thoughts rolling through my head. If there's one thing I can count on Tim for, it's him not beating around the bush when time calls for it, and time is on the phone.

He stands up, pulling me from my chair with him and embraces me in a hug.

"If you can find a way to open your heart and love Kinsley, as passionately as you love your mother, then she will be one very lucky lady."

His final words are what I leave with as we say our goodbyes. I get in my truck and hit the road back to my new home.

Chapter 38

Kinsley

Every day brings forth a different kind of struggle. Some days I wake up, wondering why I still have air in my lungs and blood pumping through my veins. Other days awake refreshed, feeling new. That is until the reality of what's been taken from me comes out of the shadows.

Each night I toss and turn praying for my brain to succumb to the slumber, yet the times I'm able to fall asleep, I'm chased by the demons who hold me captive, threatening to never set me free.

Today is not a good day and it hasn't even begun. I'm trying to figure out how I'll make it through the next twenty hours and eighteen minutes.

I will do it for Elliot. These words have been playing on repeat in my head, fighting away the desire to knock myself out until tomorrow.

Jenna stayed home last night to keep me distracted. We made sub sandwiches and took Elliot to the park. We had a picnic and played on the playground. An ice cream stop on the way home ended our perfect evening, then a bath for Elliot and a couple glasses of wine for me.

I know Jenna was trying everything in her power to keep me busy. To keep my brain in the moment instead of on the day approaching. It's incredibly hard to push something which has been such a huge magnitude in your life, from the time you were born. I truly believe that even if I lived alone, on an island, where time and days, months and years didn't mean a thing, every part of my being would still know when this day came around.

Fortunately, the couple glasses of wine, which was probably the whole bottle, knocked me out shortly after Elliot went to bed.

Unfortunately, it wasn't for long. I woke abruptly at 11:58 pm and haven't been back to sleep since. This day is so ingrained in me, I can't even drink it away.

When the clock struck midnight I dialed up his number, allowing it to ring, praying a stranger wouldn't answer. When the robotic female started speaking, telling me the voicemail box of the person I was attempting to reach was not yet set up, I whispered, "happy birthday, Ryk," then ended the call.

I wanted to call over and over again. Instead, I turned off my phone, chucked it into the drawer of my nightstand, and curled up into a ball. My vision blurred as the frayed lesions of my beaten down heart trickled from my lids, gathering in rivulets on top of my pillow.

I didn't cry hard. I just let the liquid flow on its own. I'm surprised, yet relieved, that the tears stopped an hour ago. As much as I've been dreading this day, I've made a commitment to myself that I would try my hardest to get through it in one piece for Elliot. Swollen eyes and dark circles are something I don't want to worry about.

Getting up, I head to the bathroom. I don't stop in front of the mirror or even glance at the girl in the reflection. Instead, I strip off my clothes and get in the shower. I stand under the spout as I turn the knob. I let the ice cold water slide down my body, praying for it to freeze my sorrows before the liquid turns hot enough to burn them from my skin.

After I'm done with the shower I dry myself off and put on my sleep shorts. I walk to my dresser to retrieve a fresh shirt. When I open the drawer the smell of Ryker's cologne pervades the air. I pull his favorite Shinedown shirt over my head and decide the only place I may get a few hours of actual sleep will be curled up next to my baby boy. Making my way to his room, I climb myself into his toddler size train bed and slide my body between his and the wall. He stirs just a bit, moving his body within the shape of mine.

Just listening to his soft breathing and the pitter patter of his heart reassures me I will be able to make it...through this day, through this month, through this year, through this life.

My legs are moving in swift, fast motions as if I'm running in the fastest sprint of my life. Except, I'm not running, I'm falling.

FALLING

FALLING

I land on cold, hard, earth, six feet down.

Touching the sides surrounding me, my fingers entangle themselves within smooth satin which seems to line the walls. Gripping onto the silk, I hoist myself into a sitting position only to be slammed back down with a brutal force.

What the hell?

I try to sit up again, this time the top of my head crashes into a ceiling, an invisible ceiling. How is there an invisible ceiling above me?

None of this makes sense.

I can see the dried, crusty dirt on every side of my body and I notice how it looks to be freshly dug. My eyes shift their attention to my hands. I can still feel the silk threads of the satin material gripped between my fingers. I begin to feel all around me, the sides are soft, plush, like a cushion. Like I've sliced open the center of a mattress and cocooned myself within.

All I see is dirt...to my left, to my right, at my feet, and behind my head. Four sides lined with dirt. Four sides to a dirt box. And it's not the loose, crumbly—makes a dusty wind tornado—kind of dirt. No, it's more of a mixture of dirt and mud. The compacting kind that was most likely watered recently to be molded, or in this case, dug into the desired shape and is now on its path to drying from the scorching sun.

Wait...the sun!

I look up and see the bright sun peering its ghastly carbons over the edge of my makeshift grave—my demise.

Makeshift grave, demise...makeshift grave, demise.

As the words run rampant through my mind, I come to the realization that they explain exactly what this is.

My heart is picking up pace, informing me that I need to work a little harder to figure a way out. I open my mouth to scream for help. My ears are met with silence. My hands press against my throat, feeling for some sort of vibration.

I can feel it, the vibration, I'm still screaming. Why can't I hear it?

I move my hands to my ears and start feeling them for something that could be blocking out the sound.

I find nothing. Am I deaf?

Large hands grip my biceps, shaking me slightly, yet I'm still alone.

"Kinsley!" A voice so familiar calls to me. I can tell he's shouting, only it's barely audible like he's far away in the distance.

"Kinsley, baby, I'm here. I'm right here."

Ryker?

It can't be, can it?

"Kinsley, it's me. I'm here. Open your eyes, please." His voice is begging, pleading, but my eyes are open. Why can't he see that?

Why can't I see him?

I decide to close my eyes, hoping that when I reopen them, I will be able to see him.

"Kinsley, why won't you look at me?" Ryker's voice becomes sad and heavy as though he's being weighed down by something.

I re-open my eyes and look up. The ground has begun to close, swallowing me whole, but still, no one is there. My head shifts to my left, where the last stream of sunlight exposes the form of a body lying next to me. A dead body. The body of my fiancé, my best friend, the father of our child—my Ryker. His eyes open, but they're pools of black—lifeless. I feel a strong urge to scream but a stronger urge to hold him. I grip on to his arm and pull him to me. He's heavy...too heavy. I need to be near him, to feel him for one last time. I lay my head upon his chest.

"I'm sorry. I'm so sorry baby."

My thoughts are being said out loud, only I'm not the one speaking them. I ask him what he's sorry for. I tell him I'm the one who should be apologizing. He takes a few seconds before he responds, it feels like forever. I try to shift so I can turn my head to see his face, but I'm not able to within the confines of this box. I grasp his hand finding it to be ice cold. It doesn't bother me though. I'll happily die of hypothermia as long as it means being in his arms.

He tells me he's sorry for going to her house alone, "for going there at all. For holding on to a glimmer of hope that she would have ever changed for me. For thinking she would've been excited to have a grandbaby when she could never accept the love I hold for you."

Tears are streaming down my face as I listen to his words. Hearing his voice again after so long, warms my heart, but listening to his apologies and regrets turns it to ice that threatens to dissolve. My head is shaking, telling him to stop this nonsense. "I don't want you to apologize. I don't blame you for what happened. I blame her. It's always been on her," I say as a sob claws its way out of my throat.

His arms wrap around me and I'm instantly calm. I notice he's warm as if the life which was stripped from him is now back.

He strokes my face and tells me he doesn't have much more time. I want to cry out again, but force it back so I can soak in what little time I have left.

"Kit," he whispers, "You're an amazing mommy, you know that? The way you're raising our little boy, and staying so strong for him is incredible and absolutely inspiring."

Everything he's saying makes me feel amazing and erases any doubts I hold about how I'm doing as a mother. I hate that he isn't by my side raising Elliot with me, but at least now I know he's seeing everything from up above.

"Now, I have something I need to say before our time is up and I want you to absorb it all and promise me you'll do what I ask of you."

My head nods automatically, knowing I will do anything to make him happy.

"The love we share is strong and so very real. I know it hurts so much right now and you might feel incapable to love another or to let another love you the way I do, but I'm here telling you right now that it's going to happen and I want you to let it happen. In fact, it's already happening so I need your promise to love the hardest you've ever loved. Harder than you love me, even if you think it's impossible. Feel the love given to you with your full existence. And don't for one-second doubt it, or think by doing so you are in any way replacing me or forgetting me. I know it's not possible." He pauses to let his words sink in.

"Can you do that for me, Kit?"

I barely nod my head, questioning if I want to commit to this promise like I thought I would.

He's rocking me back and forth which feels nice and reassuring.

"Sometimes I wish you weren't so hard headed even though it's actually my favorite part of you," he says with a little laugh. "Who am I kidding? I have no favorite parts of you. I love them all equally."

The rocking continues as I feel his lips press against my forehead. I've missed these embraces so much.

"Kinsley, please just promise me this. You'll know the love I'm talking about once you open up your eyes."

Ryker's words become distant. They're drifting away from me. My arms go around his body tightly, as I pray I can hold him close forever. "I promise," I say, "I'll do the best I can."

I hear the faint whispers of an "I love you."

"Kinsley, please wake up. Please, you're scaring me."

Chapter 39

Caleb

I had to see her today. After finding out the significance of what today is and what it might do to her, I had to make sure she would be okay.

When I spoke to Jenna yesterday I could hear the slight panic in her voice. She confided in me the details of this date, Ryker's birthday and Kinsley's half birthday, which I've learned meant the world to them.

I've fought with myself all night on when I should make an appearance, how I would do it, what I might say.

Right after I got off work I went straight to the store. I bought Elliot a little toy and a 'create your own picture frame' craft. I grabbed a gift bag and tissue paper, and a box of cake mix and icing. I'm not exactly sure of my plan. I figure if this has always been a day of happiness for Kinsley, then why not try and keep it that way.

I pull into her driveway and stuff the things I bought into the gift bag. Looking at the clock on my dash, I realize it's barely past seven. I tap my fingers on the steering wheel trying to decide what to do. *Is it too early to knock? What if Elliot's sleeping?* Who am I kidding? That kid hardly sleeps past six. I let myself in, expecting everyone to still be asleep. What I wasn't expecting is to find Elliot sitting on the couch by himself.

"Hey, Buddy. What are you doing?"

"Mommy's sweeping in my bed. I fink she's having a bad dweam."

As the words leave his mouth, a garbled cry comes from down the hall.

"Elliot, stay right here," I tell him, and then run down the hall to his door. Jenna comes flying out of her room at the same time.

My hand on her shoulder stops her from going to Kinsley. "Do you mind if I go in...alone?" She looks at me unsure, her gaze probing, her lip between her teeth. "Elliot's in the living room. He was on the couch when I came in." She nods her head and moves past me down the hall.

I move into Elliot's room and the sight before me threatens to take me to my knees. On Elliot's small train shaped bed, Kinsley is completely curled into the fetal position as her body shakes with turmoil.

I rush over to her and softly call her name. I want to wake her as fast as I can. I don't want to startle her while doing so. Her head shakes vigorously, a strangled 'no' comes from her as she chokes on another sob.

I maneuver myself onto the bed, hoping I don't break it, as she begins to shift. I take this moment to bring her upper body into my arms. She's ice cold against my warmth. I scan the bed for a blanket to cover her with.

I begin to rock her back and forth with my body. I smooth the hair back from her face and press my lips to her forehead.

A whispered 'I love you' falls from her mouth as she clenches onto my shirt, and its then I know she's dreaming of Ryker. I'd do anything to take away her pain. I'd switch him places if it meant she would always be happy.

I kiss her forehead again and leave my lips there as I speak, "Kinsley, please wake up. Please, you're scaring me."

Her body moves. I bring my head up and look at her. Her eyes are open and besides the redness that circles them from crying, they're clear. *She's awake.* She looks at me, searching every feature of my face as if it's the very first time. I wonder if she's aware she just had a nightmare.

She moves out of my arms and stands up, then runs her hands across her face. "I'm sorry," she says, "I must've had a bad dream."

My head nods once in response. I want to ask her if she's okay. I bite my tongue. Clearly, she's not. I want to tell her it'll be okay. What if it won't?

She sways back and forth from one foot to the other. Her hands alternate between messing with her t-shirt and smoothing down her hair. I sit frozen, watching, waiting for what she'll do next.

She seems nervous, apprehensive all of a sudden. An emotion I'm not used to seeing on her. Her mouth opens then closes. Her eyes glance around the room quickly before falling back on me.

"What time is it?" she asks.

"Seven twenty or so," I respond based off the time I got here.

"Where's Elliot?" Her attention bounces around the room again as though she can no longer look directly at me.

"In the living room with Jenna."

My voice is quiet, soft, hoping to provide her comfort. She seems fragile in the state she's in right now. I don't want to risk breaking her more than she already is.

"Um," she bites the inside of her cheek. "How long have you been here...in here...with me?" Her question is broken.

"Maybe ten minutes," I say, then take a few seconds to formulate my next words. "Kinsley?" I pause again, waiting for her eyes to meet mine. When they do, it's only for a mere second before she focuses on my forehead. She does this every time she talks to me—never completely looks into my eyes—it's something I don't think she realizes I notice. She may not even notice it herself. "If there's anything I can do to make today, and any day, a little better for you I'll do it. Please don't hesitate to ask. And I do mean anything, even if it's cleaning toilets or taking out the trash."

She nods her head as a sad smile slips on her face. "Thank you, Caleb," she manages to say before leaving the room and me behind her.

Chapter 40

Caleb

I've been sitting in my truck, parked in front of my father's house, for a good twenty-five minutes. I still can't believe I've already lived in this town for eight months and I haven't been face-to-face with my father. I've spoken to him a couple of times on the phone, but have yet to make it a priority to see him. It's a shitty thing to do. It makes me a shitty son. I'm thankful though that he hasn't pushed the issue.

Our relationship was once like a chewed up wire. The wires that remained attached to each other still made a connection on an occasion, even though they're always faulty. Then after my mother died those wires completely snapped.

I'm not saying I don't love my dad, nor think that he doesn't love me. I know he does. He's a great man and always worked so hard to provide the daily necessities for his family. My mother stayed home to raise me and my sister, which is most likely the reason my father worked so much and was never home. My sister was and, from what I can tell, still is a daddy's girl. I guess that makes me a mama's boy, which is fine and a title I don't mind wearing proudly.

My mother was an amazing woman and mother. Her belief and faith in God were so strong. Her love for her children and husband was stronger. She had a daily schedule she kept us on, but was such an easy going person that if something got off track like life often does, she didn't freak out about it. She always made it feel like whatever had changed throughout the day was just how it was originally planned.

What I've realized as I've grown older is how she most likely kept the schedule for me. I seem to be at my best when things are structured when I have a plan of attack for the days to come. This is something my father was not good at and it seemed to aide in my lack of coping with my mother's death.

Moving me to my Gramps and Grams farm was the best thing he could've done for me, even though I didn't understand it at the time. He probably didn't realize it either. When you're raised on a farm, you have to have a structure in order to feed, clean, and take care of the animals and crops. Things have to be done at a certain time and in certain ways or you could wind up with a loss. That did more for me than any amount of therapy could.

Getting out of my car, I make my way to the front door of my dad's house. Before I can even raise my hand to knock it opens revealing my dad.

"I was wondering if you were ever gonna to get in here," he says.

I figured he'd know I was sitting out here. I called and told him I would be here today at this time. I needed to make sure he would be available for a bit along with Jenna.

"Well, come on now. No reason to stand out here wasting more time," my dad says as he smiles and turns around, leading me in through the house.

His home is a ranch style house with a one car garage. Jenna told me he bought it two years ago. He walks me around, giving me the grand tour. The outside is deceiving making it seem very small when you look at it from the front. Once inside it reveals a larger interior. As soon as you walk through the front door, you're in a large open room that houses the living room and kitchen, with a four-person tall table in between. To the right is a hallway that leads into three bedrooms and a hall bathroom. If you look to the left where the kitchen is, there's a door that takes you to the garage and a staircase taking you to a finished, walk out basement.

The décor gives off a woman's touch. I wonder if my sister did the decorating or if my father's seeing someone. Like I said, I haven't seen my father in a very long time and I don't ever ask for details. I know, I'm a shitty son. I'm hoping to correct that now and work on being better.

A common theme I've noticed throughout this house is how all the walls are some shade of gray. Even the exterior is painted a dark hue of gray with black shutters. Although, I can almost guarantee they're not actually black. They're most likely the darkest hue of gray you can get with it still being considered gray.

The reason this stands out to me in such a significant way is that gray is my mother's favorite color. It's not a color people typically choose as their favorite, especially not by a woman. My mother loved every aspect, every hue, and every combination of that damn color. She'd wear it, decorate with it, and buy things just because they were that color. Then she would offset the monotonous by incorporating splashes of bright color.

This house is the embodiment of my mother. A remembrance, memorial, of her without anyone who didn't know her ever even knowing that's what it is. This house gives me warmth and makes me feel at home even though it's the first time I've stepped foot inside. This house *is* my mother, and my father is the one who brought her here.

We sit on the couch in the living room and I can feel my dad watching me as I look around, taking it all in.

He's comforting me with his thoughts and he knows I've noticed the choice of his coloration.

I've blamed him for far too long in having a hand in my mother's death, however, just coming into this house, his home, already makes me optimistic about the future.

"Sis should be here soon," he says, "She said she'd stop to grab some bagels. Do you want something to drink in the meantime?"

"I'm good, thanks."

The front door opens and in walks Jenna with a box of fresh bagels in one hand and drinks in the other. Hopping up from the couch, I meet her at the door, retrieving the items from her hands.

I place everything on the kitchen table, then grab the iced coffee with my name scrawled across. Apparently, she's learned how I like it—cold and black.

We all take a seat in the living room, Jenna and I on the couch, my dad in the chair beside us. I don't really want to beat around the bush and drag this out longer than needed. I still need to get home and try to fit in a few hours of sleep before work.

"I'm just going to get into things," I say as I look at my father then Jenna. "I need to talk about some things surrounding mom's death."

Jenna's head nods once before her eyes dart to my father for a split second. I continue to stare at my sister, knowing if I look at our dad I may never say what I need to.

"First, I want to apologize." My focus moves to my dad as I say the last word of the sentence.

He runs his hand over his balding head as his eyebrows squish together. "Caleb, son, there's nothing you need to apologize for."

I look him straight in the eyes pleading with him to just let me finish. I glance at my sister to do the same, even though there's no need. Jenna lives life quietly. She's like a sponge absorbing her surroundings before giving out her words.

"I'm sorry for the way I acted after mom's death. I may have only been nine, however, I did know right from wrong and I completely knew everything I was doing was beyond wrong." I take a second to take a drink of my coffee.

"When mom died something inside of me snapped. I know I'm not the only one who lost her. After she died I felt like I no longer belonged here, on this Earth." My throat's thick as I try to swallow down the lump that's formed. "Dad, I'm so sorry I blamed you for her death. I'm sorry it's taken me this long to finally look at things differently. To truly understand how you're not the reason she's gone."

The night my mother died, the four of us went to dinner and a movie. It was the end of summer break and Jenna's first movie at an actual theatre. Jenna was starting kindergarten and I was going into the fourth grade. My mom was having a hard time with how both her babies were going to be in school. My dad wasn't catching on to that. They'd been arguing for a while about her going back to work so my dad could quit one of his jobs and be able to spend more time with the family. They thought they kept their disagreements hidden from us. Parents always seem to think kids are oblivious to the things they say to each other. We're not.

My parents didn't argue often. They were madly in love from what I recall. My dad typically treated my mother like a queen, so much so it's what he called her, "my queen."

That evening after the movie was over after we were all seat-belted into the car and on our journey home, they began to argue. It started out small. My dad wouldn't let things go. He became distracted. The car swerved off the road, onto the shoulder, then onto the road as he brought it back.

My mother's words often play in my head, 'Mitch, can we please save this conversation for when we get home so we all make it there alive?'

My dad was distracted at that very moment. Distracted by how he'd already run off the road. Distracted by what my mom was saying. Distracted by his frustration with the argument which seemed to be played on repeat with a nonexistent outcome.

And his distraction caused him to fail.

He failed to see the speeding car, their headlights shining from the crossing road. He'd failed to notice how even though our stoplight had just turned green the drunk driver in the other car was going too fast to even make an attempt to stop at his own.

He simply failed.

I failed too, by not honoring my mother's final wish.

"Son," my dad says, "you don't have to apologize. I blame myself every single day for the very same thing."

I swallow down the sorrow creeping up my throat. It's crossed my mind a few times how he might blame himself, yet to hear him confirm it cuts me deep. It's a hard pill to swallow knowing right after your dad lost the love of his life he practically lost his son as well.

"There's something I've kept to myself from that night," I pause, taking a deep breath and clearing my throat, "I know the paramedics told you mom died on impact. It wasn't true." I look to my sister who's staring at me wide-eyed. Her hands tremble in her lap. I move my hand on top of hers, hoping to give her some comfort.

"You were unconscious, Dad. And Jenna, you were crying. I unbuckled and checked on you first to make sure you were okay. I didn't find a single scratch. Then I heard a gargled noise from mom's seat. I got out seeing if I could get to her from her door. It was too smashed up keeping her trapped inside. I got in through the back and slid myself between the front seats, sitting on the center console. She looked like she wanted to say something, but blood was coming from her mouth. I laid my head gently on her shoulder and told her not to worry, help was on the way, even though I didn't know if

I was right. She tried to speak again, so I sat up to look at her. I remember her eyes looking weird like she wasn't truly there at all. Then not a second later her vision cleared bringing back the eyes I've always known. She was able to whisper her final words."

"Caleb, my sweet, handsome boy. Our Lord Jesus is calling me to come home. Now, more than ever, I need you to help dad take care of your sister and you need to keep an eye on him. These next couple of months will be hard for you all. Just remember how much I love you three, more than anything in this world. I will always be watching over you."

Jenna squeezes my hand and it brings me back to the present. I hate to even think about that night, let alone relive it. It hurts like hell to share with them the thing which has burdened me the most. Except now I feel lighter, now that they know.

There are tears in my eyes and a lump in my throat. It's been a very long time since I've let myself cry and I'm not sure I'm ready to embrace it. I may have no choice.

"I'm sorry I couldn't save her," I choke out, "I watched her take her last breath and I wasn't able to do anything."

I feel my dad's hand grip my shoulder. "It's not your fault. There's nothing you could have done, son."

I nod my head once and glance around the room. This time I notice a shelf hanging on the wall above the television. On it sits a frame holding the last family photo we ever had taken.

I was seven, Jenna three, and the four of us were sitting on a blanket in the middle of a field of sunflowers. In this particular picture, we're not all facing forward and smiling at the camera. We are looking at each other, laughing at something funny my dad said. The happiness on our faces encompasses the pure love we had for one another.

Next to the frame is a skinny vase. In the vase are four artificial flowers—two gray daisies, two bright yellow sunflowers. Words are scrawled on the wall above everything.

You are a sunflower in a field full of daisies.

They're the very words my mother used to tell Jenna and I. In some ways I feel as though she's speaking to me now, telling me she's still here and everything will be all right.

Chapter 41

Kinsley

I flip through the pages of the photo album I forgot my parents even had and come across a picture of Ryker and I playing dress up. I lean back in my mother's recliner, propping up my feet, and reminisce about my younger years.

I loved to play dress up. I dressed up in all types of costumes; princess, evil queen, cowgirl, police officer, doctor, ballerina, superhero. I had a very active imagination, often times not even needing the costume to portray the role.

Ryker always dressed up with me. I remember he got an awesome Batman costume for his sixth birthday and after he put it on he told me I was a princess he wanted to save. Sweet, right? Well, I didn't think so. I threw such a fit. I wanted to be Batman and I told him that princesses didn't need saving, especially this one.

It was a memory I brought up often and we enjoyed laughing about. Mainly, because he gave in to me being Batman and *he* dressed up as the princess in distress.

I run my finger over the picture of us, me in the Batman costume, Ryker in a pink sparkly dress, and for once a memory of us, of him, makes me smile instead of cry.

My mother walks into the living room wearing a black floor-length, sweep train evening dress. One side has a strap, coming up and over her shoulder connecting with beautiful beadwork. Delicate beads and pleats snug tightly in the waist. There's a split in the front revealing her leg up to her thigh. She's absolutely gorgeous.

"Kinsley Mae, it's time to put on your gown," she says.

When Trexton and Mandy's family moved here Mrs. Newton decided to bring back the policeman's ball. She changed the name to the Police Gala and made it a black tie event, however, it still has the same agenda...to raise money for the families of fallen policemen and women.

Many affluent individuals from quite a few surrounding towns make an appearance as well as a lot of higher ranking officers and the officers who happen to have the night off.

I only attended the very first year, yet somehow my mother has managed to guilt me into going tonight. And on the arm of Lieutenant Jake Grand. I must've been delirious when I let her talk me into this.

Standing before the floor length mirror of what use to be my bedroom, I pull my hair to the side as my mother zips up the back of my dress.

When I finally succumbed to the pressures of both my parents I went in search of a dress that would meet my standards; floor-length, completely covering my body. My parents convinced me this wouldn't be viewed as a date in any way.

I felt like it took forever to find the piece I'm wearing. The color's a soft pink with beaded flower embellishments across the entire front. Sheer lace creates the long sleeves and high neckline making sure it's not revealing or too sexy in the slightest yet remaining elegant. The thing I didn't anticipate is how form fitting this dress truly is with its mermaid style flow.

I take in a deep breath and expel it hoping to chase a bit of the nauseous away.

"You doing okay?" my mom asks while she places pins in my hair to keep it off to the side.

I look down at my trembling hands and repeat her question to myself, *am I doing okay?*

How does one in my situation answer such a question? As much as I tell myself, and Jake, that this is not a date, it's still the first time I will be out at an event on a man's arm that isn't Ryker. We may understand how it's only a friend helping out a friend, as my mother described it, yet everyone else will see and think differently. Everyone, including the one who has begun to matter.

"Have you heard if Caleb's going to be there?" I ask as uncertainty pulses through my veins.

She steadily watches me through the reflection of the mirror. I can tell she knows exactly why I'm asking. A small smile forms on her lips for barely a second. She's concealing her happiness over what this question may mean. *I regret asking.*

"I'm unsure if he'll attend. He told dad last week how he wants to support the cause, but would rather be able to wear cowboy boots and jeans."

Laughter fills me knowing it's exactly something he would say. Caleb lives in cowboy boots. He bought a pair of Wellington's to wear while on duty since they grip better. He even bought Elliot his first pair of boots. He's known in the department as the cowboy policeman even though the only thing that makes him look like a cowboy is the boots.

Flutters of dancing butterflies warm my insides as I think of the possibility of seeing him dressed in a Tuxedo. They're stamped out quickly as the sound of the doorbell alerts us to Jake's arrival.

"Does he know I'll be there with...with Jake?"

My mother's expression softens. She takes the curling iron from my hair and adds the last strand to the rest of the curls lying over my shoulder.

She places her hands lightly on my shoulders and says, "everything will work out. Let's take a deep breath." Simultaneously, we inhale and exhale. The sound of my father and Jake's voices carry down the hall. Panic grips me by the chest.

"Kinsley Mae, I want you to focus on me right now." My mother steps in front of me, bringing my attention back to her. "You can do this. You are strong. You are brave. You are amazing. I know this feels very much like a date. I'm going, to be honest with you. Just please don't let it freak you out more. I do feel as though Jake wants to pursue you as more, however, I'm confident that he won't do it tonight. Probably not the near future either. He's a very patient man. Dad and I have made it very clear about tonight being nothing more than a friend helping a friend." She brushes her finger across my forehead. "I do feel like this will be good for you, though. A stepping stone of sorts to get you back into the dating field for whenever the time comes."

I open my mouth to resist, but she cuts me off.

"I know you feel it's still too soon. You're so young and full of life I'd hate to see you let these years pass by. I know eight months doesn't feel like a very long time since Ryker's passing, but in reality, he's been gone for over four years." Tears form in my eyes and I wonder if they're glistening in the light like hers are. "I know, without a doubt, he'd want you to be as happy as you can be. He'd want you to experience love fully and fully be loved."

A tear falls from my eye. One, single, lone tear as I think about her words. I'm unsure if it's holding happiness or sorrow or a mixture of both. What she's saying is true. Ryker wouldn't want me to mourn him this long. He'd most likely be upset to know how I haven't let anyone help ease the pain. He once told me if he wasn't lucky enough to have me, he'd request the privilege of picking the one who's worthy enough. Maybe he already has.

"I didn't mean to upset you," my mom says, "I do want you to know how I, personally, don't think Jake is the one you need." She smiles before pulling me in for a hug.

The gala's being held in Chesterland City. The Newton's rented the entire Venice Mansion—a large, old estate that was abandoned due to the great flood of 1993. Water covered four thousand acres of the area for ninety-four days. Houses, businesses, and cars were six to fifteen feet underwater, except this particular mansion.

The water made its way right up to the house, sitting about an inch away, never making it inside. It created an ambiance of the Venetian Lagoon. Hence the reason for its name.

After the flood, the family wound up selling the place in fear of a repeat occurrence where they might not be so lucky. It was bought by an anonymous buyer, gutted completely and renovated specifically for different occasions and events.

My parents rented a limo for the four of us to ride in. It's a nice jester and takes away my fear of awkward silence in a car alone with Jake.

He looks very handsome tonight. A person having vision problems could still see how much he put into making himself look fresh and new. The hair on his head is as white as the tuxedo he's wearing and longer than it's ever been. He's sporting a baby blue bow tie making the blue in his eyes look crystal clear.

As we walk through the large mahogany front doors, my hand hooked inside Jake's arm, I'm privy to the many eyes taking him in as we pass. Many women have made it obvious they'd be honored to make him theirs. It's as though they don't even see me, completely opposite of what I was expecting. I thought I'd be explaining away our non-relationship when they couldn't care less about me.

As we make our way to the table, people stop and give their hellos. Some are colleagues of Jake's or of my mom and dads. Many are strangers who have more money invested in their lapel pins then I've ever even seen in my life.

Jake's not fazed by the riches. He greets everyone the same, with confidence and class. He blends in well with the people here.

The ballroom is exquisite. Decorated with gold, white, and silver flowers and white lights strung throughout. Roundtables housed with name cards surround the edges of an open floor, with a podium on the other side. Lining the walls are paintings donated by local artists as well as information on the trips included in the auction.

With ten minutes left before the proceedings take place, Jake suggests we go ahead and take our seats. He's such a gentleman as he pulls out my chair for me.

As I lower my body down to meet my chair, I pause mid-movement, caught off guard by the silence being stowed upon the room. I only assume it's someone of importance as I watch the heads of many turn toward the entrance, curious adoration pasted on their face.

What I don't expect to see is the man I've been thinking about all day.

He stands out amid the crowd and not just from his overpowering presence. It's due in part to the way he's dressed. Where everyone here is in a black or white tux with a white shirt and colored bowtie, Caleb's wearing all black. Black matte tuxedo with a satin lapel, black shirt, and a black, skinny satin tie.

The masses flow around him as he moves through the room. His gaze searches every face as he goes. As soon as he finds who he's looking for his eyes dance with delight.

The smile he gives me is one that should be a part of the paintings, for it's the most beautiful creation I've seen. There's no stopping the smile I give back.

Caleb's a few feet from the table I'm now standing in front of when the sound of a throat clearing comes from nearby. Our attention is diverted. Only now do I remember I came here with Jake.

As I look at him my smile turns apologetic. Looking back at Caleb, I notice his eyebrows have drawn down, his lips are thin, pressed into a line. His focus bounces between Jake and me as though a match of tennis is played before him.

I pinpoint the instant he recognizes I've come here with Jake. Anger momentarily taking over his features.

"Good evening, Lieutenant Grand," Caleb greets, offering Jake his hand.

"Good evening, Officer Tierney...Caleb. You can call me Jake here." Jake grabs Caleb's hand tightly, giving it a shake. "I didn't realize you were going to make an appearance tonight."

Briefly, Caleb looks to me before responding to Jake, "I didn't think I would be either."

That's all he says, no explanation, nothing more.

My parents arrive at the table and give out their greetings. As my mother softly smiles at Caleb she says, "glad to see you were able to make it," and I wonder if she knew all along that he'd be here.

We all move into our seats as my heart beats fiercely. Jake sits to my left, Caleb to my right. I've told myself many, many times tonight is not a date. So why do I feel like I'm doing something wrong? As though I've been telling a lie.

I lay my hand flat on my chest hoping to contain my hearts brutal punch. I startle when I feel something press against my lower back. A blush sears across my skin.

"You okay?" Caleb's throaty voice whispers into my ear.

I turn my head to face him and find he's leaning toward me. He's so close I can smell the fresh mint rolling over his tongue.

"I'm fine." A falsehood, one I'm sure he knows.

"Yes, fine is one way to define you." His playfulness turns serious as he continues, "You look absolutely divine, Kinsley. I swear your beauty holds no bounds."

His words are a cloud beneath me. I'm weightless, floating above the ground. Only the feeling is stolen from me quickly as Jake's hand rests on my thigh.

Abruptly, I stand from my seat causing Caleb to straighten. I excuse myself from the table, moving as fast as my snug dress will allow. I make my way to the hall, in search of a restroom as strong footsteps follow behind.

I keep myself faced forward, unsure of who it'll be, afraid of what's to come.

The footsteps come closer, a hand lightly surrounds mine. A simple tug is all it takes to turn me around in his arms. Arms which have embraced me before. I place my hand on his chest as he swings his arm around my waist, pulling me into him. His eyes try to search mine. I don't allow them to for long, diverting my attention to the satin of his lapels.

"Why are you here with him?" he asks.

I swallow my answer. Excuses are all they feel like, even though they're not.

"Kinsley...please tell me. Do you want to be here with Jake? Is this a date? Do you like him?"

All these questions flying my way, I can't move to dodge them. I apply pressure with my hand creating the much-needed space between us. His hold loosens but doesn't leave.

"I don't mind. No. Not in that way," I lay out my answers for him to read.

I see him thinking over my answers then the first question repeats.

"Why are you here with him?"

"Why does it matter?" I focus on his lips.

His hands move to my cheeks, steadying me as he tilts my head to his. His mouth is so close to mine, the heat from his breath feathers across my skin. Conflicting emotions collide in my veins, while his are written clearly in the brown of his eyes.

Barely allowing myself a second to look deeply into his eyes, I move my focus to lips.

I can't let this happen. I'm not ready for this...am I?

"Ryker," I breathe out.

My hand's moves over my mouth as the name I've said repeats in my head. My eyes shut tight, praying there's some way he didn't hear me.

Please ground, swallow me whole.

I should look at him and apologize, yet I won't. I can't look at him. I'm not sure I want to look at him and see the pity he may be holding. I turn quickly and run into the ladies room, finding a chair to sit on within the doors.

Maybe this was a good thing. Maybe this is how things are supposed to be. This will help Caleb understand the grief I still drown in on more days than I can handle. A heavy burden he shouldn't have to carry. Maybe...just maybe he'll realize how I don't have enough of me to give to him.

My skin is blotchy. *What have I done?* I'm trembling, sick to my stomach. *Why did I call him Ryker?*

I've *never* called another person Ryker, ever. Not even accidentally. And it happened while he was attempting to kiss me.

I'm a fool. To think I'm remotely ready for something. For wasting Caleb's time.

A tear slips from the corner of my eye and down my cheek. Before I can wipe it away, another's hand removes it for me.

Somehow Caleb's in front of me, kneeling before me.

"Kinsley, look at me, please," he says, desperation trickling from every word.

Both of my hands are being held by his, face up, his thumbs massaging my palms. I've yet to look at him and as the minutes tick by I wonder how long he'll stay. How long he'll wait for me.

Deep breath.

"Please," tumbles from his lips, crashing into my lap.

That one word somehow sounds so sturdy, yet broken into tiny pieces.

My head moves first then my eyes. They travel ever so slowly until they're met with deep pools of brown that look like they could drown me, however, I feel certain they could bring me back to life.

It's hard to look at them, which is why I never do. In some ways, I fear to look at Caleb's eyes. Even though his are entirely different from Ryker's, they're just as beautiful and that wherein lies the problem.

I don't want to look into Caleb's eyes, because I'd hate myself if I let the memory of Ryker's fade away.

Another tear falls. Caleb catches it with his finger.

"What just happened?" he asks. Silence greets him. "Please talk to me. Let me in that beautiful head of yours. I can see how you're fighting a war inside." His thumb glides gently across my cheek. "Baby let it out. Let me fight it with you."

I close my eyes and let out the air I've been holding. "I'm sorry," I say, which sounds weaker than intended.

"Don't apologize. Not now, not ever."

I flinch when he speaks even though his voice is soft, assuring. I'm humiliated by what I've done.

"Of course I'm going to apologize. I...I called you..."

"And that's all right," he says.

He stands up off the ground and moves the other chair to sit directly in front of me. He's so close his legs seal against the outside of mine. My hands clasp together in my lap and his hands surround them.

"Did you hear me? Look at me, please," he pleads.

I look at him briefly never making it to his eyes.

"I'm okay that you called me Ryker. In fact, it doesn't bother me at all," he pauses to gauge my reaction.

"Your eyes said different," I whisper.

His lips tighten for a second and then the right side of his mouth turns up into a cocky grin.

"For someone who can't stand to look at me for more than a second, especially in my eyes, you sure are confident you know how to read me."

I tuck my chin into my chest, the feeling of shame washes over me. His words sting, even though they're very true and I deserve to hear them.

"It's not that I don't want to look at you," I softly say.

"You don't need to explain anything to me. Just please let me finish."

His hand moves under my chin bringing my head back up to face him. His thumb feathers over my bottom lip before he speaks again.

"Kinsley, who was the last person to truly make you feel, Ryker?" My head nods automatically. "You calling me by his name simply assures me that I made you feel something. Which brings me more joy than you'll ever know."

Everything he's saying is true, even if I would've never looked at it that way. Caleb makes me feel things in more ways than I ever thought possible.

His hand slides to the back of my neck and pulls me forward just enough for him to rest his forehead against mine. My mouth goes dry causing me to lick my lips.

"Dammit," he says with a throaty growl, "Does Jake know you two are not on a date?"

"Yes," I say. Before it's completely out, his mouth crashes over mine.

This kiss is intense, on fire. I'm copying him move for move reciprocating everything he gives me. My hands find the lapels of his tux. I grip them tightly. I want him closer to me, pressed up against my body, but this damn dress has my legs pinned together.

Slowly our movements dwindle and life hits me square in the face. I pull away as my hands push him back into his chair.

Standing, I make my way toward the mirror. My name floats in the air behind me. I move quickly to fix my lips, wishing I'd brought in my clutch.

Oh my god! Oh my god! Why is this happening? It's too soon for this to happen. I'm too broken to try and move on.

I hear movement where I left Caleb and wonder if he's hightailing it out of here. I know I probably should before my mother, or heaven forbid Jake, come looking for me.

As I fix my hair in the mirror, I notice Caleb standing off to the side. His head's down and his hands are on his hips.

I keep my focus on myself and try to swallow down the knot stuck in my throat. I feel it when he looks at me. It's only for a moment before he turns around to leave the room.

I take a deep breath thinking I should feel relieved.

I don't.

Instead, added guilt piles on top of what I already harbor. The thought of scaring Caleb off forever starts to make me feel ill.

A mumbled profanity comes from the other room and before I can blink, Caleb's standing directly behind me. His eyes keep mine captive in the reflection of the mirror. It's easier to look at them this way.

"I'm sorry for what just happened, but only because of the timing." His lids pinch tight for a moment. "When I make a move on you," He pauses, his voice is deeper and barely above a whisper. "That's when, not if. It won't be in a women's lounge at a charity ball while your *date* awaits you down the hall." He's moved himself closer, his breath feathers along my neck. "It will be just the two of us in a place where I can take my sweet time worshipping every inch of your delectable body."

I'm absolutely still, no blinking, no breathing. Caleb's hand reaches up like he's going to touch me, but stops mid-air. Instead, he leans down placing his lips on my shoulder. He leaves them there for a moment before sliding them along the edge of my neck to the base of my ear.

As he pulls away he almost looks sad. "I'm leaving," he says approaching defeat, "I'm afraid I won't be able to control myself seeing you on his arm, regardless if it's not a date. I guarantee you Jake wants more."

I narrow my eyes. There's no need to respond. I know Jake wants more, however, the feelings are not mutual.

"I'll see you around, Kinsley," he says, walking out of the room, leaving not a trace of his existence behind. I have to pin myself to the floor so I don't chase after him.

Chapter 42

Caleb

"Caleb, man. It's pretty pathetic how you're sitting at home alone on a Saturday night, drinking by yourself." Tim tells me through the screen of my IPad.

"Fuck you. I'm having *a* beer and you're here." I retort.

"Dude, me being there verse me being on FaceTime are not one in the same. Plus it doesn't negate the fact I had to threaten you before you would even call me on FaceTime."

I take a swig of my beer as I watch him attempt to analyze me from the other side of a screen. Placing my beer on the table next to my propped up iPad, I rest my elbows on my knees and lean forward. If he wants to check in on me so bad, then I want to make sure he can see it all.

"So whatcha see Doc?" Hatred pours through my words even though I don't mean it.

Tim's hand swipes down his face, making me instantly regret my words.

"Shit Leb. It's not like that. I don't want to see your face to analyze you. What kind of friend would I be if I couldn't turn the doctor off at times?" He gives me a straight face for a second before he smirks and winks. *That jackass!*

"Good thing you're not actually here or you'd have a sore arm right now," I laugh at him.

"Oh, believe me, I know." He laughs for a second before he becomes serious. "It's been five weeks since you last saw her at the Police Gala. You've called me every day since, except for these last three. What gives?"

"I'm going to her house in an hour." Tim's eyes widen a bit. No sense in beating around the bush anymore. He may be calling to check on me, but I know what he wants to hear.

"You talked to her? You guys good?" He leans forward, mimicking my position. I stare at him and count to three in my head before I grab my beer, throwing back the rest. I know better than to look away too quickly after being asked a question. It's a tell that you're lying, or at least not giving the full truth.

"You're kidding," he says like I've given him an answer. "She's not even going to be there, is she?"

Holy fuck, how does he do that?

I turn off my truck and get out, gathering the tools I need to take into her house. Once Tim figured out how I was being a coward, he told me I needed to grow a pair and make things right again. I ended the call on his ass.

As I unlock the front door and make my way inside, I'm caught off guard by loud music blaring from the kitchen. Jenna assured me they wouldn't be here. She was taking Kinsley out for a girl's night.

I examine my surroundings and don't hear any other sounds. I'm sure they accidentally left the radio on. I walk to the kitchen and discover how wrong my assumption was.

Kinsley is singing along to the song playing, her hips moving in sync with the rhythm. Her back is toward me and it gives me the opportunity to lean against the wall and drink her in.

Her hair's longer than the last time I saw her, lying down in the middle of her back. A back that's exposed from the barely-there dress she's wearing. The dress looks more like an exquisite piece of scrap material which ties around her neck, cascades down the front of her body before gripping onto her luscious hips and flowing across her mid-thigh. It's black with large hot pink flowers placed in various places.

What I would give to be part of every single thread of the fabric brushing over her skin right now.

"Why wasn't I invited to the party?" I ask, hoping she doesn't notice how low and rasped my voice sounds.

She jumps and spins around so fast she almost loses her balance but catches herself on the counter.

"Dammit, Caleb! You about gave me a heart attack," she says while clutching her chest. "What are you doing here?"

"I thought I'd try and work on the basement some more." *I don't think I'll be getting much work done now, though.*

"Next time give me a heads up, so I don't think I'm about to be murdered." Her dramatics are amusing.

Her tongue darts out to wet her lips and I find it hard to swallow.

"Sorry," I say, "I thought you were out with Jenna or I would've let you know. Is she here?"

My gaze does a consuming sweep over her entire body instead of looking around to see if Jenna's actually here.

Kinsley's hand moves to the bottom of her throat as her pupils expand. Her mouth opens slightly and her breathing shakes. There's a rose tint brushed across her skin making me curious to know if it was produced by me or from the wine she just retrieved from the counter.

"She ended up going to work." One large gulp rids the contents from her glass. "A few people called in sick and Thor called her, begging," she says 'begging' with added emphasis, "Thor *never* begs for anything, so it must've been bad."

She sets her glass on the counter next to the empty wine bottle. *Was it full before I arrived?*

"Where's Elliot?"

She gathers her hair to the top of her head and ties it into a messy bun before turning to open the fridge.

"He's with Heath and Colleen. I'd already dropped him off and didn't want to take their time away from them."

Her hips begin to sway to the music still playing. I groan, unintentionally, and attempt to cover it by clearing my throat. If Kinsley was any other woman I would already have her pushed against the wall taking everything she could give. Yet if she were any other woman I wouldn't still be coming around at all.

"Kinsley, ya really gotta stop dancin'."

She gives a brief pause, however, instead of stopping she accentuates her movements while holding onto the handle of the fridge.

"Kinsley," I growl out in warning. A warning she fails to heed. She, oh so slowly and all too sensually, turns around to face me.

Fuck. Me.

"What's wrong Caleb?" she says innocently, "You don't like my dancing?" She sticks out her bottom lip to match the pout in her voice, before taunting me some more with her movement.

I take a couple steps, bringing myself closer to her, making her still. Her eyes lock onto my chest and I watch with amusement as she syncs her breathing to mine. I wonder if her heart is beating as wildly as mine too.

"Your assumption of me couldn't be more wrong. I like everything about your dancing. *Ev-er-y-thing*. That's why I *need* you to stop."

Tiny bumps cover her flesh with every word I speak. She takes a step closer to me, almost in a challenge. She continues until she's so close, there's hardly any space left, and then walks two fingers up my stomach to my chest.

"What're you going to do about it?" she asks, seduction laced through each syllable.

Before I have a chance to respond the words, "Kiss me," faintly falls from her lips.

All thoughts have left me as my mouth captures hers. Her mouth opens automatically, her tongue waiting to have a taste, and I don't make her wait long.

Her hands fist into my shirt as I grip her waist. We simultaneously pull each other together, making us closer than we've ever been before.

The flavor of sweet strawberries lingers on her lips reminding me of the wine she's consumed.

I can't let this go too far.

I end the kiss with a nip to her lip and then give her a kiss on her forehead. This is one time I wish I could read her thoughts. *Does she hate that I stopped as much as I do?*

My emotions begin to choke me. I need to put distance between us. I let her go and turn, moving across the room. My hands grip my hair as I take a deep breath, trying to clear my mind.

As I look back to her, to give her an explanation, I'm wounded with what I see. She no longer faces me, her shoulders are hunched forward, and she's holding herself with her arms.

"Shit," I say, moving swiftly to her. She looks like she's going to be sick. I hope I didn't make her feel this way. *Maybe it's the wine.* I lean over and switch off the radio. The music now becoming an annoyance.

I'm close enough I can feel the warmth of her body bleeding into mine. As much as I want to wrap her in my arms and make sure she's okay, I only allow myself to touch her shoulder.

"I'm sorry, Kinsley. I shouldn't have done that."

"Don't worry about it," she says, barely above a whisper. "I shouldn't have told you to kiss me."

She thinks I'm apologizing for the kiss?

My hand nudges her shoulder, urging her body to turn around. I'm relieved when I feel her move without pause. Her arms are still wrapped around her middle and her head's hung with shame. I place my finger under her chin, pulling up until she's forced to look at me. I wait until her eyes lock with mine.

"I'm not sorry for kissing you," I tell her, "God, Kinsley, you standing here in this dress, moving your body the way you do has me so strung up inside. Hell, you could be covered from head to toe in thick clothing and every fiber of me would still ignite in flames just from being near you. I want you...so bad it hurts. I couldn't let us go on."

Her eyes are wide with slight bewilderment. She raises one brow and it dawns on me how I still haven't completely explained the reason. "You've had a whole bottle of wine, maybe more, and it would tear me apart if you were to regret any moment we have together."

I give her a moment to think. She has to understand how much I want her. How badly I want things between us to work. It's something I've never wanted before.

As if an idea has sparked her interest, she turns back to the counter, opens a loaf of bread and takes three pieces out. The first piece she shoves entirely into her mouth, almost making herself gag, yet somehow she remains composed. Piece two gets folded in half and mushed flat. As soon as she has room in her mouth she tears off little bits and eats them. Piece three gets rolled into a ball before she takes a rather large bite.

I move to the side of her and lean against the counter. She takes another bite then turns her body to face me.

Her eyes stake claim on my mouth as I bite my lip, trying my damnedest to suppress the smile forming underneath.

I watch her mess with the wad of bread that's left. I give her a quizzical look and ask, "what are you doing?"

Her eyebrows and her shoulders rise simultaneously as she tries to smile with her mouth full.

"Just trying to sober up."

Huh?

"You serious?" I ask as a chuckle rumbles from my chest.

"I've never been more serious in my life." Her voice is an octave lower than before.

I move directly in front of her, placing both hands on each side of her body, caging her within. "Are you sure about this? This is what you want?" I stare at her as she stares at my mouth. "Cause I'm going to tell you now if we do this, it changes things. It will change everything between us. It will be all or nothing for me. I'm not saying we have to rush, but I won't be able to sit back and watch you live your life without me. And definitely not with another guy."

She looks at me in silence, drinking me in with her eyes. She assesses my entire body like it's the deciding factor for her answer. I wonder if all that bread actually helped sober her up or if it did nothing at all.

She moves closer, pressing her body against me. Every single one of my muscles tense with hopeful anticipation. She lays both of her hands flat on my stomach then slides them up, ever so slowly, until they're pressed against the back of my neck. She rises to her tiptoes and pulls my head down toward her.

Her words are soft yet powerful as she tells me, "do not move...don't even blink."

So I don't.

I watch as her tongue slips past her lips and slides across mine.

I feel it when her teeth go around my bottom lip and bites, just enough to wreak havoc on my insides.

The moment her tongue moves into my mouth is when I lose all control. My hands grip her ass and lift, moving her legs around my waist. The warmth between her thighs presses against my erection making moans tear from both of our chests.

I turn and press her against the wall, our tongues never stopping the dance they're in with each other. I rain kisses on her cheek and on to her neck.

As she tilts her head to give me more access, two words come from her mouth which stops me.

"Not here."

Not here? Not here in this kitchen, not here in her house, or even not here at this time of her life?

Her silence is resounding as I leave my lips pressed against the sweet skin of her neck. I lift my head and look at her, straight into her eyes. Her expression is unreadable making me question if I actually heard anything at all.

It's been longer than a second and our gazes are still locked together. She allows me to witness how clear they look, how vibrant the colors shine, and how open they seem to be. It's as if those concrete walls she built have been completely annihilated and she's giving me a small glimpse into her soul.

Her hands push against my shoulders as her legs unravel from my waist and drop to the floor, taking my heart down with them. I'm confused as hell and curious to know where things went wrong.

I shouldn't have pushed.

I call out her name when she turns to leave the kitchen. She keeps moving as if she never heard me. *Where is she going? Should I follow?* The quick glance she throws me accompanied by a smile answers my unspoken thoughts.

She walks into the living room and makes her way down the hall. When she reaches the end she pauses for a brief second seeming to listen for something, my footsteps maybe? Then she moves on into her room.

I stop within her doorway, leaning against the frame. Her back is facing me as she stands near the edge of her bed. She pulls the tie from her hair letting the strands cascade down her back.

I glance around her room, noticing how the walls are vacant. Not a single memory or decoration as before.

"I haven't done this in a very long time," she says as she turns to face me.

"Kinsley, we don't have to…"

"Wait," she cuts me off, "I want to do this, more now than ever. When I'm with you every part of me feels peaceful, calm, and I know it has to mean something significant." Her posture is straight, strong. Not a single movement or fidget. "I can't and won't fight these feelings any longer."

Confidence and honesty wrap around her words.

I'm ready to go to her and accept what she's willing to give, but as I take a step forward she moves her hand out in between us, securing me in my place.

A playful smile spreads across her face as she takes her hand and runs it up her body. She continues until she's at the back of her neck, gripping onto the tied fabric which is the only piece securing her dress in place.

Slowly, she pulls, releasing the knot and then lets it go. The pink flowers printed on the dress, skim across her skin as they float down to the floor.

She's completely bare and unequivocally beautiful. The fact she isn't wearing anything underneath arouses me more as I feast upon her body with my gaze.

The woman standing before me is beyond strong and utterly exquisite...there are not enough words to describe the goddess who has graced me with her presence.

I take a few steps until I'm in front of her then fall to my knees. The position I'm in is how I feel a person would look when they worship their God. On their knees, arms slack to their sides, head bowed in prayer.

I've never been much of a praying man. I've questioned my belief in God too many times to know if I even do believe. I remember screaming and spitting at the sky asking if there really is a God then why would he let all the bad things in this world happen. Why would he strip me of my selfless, God-loving mother? And why would he drag Kinsley through hell and back?

But right now, at this very moment, my belief in God is strong. He's giving me another chance, breathing life back into me when I already thought I'd been living. He's opening my heart to a love he thinks I deserve while giving me the strength to love this woman whole again.

My hands graze against her feet and up her legs as my sight follows. Gliding to her hips, the tips of my fingers move lightly over the scar she was rewarded as she brought her amazing son into this world. There's a tear-drop shaped birthmark to the left of her belly button. Faint stretch marks are dusted across her stomach.

She's perfect in every sense of the word. Her imperfections, her flaws, the very things most women hide from a man are the very things she's allowing me to see. It makes her even more desirable.

"I know I've seen you bare before, but then, in that shower, your heart was gone and your soul was bleeding. It hurt every fiber of my existence to see you so broken. I so desperately wanted to help, I didn't know how. I was grasping at your torn pieces, trying to form them back together, and they kept shattering faster than my hands could mend."

I end my words with a kiss to her skin, and another, and another. I make a promise to myself that if she'll have me, I'll do everything in my power to help piece her back together.

Chapter 43

Kinsley

Standing here, I take in the beautiful man kneeling before me. The words he just spoke seep into my skin, move through my muscles and flow in my veins straight to my heart. I feel a bit stronger than I was before.

Once again, he seals his lips against the cesarean scar running along my lower abdomen. He repeats the same motion, kissing every inch of my jagged skin.

I run my hands through his hair and down to his shoulders. Gripping onto the neckline of his shirt, I pull until it's completely off then toss it on the floor.

He nudges me back until I'm sitting on my bed. He gets up and rids himself of his boots and socks, leaving on his jeans.

I fiddle with my hands in my lap while the confidence I had escapes me. Doubt-filled thoughts begin to fill my mind. *Is it selfish of me to want this, to want him, so badly when I don't even have all of myself to give?*

When he looks at me I know he can sense the change.

"Caleb?" I croak out as he takes a seat next to me. "I'm still shattered." I look at him with tears filling my eyes. "Some days I feel like I'll never be fully put back together. Some days I wonder how I'm still alive."

He reaches out his hand sliding his thumb across my cheek then cups the back of my neck. His eyes squeeze shut as he presses his forehead to mine. "I've never completely healed after my mother died. It was a different loss but one that still makes me less whole." His eyes open revealing his truth. "What if our broken pieces are meant to fit together? Mine with yours, yours with mine. Intertwined with each other to make us complete. Make us whole. The connection we have is something I've never felt before." I nod in agreement because it's true. Even my connection with Ryker was different than the one I feel now, with Caleb. "Kinsley, let me be your other pieces. Let me love you whole."

His words are a symphony, playing the sonata of his heart. As soon as they're processed, I do just as he's asked.

I let him love me whole.

The End

Epilogue

I turn the water to warm and then pump soap into my palm. As I wash my hands in the sink a light knock comes from the other side of the door.

"Babe, you almost ready to head out?" Caleb asks.

I smile at my reflection in the mirror. "Two more minutes then I'll be out."

Grabbing the small towel, I dry my hands. I pick up the test from the counter and dry it as well, making sure the cap is on tight before placing it in the gift bag.

I can't wait to watch his reaction.

I make my way to our living room finding Caleb patiently waiting near the front door. He looks so sexy dressed in black slacks and a maroon button-up shirt with the top two buttons undone and the sleeves rolled back to quarter length.

I push up on my tip-toes and give a quick peck to his lips.

"Happy anniversary," he says.

"Happy anniversary! I love that you wore the color from our wedding."

"Great minds think alike," he says as he gives the material of my dress a slight tug.

Today is our wedding anniversary and as Caleb drives us to dinner all I can do is stare at the sexy man beside me and think about what an amazing year it's been.

"Was Elliot excited when you dropped him off?" I ask as the hostess leads us to our table.

Elliot's staying the night with Jenna at her new house. When Caleb and I became engaged, Jenna took over the lease on his apartment so he could move in completely with me. He had already pretty much been living here, but the switch made it official. Last month Jenna bought a house of her own and Elliot hasn't stopped talking about wanting to stay the night with her.

"Excited is an understatement," Caleb says, "He went screaming through her entire house then jumped on her bed trying to claim it as his for the night."

Elliot is a wild child. I was kind of hoping he would begin to wind down as he became older. No luck yet. He starts kindergarten in the fall and I feel like I should apologize to his teacher now.

"He sure is something else, isn't he?" I say with laughter.

"He sure is. I wish you could've seen the look on Thor's face though. It was priceless. I don't think he's prepared for Elliot the Elusive." Caleb shakes his head at the thought. "Thor quietly told me he may be 'called' into work tonight."

"I'm shocked he was even there, knowing Jenna was keeping Elliot."

Jenna and Thor have been in some sort of relationship for a while now. I say it that way because no one really knows what it is. They obviously like each other, a lot, but say they don't want to mess things up with labels, whatever that means.

We finish our dinner and Caleb orders a volcanic brownie with one scoop of vanilla ice cream to share. It's my favorite dessert.

Pulling a small gift bag from my purse, I set it on the table. Caleb looks at it and then looks at me.

"I thought we were saving gifts for when we get home? I didn't bring yours."

"We are. I just wanted to give you this one now," I say.

He opens the bag and glances in it. The item inside is a piece of paper so he has to get it out to know what it is. He pulls out the paper and opens it. A smirk appears as he lifts one eyebrow at me.

"You're giving me a massage certificate addressed to you?" he asks.

"Uh, no. Read it entirely. It's a couple's massage. It's for both of us." I wink at him.

"Yes! I've always wanted one of those happy endings." I stare at him incredulously. "What? You think I'll be able to lie next to you naked and behave? This is your idea."

I laugh at him, *and think of how to bribe the massage therapists to give us twenty minutes alone on that day.*

As I walk through the front door I text Jenna to see how things are going. She sends me back a picture of Elliot on Thor's shoulders with a foam sword in his hand and a giant smile on his face. Thor's actually looking like he's having a good time.

I grab the other gift bag out of the bedroom and make my way to Caleb in the living room. He's sitting on the edge of the couch, his elbows resting on his knees and his hands clasped together. His leg is bouncing up and down.

"You all right?" I ask as I sit next to him.

He looks at me with wide eyes as though he didn't realize I was sitting next to him. "Huh? Oh, uh, yeah. I'm fine."

Clearly, he's not, but I'll have to pull it out of him later. His nerves are starting to freak me out over the gift I'm about to give him.

I set the gift bag that's in my hand on top of the coffee table. Caleb wipes his forehead with a shaky hand. I place my hand on his knee to stop it from bouncing.

"Sorry," he says, looking at his knee and then at me. "I'm working myself up. Do you mind if I give you my gift first?"

"I don't mind," I say, wondering if It's his gift he's worried about. He pulls a big package out from the side of the couch and sets it in my lap. I grab the side ready to tear off the paper when he places his hand over mine.

"Before you open it..." He stops to swallow, "I just want you to know that I thought of this idea and kind of ran with it without thinking about anything else. I hope I'm not crossing any lines and I apologize if I am."

I stare at him. He's sweating profusely. *What in the world could this be to make him so nervous and apologize already?*

"Caleb, I'm sure I'll love whatever it is."

He nods his head once and then let's go of my hand. I carefully tear off the wrapping paper and toss it to the floor. I'm holding a large picture frame. There's a piece of white paper on top of it keeping me from seeing the picture.

I move the paper and my breath draws in sharply. My hand covers my mouth. Tears spring to my eyes as I stare at the image before me. I can feel Caleb's gaze resting on my face. I hope he realizes these are tears of happiness.

"How?" I say in barely a whisper.

"There's this guy at work who is really good with computers and Photoshop. I know you only have a few pictures of the two of you together when you were pregnant. I just...I thought..." I grab Caleb's hand and give it a light squeeze.

I look at him and stare straight into his eyes. "I love it. It's amazing and beautiful and looks so real. It's absolutely perfect."

I set the frame on top of the table and crawl onto Caleb's lap. My hands move through his hair as I devour his mouth.

The gift he has given me is a photo of Ryker and me. The picture was taken shortly after we found out I was pregnant. He's standing behind me slightly off to the side with his arms wrapped around my middle section and my arms resting on top of his. Except now, instead of our arms being empty, lays a sleeping Elliot as an infant.

The image is so perfect you can't even tell it wasn't taken this way. And the best part is Ryker is staring down at Elliot with the brightest smile on his face.

"How did I get so lucky with you?" I say as I rain kisses all over Caleb's face. *I've been blessed with such a selfless man.*

A deep chuckle resonates from his chest sending vibrations straight to my core. "So you like it?" he asks knowing the answer. "Do I get to open my gift now?"

I don't move off of him. I simply twist my waist and grab the gift bag sitting on the table. He takes the bag from my hand and I resume kissing his face.

"You're not going to stop, are you?"

"Nope," I whisper next to his ear before nipping on the lobe.

"Kinsley," he warns, his erection pressing between my thighs.

"Just open the damn bag so you can take me to bed and finish what I've started."

He laughs again, but finally, tears open the bag. I feel the test fall to the floor. *Dammit!*

I move onto the couch beside him. He reaches down and picks up the pregnancy test. Before he even looks at it his attention is on me.

"You're pregnant!"

I nod my head and bite the inside of my cheek. Before I even know what's happening he has me in his arms, my legs around his waist, as he marches down the hall to our room. He lays me on the bed and climbs between my legs. Sliding the tips of his fingers up my legs, he pushes my dress up until it's off my body. He stares at my stomach with adoration in his eyes. He kisses it over and over as he speaks, "best anniversary ever."

He continues his kisses up my body and stops at my mouth. "How did I get so lucky with you?" he says, repeating the words I used in the living room. "Seriously, you make me the happiest man in all of the planets. I love you, Kinsley Mae Tierney...for the rest of our lives."

"I love you, Caleb Joseph. Thank you for loving me whole."

I had the greatest love one could feel, the love of my best friend...my soulmate. To be able to recognize and experience this type of love at such a young age is simply remarkable.

I thought the love I felt with Ryker was it for me. I thought that when he died I would never be loved or be able to love in such a way again. I was certain we could only be granted one all-consuming love during a lifetime.

I was proved wrong.

Acknowledgements

Wow! Are we really to this point? I can't believe this story is already over. It's been a part of me, deep in my soul, for what seems like forever. Although at times I wanted to throw it all away, I can now say I'm sad to see it come to an end.

February 22, 2016, is the day this story came alive. I was at my mother's house taking care of my son, newborn niece, and grandpa when the words began bleeding from my fingertips. That's how it felt at least. I grabbed an old, empty notebook of my sisters and a pen and began writing. It felt like an out-of-body experience. My hands couldn't move fast enough, my mind wouldn't slow down. I wanted to go into hiding, take away my responsibilities for a week, just so I could get all the thoughts out without losing them. Unfortunately, that wasn't able to happen, which is the main reason this has taken so long.

I've learned so much during this process. I didn't know a single thing about how to write a novel, the proper way to do things, or the actual craft itself. I've become a part of amazing, informational groups. I've met so many amazing people, other soon-to-be authors or already published ones, who have answered all my questions and encouraged me to keep going. And I couldn't be happier to say that I found my tribe amongst them.

There are so many people I want to thank for sticking by my side throughout this crazy ride. First and foremost, I want to thank You, the reader. Thank you for reading my story. For taking a chance on a newbie author who knows nothing about nothing, who felt a story in her heart and worked hard to bring it to fruition. Thank You.

To my husband and my boys, you've been nothing short of amazing and patient with me, giving me many opportunities to sneak away to the quiet library for hours to get in some writing time. I love you.

To my family, each and every one of you has encouraged me, bragged about me, and cheered for me. I'm grateful to have such an awesome support system behind me in everything I decide to do.

To my ride or dies, the other half of my brain (Kelly), my bestie (Heather), and buffalo (Nikole). To think that all of you have been friends with me longer than you have not is a true testament to your character. : Shrugs in laughter: All jokes aside, thank you for being my biggest cheerleaders. For letting me send you snippets here and there to make sure it sounds all right. I love each of you and appreciate you more than you'll ever know.

To Diane and Nichole. Diane, I couldn't be happier that you reached out to me and rekindled our dormant friendship. You were the first person to read this story when it wasn't even finished and in all its first draft glory. The beginning wasn't good at all, but somehow I was still able to make you love it and cry. I hope you like this version much better.

Nichole, the best day of 2017 became even better when I met you. Spending the weekend at our favorite author's house, an experience of a lifetime, with you was a time I'll cherish forever. Thank you for letting me torture you chapter-by-chapter with my story. I hope you're ready for more because you're stuck with me for life.

To my beta readers Kathi, Kirsten, and Cassie. Thank you for your honesty and input, for helping me make this the best story it could be.

Thank you, Sam, for reaching out to me and graciously editing my words.

Thank you, Kris Pittman, for your beautiful artwork. You took the image I had in my head and brought it to life.

Thank you to the authors who have inspired me to find my passion and reach for my dreams. My top four: Colleen Hoover, Tarryn Fisher, Molly McAdams, BB

Easton. Your words have made me feel every emotion known, but your heart has shown me so much more.

Last, but far from least, thank you TiCs. You five are my tribe, my confidants, my foundation, and support. You pick me up when I have fallen. You remind me to take a break when one's needed. You share your knowledge and your love. We may be placed all over the globe, but our red threads will never break. This story would never be what it is today without each and every one of you. You've all had a huge hand in helping me bring it to life. I love you all and thank you from the bottom of my heart. #TiCsUnite

About the Author

Crystal A Blanton lives in the Show Me State with her sarcastic, yet loving husband of fifteen years and two wild, crazy sons. She has a love for reading, writing, warm weather, Zero Ultra Monster Energy drinks, massages, traveling, spending time with her family and friends, writing in third person, and chocolate; in no particular order.

You can connect with her here:

www.facebook.com/crysblantonauthor

www.instagram.com/crysblantonauthor

www.goodreads.com/crysblanton